# "I Can't Be The Nine-To-Five, Lawn-Mowing Man Next Door, Lydia.

"But I'd like for you to be my lover," Evan said.

"What about love?" Lydia asked.

"Love is just a pretty lie that men and women tell each other."

Lydia tilted her head and stared up at Evan, her wide blue eyes making him feel as if she were probing past his defenses and finding the heart he'd hidden deep within his soul.

"I'm going to show you that love is more than lies and pretty words."

"And if you don't?"

"Oh, I will, Sheriff. Even *your* heart isn't buried that deep." Then Lydia turned and walked away.

As he watched her go, he found himself hoping for the glimpse of heaven she'd just so confidently offered him....

Dear Reader,

Welcome to the world of Silhouette Desire, where you can indulge yourself every month with romances that can only be described as passionate, powerful and provocative!

The always fabulous Elizabeth Bevarly offers you May's MAN OF THE MONTH, so get ready for *The Temptation of Rory Monahan*. Enjoy reading about a gorgeous professor who falls for a librarian busy reading up on how to catch a man!

The tantalizing Desire miniseries TEXAS CATTLEMAN'S CLUB: LONE STAR JEWELS concludes with *Tycoon Warrior* by Sheri WhiteFeather. A Native American ex-military man reunites with his estranged wife on a secret mission that renews their love.

Popular Peggy Moreland returns to Desire with a romance about a plain-Jane secretary who is in love with her *Millionaire Boss*. The hero-focused miniseries BACHELOR BATTALION by Maureen Child continues with *Prince Charming in Dress Blues*, who's snowbound in a cabin with an unmarried woman about to give birth! *Baby at His Door* by Katherine Garbera features a small-town sheriff, a beautiful stranger and the bundle of love who unites them. And Sara Orwig writes a lovely tale about a couple entering a marriage of convenience in *Cowboy's Secret Child*.

This month, Silhouette is proud to announce we've joined the national campaign "Get Caught Reading" in order to promote reading in the United States. So set a good example, and get caught reading all six of these exhilarating Desire titles!

Enjoy!

*Joan Marlow Golan*

Joan Marlow Golan
Senior Editor, Silhouette Desire

Please address questions and book requests to:
Silhouette Reader Service
U.S.: 3010 Walden Ave., P.O. Box 1325, Buffalo, NY 14269
Canadian: P.O. Box 609, Fort Erie, Ont. L2A 5X3

# SHADOW OF THE
# MOON

## REBECCA YORK

**BERKLEY SENSATION, NEW YORK**

**THE BERKLEY PUBLISHING GROUP**
**Published by the Penguin Group**
**Penguin Group (USA) Inc.**
**375 Hudson Street, New York, New York 10014, USA**
Penguin Group (Canada), 90 Eglinton Avenue East, Suite 700, Toronto, Ontario M4P 2Y3, Canada
(a division of Pearson Penguin Canada Inc.)
Penguin Books Ltd., 80 Strand, London WC2R 0RL, England
Penguin Group Ireland, 25 St. Stephen's Green, Dublin 2, Ireland (a division of Penguin Books Ltd.)
Penguin Group (Australia), 250 Camberwell Road, Camberwell, Victoria 3124, Australia
(a division of Pearson Australia Group Pty. Ltd.)
Penguin Books India Pvt. Ltd., 11 Community Centre, Panchsheel Park, New Delhi—110 017, India
Penguin Group (NZ), Cnr. Airborne and Rosedale Roads, Albany, Auckland 1310, New Zealand
(a division of Pearson New Zealand Ltd.)
Penguin Books (South Africa) (Pty.) Ltd., 24 Sturdee Avenue, Rosebank, Johannesburg 2196,
South Africa

Penguin Books Ltd., Registered Offices: 80 Strand, London WC2R 0RL, England

SHADOW OF THE MOON

A Berkley Sensation Book / published by arrangement with the author

PRINTING HISTORY
Berkley Sensation edition / June 2006

ISBN: 0-425-20961-X

BERKLEY SENSATION®
Berkley Sensation Books are published by The Berkley Publishing Group,
a division of Penguin Group (USA) Inc.,
375 Hudson Street, New York, New York 10014.
BERKLEY SENSATION is a registered trademark of Penguin Group (USA) Inc.
The "B" design is a trademark belonging to Penguin Group (USA) Inc.

PRINTED IN THE UNITED STATES OF AMERICA

10  9  8  7  6  5  4  3  2  1

# CHAPTER
# ONE

**THE THICK UNDERBRUSH** of Rock Creek Park made the perfect cover for the gray wolf who hunted in these woods where no wolf should be.

He wasn't stalking deer or rabbits. He was a werewolf, and he was after much more exotic wildlife.

Laughter drifted toward him through the darkness, and he moved closer to a hulking building perched at the edge of the woods. A fantasy of stone and concrete, it was built like a medieval fortress with turrets and small, arched windows designed for privacy—or to prevent escape.

To his right, he picked up footsteps and the strong scent of a man who hadn't bathed in a couple of days.

Blending back into the shadows, the wolf watched a

security guard pass on his rounds, then crept toward the front of the building.

It was called the Eighteen Club—or, more familiarly, the Castle—and he knew the main floor housed a couple of nightclubs. Above and below it were much more interesting private rooms—set up to accommodate any sexual fantasy that the elite of the nation's capital could imagine.

A long black limousine pulled up and disgorged a U.S. senator, his broad smile and craggy eyebrows instantly recognizable. Tonight he bent his head as he hurried toward the front door.

The wolf watched as the senator was swallowed up by the massive stone building. Then something subtle caught his attention.

He looked to his left, peering into the darkness, then blinked as he saw a shadow detach itself from a tree. A woman, judging from her body shape and feminine scent. She wore black leggings, a long-sleeved black top, and her hair was tied up in a black bandanna.

Like her body, her face was delicate. With his night vision, he could clearly see her light eyes, her little nose, her lips that might have been sensual if they hadn't been pressed into a thin line.

A wisp of blond hair had escaped from her bandanna, adding an endearing touch.

But the overall effect was no-nonsense. He saw anger, determination, and more.

What had the Eighteen Club done to her? Alienated the affections of her lover?

Something dangled from a strap around her neck. A camera.

Was she part of a special security patrol? Had she come to take pictures of the people who entered the club, so she could blackmail them? Or was she stalking this place for the same reason as he? And what were the odds of that?

More cars pulled up, and she began snapping pictures. First she caught a man and a woman. He wasn't a political celebrity. Far from it. This guy kept his face out of the media. But he had a reputation for getting things done if the price was right. The woman with him was a looker, wearing a barely there little red dress. She was slender, except for the large breasts that had probably been purchased from a plastic surgeon's catalog.

The woman in black snapped another patron. A matron in her late forties or early fifties with auburn hair and a face that looked like it was just on the verge of sagging.

When the photographer moved closer to get a better angle with her camera, he might have growled a warning—but it was already too late. One of the security men had spotted her.

"Hold it right there!"

She whirled as the guard moved quickly toward her.

"Freeze. Hands in the air—or I'll shoot."

# CHAPTER
# TWO

**THE WOLF COULDN'T** see the woman's face, but he felt her terror—smelled it wafting toward him in the night air.

"Take off your camera and put it down on the ground." The guard's voice was edged with steel.

With unsteady hands, she followed directions, standing helplessly by as he slung the strap over his own shoulder.

"Come on," he ordered.

"Where?"

"Inside."

She looked like she wanted to run. But the gun kept her standing in place.

"Let me go. I didn't mean any harm."

"Then what were you doing?"

The wolf waited for the answer, and gave her points for guts—and fast talking. "I'm an amateur photographer. I was in the woods taking pictures of the natural environment, and I was curious about the lights. I didn't see any No Trespassing signs."

"Do you expect me to believe that? When you sneak up on us at night dressed like a damn ninja? Move. Down there. Around the back."

The man started toward his victim, obviously enjoying himself.

The wolf watched the drama. This woman's fate was none of his business, he told himself. But he couldn't make himself buy into it.

Over the past weeks, he'd discovered a lot about the Castle. If the guard took her inside, she might never come out again alive. And death might not be the worst thing that happened to her.

The wolf could feel his heart pounding, his adrenaline pumping as his body tensed to strike. Once the thought of attacking entered his mind, the savage need built.

He was in back of the guard, and the man was focused on his victim, sure that a lone woman in the woods wasn't going to get the drop on him.

He pulled out a pair of handcuffs. "Hands behind you," he ordered.

With a snarl, the wolf sprang, leaping on the man's back, taking him down. The handcuffs clanked to the ground, and the guard's finger squeezed the trigger of his gun.

As the wayward shot rang out, the wolf went for the gun hand, chomping down until the man screamed in agony and fear as he lost his grip on the weapon.

The woman screamed as well, then turned and dashed into the trees, as the security force came pounding toward the sound of the shot.

Snatching the camera strap in his teeth, the wolf pulled it free, then took off after the woman, his body bracing for the thud of a bullet piercing his flesh.

But he was lucky. The guard was in no shape to fire his weapon, and the other men were too far away for an accurate shot in the dark.

The wolf disappeared into the forest, following the woman's scent, the camera thudding against his chest.

"What the fuck?" he heard someone shout.

"Get the damn girl," another voice gasped.

"And the dog."

He kept moving. He couldn't see the woman now. But he could hear her crunching across dry leaves, desperate to get away from the men with guns. And from the creature who had come to her rescue. He knew that as well as he knew anything else.

She was in good shape; she could run fast. And she must have made sure of her escape route, because she seemed to know where she was going.

Too bad she hadn't done a little more research before coming here in the first place. The Castle was a well-guarded playground for the rich and powerful. Anyone who tried to get too close was taking an enormous risk.

She fled through the woods, up an incline, then slipped partway down again. Scrambling for purchase, she righted herself and kept going toward the houses on the other side of the stream valley.

He saw her hand go into her pocket, probably fumbling for keys. She pulled out a remote control, pressed the button, and lights blinked as a car lock opened.

As the wolf reached the edge of the woods, he heard the vehicle's engine roar to life. Leaping onto the black-top, he put on an extra burst of speed. The car jerked, and pulled away from the curb. Exhaust roared in his face, making him cough.

But he focused on the license plate, taking in the letters and numbers, committing them to memory as the woman sped into the darkness, not bothering to turn on her lights.

The guys in back of her didn't know she'd escaped. They were crashing through the woods behind him like crazed elephants, unwilling to give up.

What were they going to do—start shooting in the middle of a residential neighborhood?

He dashed past the homes across the street and into an alley. Two dogs heard him streak past and started barking. He could hear people behind brick walls warning them to cut it out.

He ended in the backyard of a house that was currently vacant, trotting past beds of blooming black-eyed Susans. He'd called them chocolate daisies when he'd been a kid. In the breezeway between the house and the garage, he carefully set down the camera, then began the chant that he had learned when he was sixteen.

The words of transformation. As a wolf, he couldn't say them aloud. But they echoed in his mind, in his very bones.

*Taranis, Epona, Cerridwen,* he silently intoned, then repeated the same phrase and went on to another.

*Ga. Feart. Cleas. Duais. Aithriocht. Go gcumhdai is dtreorai na deithe thu.*

Before he finished, he felt the familiar pain as his body began to morph from wolf to a man named Lance

Marshall. The change from one form to another was in his genes, in the fabric of his existence.

Back on the night he'd first changed from boy to wolf, he'd been giddy with relief when he'd found himself lying in a forest clearing with his head throbbing. His father, a shaggy gray wolf, had been standing over him, no doubt exhilarated to find that his fourth son wasn't going to die during transformation as two of his older boys had.

Tonight, he pushed through the change, then quickly reached for his sweatpants, pulling them on over his naked butt because speed was the important thing about dressing and undressing out in the middle of a city.

It was always hard to cope with the senses of a mere man when he had been blessed only moments before with a wolf's wonderful faculties. But there were compensations, he thought as he picked up the camera in his hand and stuffed it into his knapsack.

After waiting in the shadows for a few minutes, he stepped into the alley, walked to where he'd left his car, then drove out of the city toward his property bordering the Patuxent State Park in Howard County, Maryland.

His brother, Grant, who owned a construction company, had built him a house. Nature lover's rustic, he'd called it. A wood and stone structure, nestled into the side of a hill, with lots of space where he could shelve his books and spread out his research materials.

Although he'd gotten exactly what he wanted, it had been difficult for two werewolves to work together because they were all alpha males. But they'd each tried to keep from attacking the other—because they were determined not to end up like their father and uncles, exhibiting all the old family traits of brotherly love. Not.

When he stopped at a traffic light, he picked up his cell phone and punched in a speed-dial number—for his cousin Ross, who was a private detective.

Until three years ago, Lance had never met his cousins, but Ross had gotten in touch with Grant and then with Lance, partly because he had some important information about preventing the death of werewolf children. Now they had a gentleman's agreement to help each other when help was needed.

"Lance, are you keeping out of trouble?" Ross asked.

"As much as you are."

His cousin made a dismissive sound. "My life isn't exactly like the old days, before I acquired a wife and kids and responsibilities."

"Yeah," Lance answered, thinking none of that was on his personal agenda. But he hadn't called to spout his philosophy of life.

"I read your story on that heroin ring in Baltimore. That was good work," Ross said.

"Thanks."

"I guess you sniffed out the drug dealers."

Lance laughed. "Yeah."

"You're a damn good writer—for a guy with your genes."

"Thanks, I think."

"What can I do for you?"

"I need some information for another project—something that I've moved to the front burner."

"For the *Washington Post*?"

"It's still in the preliminary research stages. Maybe it's going to be a book."

"Fantastic."

Lance dragged in a breath and let it out. "Can you get

your police detective friend to run a Maryland license plate for me?"

"Sure."

He gave his cousin the letters and numbers, wondering what he would find out about the woman dressed like a ninja.

He was excellent at digging for details—and lying his brains out if he had to. And especially adept at taking risks. There was no point in being modest. He was born to sniff out information that eluded other journalists—which was why he'd gotten so far so fast. It wasn't his writing ability. That was adequate. Or his journalism degree from the University of Maryland. At school, he'd been more interested in hooking up with girls than getting good grades. But once he'd started doing freelance pieces for local newspapers and magazines, his wolf persona gave him an edge nobody else could beat—whether in his blockbuster exposé of hidden government labs salted around the region or his inside view of the puppy mills in the Virginia suburbs.

Right now, as he drove home, he thought more about the woman. She certainly had more guts than brains. She'd be in deep kimchi if a wolf hadn't leaped out of the shadows and disabled her captor.

How did she fit into the puzzle of the Eighteen Club? He meant to find out.

A blast from a car horn startled Savannah Carpenter. Glancing to her right, she saw a motorist flashing his headlights—and realized hers were still off. Good thing a cop hadn't spotted her.

After turning on her lights, she glanced nervously in her rearview mirror again. It didn't look like anyone was following her up Connecticut Avenue. Thank God.

As far as she knew, nobody had been close enough to see her license plate—except the big dog or wolf, or whatever it had been. And animals didn't take down numbers.

But there was no use lying to herself. The dog had saved her bacon. She shuddered, remembering the look in the guard's eyes. He'd been excited about capturing her. And eager to turn her over to whoever ran the Eighteen Club.

Her very expensive camera was still back there. Thank God that was the only casualty of the encounter. And thank God she hadn't slapped a name tag on the damn thing!

She headed uptown, toward Bethesda, Maryland, to the small house she'd rented a year ago.

The brick rancher was in a settled neighborhood on a quiet tree-lined street, where all the homes were well kept. The garage had been converted into a recreation room. It had massive windows facing north, perfect for an art studio.

She'd moved to D.C. to be closer to her sister. But Charlotte had kept their contact limited. They'd talked on the phone more than they'd seen each other—until her sister had ended up in the George Washington University Hospital. In a coma. And the police had found Savannah's name in her wallet.

Since then, Savannah had felt cast adrift in a sea of uncertainty, struck with a terrible sense that she didn't know much about Charlotte's life at all. Starting with her expensive apartment.

How could someone who worked as a dance instruc-
tor in a studio above a restaurant afford a place like
that? Well, since reading Charlotte's diary, she was
pretty sure someone else was paying the rent.

After pulling into the driveway and cutting the engine, she started to get out of the car. Then she stopped
and glanced around.

When she realized she was looking for a large,
vicious dog, she made a snorting sound. What did she
think—that the animal she'd seen in Rock Creek Park
had somehow followed her home, running like the wind
to keep up with her car? And that he was hiding in
the azaleas, ready to jump out at her when she got out of
the car?

Still, she was unable to shake the feeling that someone was watching her. Not just tonight. Since her sister's accident.

She sighed. That had to be paranoia.

And ditto for her worry about the dog. Even if he
were here, why would he attack her? She'd initially
thought he was part of the security force. Then he'd
rescued her, and she'd run for her life.

Unanswered questions swam in her head. Could a
dog understand the concept of a gun? Or was he just responding to the threatening tone of the guard's voice?

She couldn't explain what had happened back there
in the woods. Still feeling creeped out, she exited the car,
locked the door behind her, and hurried up the walk.

Once she had closed the door with a satisfying thud,
she let out a sigh of relief. Coming home to her own
environment always did wonders for her stress level.

The house was decorated exactly the way she
wanted it—with artwork she'd collected on her travels,

upholstery in soothing earth tones, and a minimal amount of furniture.

She lived and worked here. Her usual routine was to paint during the day, then relax in the evenings, although she hadn't done much painting since Charlotte's accident. She'd started a picture of her sister, but it was still sitting on the easel.

Luckily, her one-woman show at the Wordsworth Gallery downtown in D.C. had just about sold out. So she had ample cash on hand. But sometime soon, she would need to get back in gear.

She'd spent the first few nights after the accident at the hospital, talking to her sister and holding her hand—when the staff would let her into the intensive care unit.

The sight of Charlotte lying in that narrow bed, pale and lifeless and surrounded by machinery, made her throat close.

In response to her murmured words, Charlotte had stirred—as though she knew Savannah was there.

"What is it, sweetheart? Do you want to tell me something? What were you doing in Rock Creek Park at night? Did you really fall off an outcropping of rocks? Or did something else happen? Did someone push you?"

Charlotte hadn't answered. But Savannah sensed that her sister desperately wanted to tell her something, and as her own frustration had grown, she'd gone to Charlotte's apartment and started poking into her sister's life.

She'd gotten her first shock when she'd stepped into the living room and seen the decor of bright clashing colors and fifties retro furniture.

It had been a long time since she and Charlotte had lived in the same house. Was this really her sister's taste? Or had someone set her up in these garish surroundings?

They had grown up in an upper-middle-class environment in a small town called Catonsville, just south of Baltimore, where their parents had been into real estate and an ultraconservative mindset. Savannah had been the good girl—the one who toed the line because she'd wanted her parents' approval. She'd gone to the college they'd selected for her. She'd even married the man they'd picked, for God's sake.

She shuddered when she thought of that disastrous episode—before she'd turned her life around.

But what about Charlotte? Her sister was the one who'd dared to be a rebel from the first. She'd gotten caught smoking on the playground in sixth grade. She'd gotten caught at a couple of drug and alcohol parties the next year. She'd gotten expelled for cheating more than once.

Since moving to Bethesda, Savannah had been picking up strange vibrations from her sister. She'd felt like Charlotte was playing with her, dangling a delicious secret she wasn't going to share. Not yet.

Then Charlotte had ended up in a broken heap at the bottom of those rocks.

She'd had a blood alcohol level of point one five. Enough to impair her judgment, but did that explain why she'd been rock climbing in the park at night?

Savannah strode to her bedroom, where she opened a dresser drawer and took out the book she'd found hidden at the bottom of a laundry basket.

She had seen similar volumes in the gift section of
large bookstores—blank notebooks that you could use
for a journal or diary.

This one had a picture of Van Gogh's *Starry Night* on
the cover. With swirls of blue in the sky and bright stars
spread above a sleeping village, it looked mystical.

But there was nothing mystical about what her sister
had written in this private journal. It was very physical.

After the first few moments thumbing through the
notebook, Savannah's heart had started pounding. And
the reaction hadn't lessened as she'd read some of the
entries in detail.

Was this journal really supposed to be private? Or
had Charlotte intended all along to turn it over to her
sister?

And what would be the purpose of that? To show
how much more in tune with her own needs Charlotte
was than Savannah? To make her jealous? To gross her
out? What?

She didn't know. But once she'd opened the book,
she'd felt compelled to bring it home. And she kept
coming back to it. Perhaps because it was an important
link with her sister. Or perhaps because the scenes
Charlotte had written in such vivid detail stirred something inside her.

# CHAPTER
# THREE

SAVANNAH TURNED ON the light, sat down in the comfortable chair where she liked to relax, and flipped through the diary, stopping as a word leaped out at her.

*Handcuffs.*

She squeezed her eyes shut, then forced herself to focus again on the word—and the text surrounding it.

*Me and him played another really exciting game tonight. A game that made me so hot. It started off the way it does a lot of the time. I was waiting for him in one of the special rooms they have at the Eighteen Club. Rooms where you can act out any scene you want to play.*

*That place is so exciting. We had decided I would*

be dressed for bed. With my hair all done up really pretty. They have a beauty shop right there, and they can make you look so elegant.

They never let me go into the wardrobe rooms. But there's this lady who works there. She looks at you, then goes into the back and comes out with wonderful outfits. Stuff that must cost hundreds and thousands of dollars from somewhere like Saks. And some of it must come from places where they do costumes for Hollywood movies.

She found me this fabulous nightgown. Cut high under my breasts with a nipped waist and a full skirt. The fabric was so sheer that you could see everything through it. My nipples, my snatch.

That's all I had on. Once I was dressed I went into a beautiful bedroom, all antique furniture and brocade fabric.

I was at the dressing table, supposed to be taking off my makeup. Only really I left most of it on. My hand was shaking. And I was sitting there creaming my pussy because just thinking about what we were going to do made me so hot.

Then he came bursting through the door, and I couldn't help gasping. He was dressed like a police officer, with a blue uniform and a cap and boots. And he had a gun in his hand.

"You're under arrest," he growled.

"What have I done?" I gasped.

"Don't give me that innocent act. You know you've been a bad girl."

"Yes," I whispered.

He looked so fierce, I was kind of afraid of him. But I played the part I was supposed to play.

"*Are you going to take me down to the police station?*" *I asked.*

"*Not if you do exactly as I say.*"

"*All right. If it keeps me out of jail.*"

"*I have to search you. Stand up. Turn around. Put your hands on that table. Spread your legs.*"

*I did what he asked, standing there with my breasts hanging down and my bottom sticking out. He slapped his gun down on the dresser, then stood behind me, running his hands down my body, touching my breasts and my hips, stroking over my butt.* "*Pull up your skirt. Bunch it around your waist.*"

*I did it. And his fingers probed between my legs. When he found I was already wet, he made a sound like he was hot and satisfied.*

*His finger glided over my naked bottom.*

*Then he spanked me. Five or six sharp slaps that made my skin tingle.*

"*Take off that gown and lie down—on your back,*" *he muttered.*

*I pulled the gown over my head and laid it on the chair, folding it carefully, because I knew he would punish me for that if I didn't do it right.*

*Then I laid down on the bed. When he took out his handcuffs, I felt my stomach clench.*

"*Raise your hands above your head.*"

*I did, and he snapped a cuff around one wrist, then passed the chain through the bars of the brass headboard before cuffing the other wrist.*

*I stared up at him, feeling my heart pound. He looked like he could really hurt me. And I had to keep telling myself this was just a game we both* liked to play—and that I was the one who had suggested it.

He sat down on the bed beside me. "Are your arms okay?" he asked.

My mouth was so dry I could hardly speak, but I managed to say, "Yes."

"Good." His expression turned intense. He reached to cover my breasts with his hands, shaping them to his touch, then pinched the nipples—hard.

It hurt, but it made me tingle, especially between my legs and on my butt where he had spanked me.

My hair was pinned up in sweeping waves. He reached up and took out the pins one by one, setting them carefully on the night table, then combing his fingers through my hair, spreading it out on the pillow around my head.

"That looks so beautiful," he whispered as he climbed off the bed. He looked toward the mirror on the wall, and I followed his gaze. Was someone on the other side of that mirror, watching us?

I didn't like to think so, but there was nothing I could do about it.

He took off his hat and his uniform shirt, baring his broad chest covered with salt-and-pepper hair.

Then he circled one of my ankles with his hand, holding it captive before he brought up a strap attached to the side of the bed. After he secured that ankle, he moved around to the other side of the bed and did the other leg.

My legs were spread apart now. I couldn't move my arms or my feet.

I wanted to close my eyes. But I knew he wouldn't allow that. So I kept them open. He stroked his *fingers along the line where my thighs met my torso. Then inward. His touch was light and teasing. I needed more. Needed him to press against my clit. Stroke me there.*

*Silently trying to tell him what I wanted, I arched my hips.*

*"Naughty, naughty. Don't move," he growled, slapping my breasts, making them sting. He kept looking down at me, his gaze thoughtful. "You don't like to make yourself come in front of me, do you?"*

*"No," I whispered.*

*"Then maybe we'll do it that way. I'll unhook one of your hands, and you can bring yourself off."*

*I wanted to tell him I couldn't do it. That I was too embarrassed. But he kept at me with that maddening, stroking finger, and finally I felt like I was going to explode.*

Savannah had read the rest of the entry in her sister's diary before. She didn't need to read it now.

The whole thing made her skin crawl. She didn't like to picture Charlotte at the mercy of some man, although the scenario had obviously turned her sister on. Savannah told herself she would never enjoy anything like that, but, if she was entirely honest with herself, the fantasy made her hot.

She slapped the diary down on the lamp table and stood up with a jerky motion.

Part of her wanted to throw the book into the trash. But it was evidence and her sister's property. She had combed through it for clues. And she had acquired some information—like about the Eighteen Club and the elaborate arrangements you could make inside.

She'd tried to look the place up in various reference sources, starting with all the usual Internet search engines. There was nothing to latch on to. As far as the written word was concerned, the place didn't even exist.

Tonight, with her frustration reaching boiling point, she'd gone over there to have a look at the place—and see if she could identify some of the people going in and out.

Bad mistake.

Savannah moved restlessly around the bedroom. What had happened to Charlotte? Had her lover gone too far and injured her, and then tried to get rid of the evidence? If so, he'd botched the job.

If you wanted to kill someone, pushing them off some rocks in the park was a stupid idea. But maybe that wasn't how it had happened. Maybe they'd been playing some kind of dangerous game, and she'd lost her balance.

Savannah squeezed her hands into fists. There were too many variables. Too many ways it could have happened. But she wasn't going to give up. She wanted to know the identity of the man her sister had written about in such vivid language. And she wanted to know what he had done to her.

LANCE set his knapsack beside one of the leather chairs in the great room and pulled out the camera.

It was a good-quality digital with a flash card inserted in the side.

He flipped the switch that put the camera on viewing mode and began looking at the pictures. Most had a very similar theme—gardens.

She had pictures of formal gardens. Woodland scenes. Banks of azaleas that he thought must be at the National Arboretum. The secluded garden in back of the Smithsonian Castle.

The woman was a garden freak. There were no people. Only flowers and trees. And none of it was in the least helpful—until he came to the last few shots.

They had obviously been taken at the Eighteen Club. In the light outside the entrance to the Castle, she'd caught some of the guests arriving. One was a wise guy. No way was Lance going to contact him. Senator Carlton was a possibility. But he was well connected and probably dangerous. The last was the matron he'd seen standing beside her Mercedes. He was pretty sure he could get some information out of her. If he could figure out who she was.

Her face was familiar. So who the hell was she? Someone he ought to know. Someone he had seen before. But he couldn't place her. Not yet, anyway.

MILES away, in Seagate, New Jersey, a woman sat in the dark in a wingback chair, laying out tarot cards on the table in front of her.

A floorboard creaked, and she lifted her head knowing it was her husband, Grant Marshall. Once she'd run the old Victorian house where they lived as a bed and breakfast. But since her husband had gone back into the contractor business, they didn't need the money. And they'd both agreed that privacy was more important than the extra income.

However, Antonia still read tarot cards for customers

during the afternoons, because she liked staying connected with the work.

Her husband came up beside her and brushed aside
her long dark hair. Bending down, he nibbled his lips
against her cheek, then touched the silver streak at her
forehead.

"Come back to bed."

She smiled. "To sleep?"

He chuckled. "Not if I can tempt you into something
more aerobic."

"Grant, I have to finish this."

"You're doing a reading? For us?"

She caught the tightness in his voice and reached for
his hand. "Everything's fine with us—and the baby."

She was carrying his child, and they had both been
anxious until they'd found out it was a boy, because
only the male offspring of a werewolf had a chance of
survival, at least until this generation. But she knew he
was still nervous about the unborn werewolf growing
within her.

"You wouldn't keep anything from me?" he pressed.

"Never." She cleared her throat. "It's about Lance. I
started thinking about him tonight, and I had to get up."

He sucked in a breath. "Why Lance?"

"He's in trouble."

Grant leaned over, and she knew he was studying the
cards she'd laid out. Since their marriage, he'd learned a
lot about the tarot. Because he was interested in what
she did, she always explained her thinking about the
cards.

"What do you see?" he asked in a gritty tone.

*See* was a relative term.

She was blind. But she had worked with the tarot for many years before she'd lost her sight. Now her many decks had braille markings in one corner. When she rubbed her finger over them, she saw the picture in her mind.

Two years ago, when Grant Marshall had been on his way to Seagate to kill a murderer, a wolf had appeared in a lot of the pictures she saw in her mind—so she'd been prepared for him when he arrived. And prepared to stop him from doing something he'd regret.

Now she was focused on his brother.

There were various ways of doing a reading. Tonight she had laid out three cards. She pointed to the one on the left—the Ten of Swords. It showed a man lying facedown on the ground, with ten swords piercing his body.

Grant shifted his weight from one foot to the other. "I know that looks gruesome. But you've told me that represents the end of a cycle," he said. "Like quitting a job or getting divorced."

"He's not married. And he works freelance."

"Yeah."

She stroked her finger over the card. "This picture could mean sudden misfortune. Especially when it's combined with this one." She pointed to another card— the Tower. "He's facing the unexpected. A sudden change."

He winced when he looked at the last card. "The Devil."

"It could represent sensuality, bondage to fear, or sexual energy," she said quickly.

"Nothing wrong with sexual energy," he said, his hand drifting down the front of Antonia's body to stroke the top of one full breast. Dipping lower, he discovered that the nipple was hard.

"Maybe he's met his life mate," Grant muttered. "He's past the usual age."

"And determined not to let it happen to him."

"He may not have a choice," her husband said, reminding her of the way he'd fought their relationship.

After almost two years of marriage, they couldn't get enough of each other. And she felt herself drifting into the fog of sensuality he was weaving around her. But she fought the sexual pull. Reaching for his hand, she moved it away from her breast. "I was trying to explain about Lance."

He sighed. "The cards. Yeah."

"I go as much by feelings as by each individual card. Like the insights I had about you when you got here. I could tell you were in trouble—big trouble."

"I know."

"I feel a dark presence hovering over Lance."

"Is that something literal or figurative?"

"I don't know. But will you call him tomorrow and ask if he's started on a new project or met a new woman?"

"I can ask, but he may clam up. You know we need to feel like we're in control of our own lives."

"I know, but tell him I have a strong premonition," she said, hoping Grant could get through to him.

# CHAPTER
# FOUR

•

RAYMOND CONRAD STOOD on the balcony behind an ornate screen, watching the late-night crowd enjoying the more public of the Castle's nightclub rooms.

Everything was as it should be now, although they'd had an incident outside earlier in the evening. The guards had caught a woman in the woods, snooping. Unfortunately she'd gotten away.

Individuals had tried to spy on them before. A few times, they'd even caught reporters mingling with the guests in the room below. That was the price of doing business in the nation's capital.

The incident with the woman had put him on red alert.

He wasn't even sure how she'd gotten away. Warner

had said he'd had her in custody. Then a big dog, prob-ably a German shepherd, had attacked him, and she'd made a run for it. And they'd both gotten away.

Raymond had doubled the guard in case she or someone else came back. He made a mental note to discuss the situation with his silent partner, thinking about how he'd phrase the explanation. Of course, that wouldn't be any problem. He had plenty of practice steering conversations in the direction that was most advantageous for him. With his partner and with his clients.

He turned his attention back to the nightclub spread out below him. From his vantage point on the balcony, he could see most of the tables, although nobody could see him because he was standing in a darkened corridor behind an ornate grille.

The room below was decorated in an "Arabian Nights" theme with lots of low brass tables, Oriental rugs, plush chairs, piles of cushions, and diaphanous cur-tains softening the effect of the massive stone walls. The lighting was low, with huge metal chandeliers hung from forged link chains simulating the effect of candlelight.

The waitstaff looked like Middle Eastern slaves, the women in costumes a belly dancer might have worn, the men bare-chested and wearing baggy pants with a wide sash at the waist. All of them were barefoot. And all of them wore a leather collar around their neck with a brass nameplate.

The guests were more eclectic. One of the mayor's aides was here. And a deputy chief of police lounged only a few tables away from one of the most notorious drug dealers in the city. Other guests were from the highest reaches of the federal government.

His gaze swept the room and found a woman who didn't look quite so comfortable. She'd been referred here by a dear friend. But she was still afraid to plunge into the fast-moving waters swirling around her.

Well, he knew how to make her feel more at ease.

She was Erica Wentworth, a widow in her early fifties, with hair dyed light brown and just the suggestion of a double chin. So far she had enjoyed the relaxed atmosphere of this nightclub, but he thought she was ready to try something a bit more daring.

He watched her for a few moments longer, then walked to the other side of the viewing area where he could see the more risqué club room. This one had a medieval theme, with stone walls, rich tapestries, and the female slaves dressed like serving wenches with gowns cut so low that their nipples were barely covered.

Turning away from the window, he descended the steps and paused to check his reflection in the full-length mirror.

If he were evaluating one of his customers, he'd call himself handsome, well built, vigorous, with just a touch of gray at his dark temples. And he was definitely well heeled in his Savile Row suit, off-white shirt, and Armani loafers.

He wasn't a vain man. But he knew he was attractive—to both men and women, which was an important asset in his line of work.

In the nightclub, he stopped to chat with several customers before wending his way to Erica Wentworth's table.

"May I join you?" he asked.

"Of course."

He lowered himself to the wide, pillow-covered bench beside her. "I hope you're enjoying yourself."

"Yes."

"I was thinking you and I might discuss some of the special features of the Eighteen Club."

"I was thinking that, too," she answered quickly, yet he detected the edge of nerves in her voice.

"Why don't we go to my study, where we can be perfectly private."

"All right." She rose gracefully and followed him out of the room and down a hall to the plush den that he used for interviews. He'd always thought of it like a psychiatrist's office, where he teased the most intimate secrets out of people.

"Please, make yourself comfortable."

He'd done a background check on her. He knew she was used to life's luxuries. He knew her husband had made a lot of money with a drugstore chain that he'd sold in the seventies, then he'd invested his funds in a variety of businesses around the city. Her two children were grown and married. She was rattling around in the house in Potomac that she'd lived in for the past fifteen years—and bored with the life of a society lady. That she'd come to the Eighteen Club several times over the past week meant she was willing to entertain the idea of a sexual adventure. But she needed a little push in the right direction.

When she'd taken a comfortable chenille-covered chair, he said, "I've been enjoying an excellent Merlot. Can I offer you a glass?"

"Yes, please," she answered.

Her extreme politeness announced that she wasn't exactly at ease.

He brought them each a drink, then sat in the chair on the other side of the lamp table and gave her his most sincere smile, projecting friendship and camaraderie. "So what do you think of us so far?"

"I think you run a very . . . comfortable establishment. A place where patrons can . . . let down their hair."

"I'm glad we've made you comfortable. But you've barely scratched the surface. If you're ready for an adventure, we can give it to you."

She shifted in her chair. "What sort of adventure?"

"That depends on you. What fantasies have you thought you'd never get a chance to fulfill?"

A flush spread across her cheeks. "It's hard to tell someone your secret fantasies."

"Believe me, I know. But many people have shared their yearnings with me—because I can make their most secret desires come true. The staff of the Eighteen Club and I are here to serve you. You're the one in charge here. We can give you anything you want."

He gave her a gentle prod, using a question that often helped people open up with him. "Do you ever wish you lived in another time?"

"Sometimes."

"When?"

"I've studied the Roman empire. It has a lot of appeal for me."

"A very dynamic era!"

"Yes."

"If you lived then, you'd be a wealthy matron—the mistress of a villa looking down on the Mediterranean," he guessed.

"Yes," she said in a faraway voice.

He had a good imagination, and he had a pretty good notion of this fantasy. "You'd be in charge of a household full of slaves," he murmured.

She looked up at him, then down at her hands again, and he could feel the tension radiating from her.

"Your husband is away at war. And you have your pick of some very handsome and desirable male slaves brought back from the far reaches of the empire."

She took her lower lip between her teeth.

"You can take any one of them you want to bed— where he devotes himself to your pleasure."

She nodded.

He was guiding her through the fantasy, making it easy for her to tell him her desires. Yet he still didn't have the whole picture. He hazarded a guess. "And sometimes you need to punish them."

"Yes," she whispered.

Her eyes were bright, and he now had an excellent idea of what she would like to do, given the chance.

"Here in the Eighteen Club, we can give you that experience. If you like, we could start with a very private slave auction, where you could pick the man you want. Then you can take him to your villa and do anything you want with him."

He watched her consider that, watched her react to the fantasy. It was turning her on. But she was still cautious.

"This is a very safe environment," he said, "where you can try out anything you can imagine. And if you find you don't like the scenario, you can always walk right out of the room."

He was enjoying her hesitation. Enjoying the feeling of her teetering on the brink of discovery.

She swallowed. "How would I set something like that up?"

"You just have to tell me what you want, and I'll make all the arrangements."

He knew when to press his advantage, when not to let a flapping fish off the hook. "Why not slip into a fantasy this evening? You can go to our beauty and wardrobe salon and get ready. And I'll have the rooms set up."

She looked slightly dazed. But when she spoke, her voice was firm. "I'd like to think about it."

"You're sure you want to wait?"

"Yes."

"All right. If you'd like to go ahead, you can come back tomorrow afternoon."

"Tomorrow evening."

He managed to keep any disappointment out of his voice as he said, "You're the one in charge. The evening it is."

He smiled and ushered her out. If he could get her into the beauty salon, she would go for the rest of the package. The salon was in the lower reaches of the Castle, two stories below ground level. Down there a kind of magic operated. People forgot their conventional morality. They felt liberated, and they did things they might not do in the real world. Afterward they wondered what had come over them, but they paid the hefty bills from the Eighteen Club and came back for more.

They also responded to his personal style since he was a model of calm and reason. Unless someone threatened to make trouble for him, he never lost his temper. Instead, he would gently show them why they didn't want to go public with any information about him—starting with the pictures he'd secretly taken of their indiscretions.

Some of them would cave in, acknowledging that he was holding the winning hand. Others would threaten to have him killed.

He'd only shrug and tell them to go ahead and try it. He had protections they didn't know about. Because his silent partner was dedicated to making sure that the Eighteen Club continued to run smoothly.

He felt a little shiver travel over his skin. Sometimes he felt like he was in over his head. Then he'd remind himself that if you sat back and hoped for the best, you'd get screwed.

He'd learned that as one of five children in the Coddington family. You had to grab a chicken leg or a breast if that was what you wanted—otherwise you'd end up with the stringy back.

So he'd worked hard to get a college scholarship, and waited tables the whole time he was in school. After getting a degree in hospitality management at the University of Florida, he'd changed his name from Coddington to Conrad, then worked at several prestigious hotels to get some experience. It was through a former employee that he'd heard about the Eighteen Club. And he'd been fascinated. Still, he'd given himself a couple more years of career building before applying for a job.

Back then, the Castle had been owned by Dave O'Hare, who had been doing okay. He'd helped O'Hare bring the operation into the twenty-first century. And they'd signed an agreement making him a partner.

The next bit was a little confusing. Mr. Boralas had come to O'Hare wanting to buy into the business. But O'Hare had turned him down.

A few days after that, O'Hare had died, and Raymond had taken over—with the help of his new partner.

He pressed his fingers to his temples. When he tried to think about that few weeks of his own history, it was never quite clear in his mind. It had happened a long time ago.

A long time? No. Three years wasn't all that long.

A little kernel of doubt gnawed like a tumor inside his chest, and he drew in a deep breath. Taking a sip of the Merlot, he grounded himself in the reality of his life. He was doing just fine—fantastic. And he had to keep believing that, or he was lost.

# CHAPTER
# FIVE

LANCE MARSHALL HELD a mug of pungent tea in his hands. After taking a sip, he grimaced at the taste.

The brew was pretty awful. He'd like to toss the plastic bag of leaves and stems in the trash. Instead he kept drinking it, the way he had every day for the past two-plus years.

He stared out one of the large picture windows, his eyes barely focusing on the park land bordering his home. He'd gotten two phone calls from his family that morning, one from Ross and one from Grant.

And he was feeling hemmed in, as he always did when he had to deal with other werewolves. He and the other Marshall men weren't cut out for working together.

But Ross Marshall, his cousin, was trying to change

the pattern. Which was why Lance had felt comfortable enough to ask him about that license plate last night.

The car belonged to Savannah Carpenter. Lance had been at the computer looking her up when Grant had called—with a warning from his tarot card–reading wife.

He'd heard the strain in his brother's voice. As far as he could tell, Grant hadn't wanted to make the call. But it sounded like Antonia had insisted. Is that what happened when a werewolf found his life mate—he started letting her boss him around?

Lance knew there was a certain give-and-take in his parents' marriage. His father was the head honcho, but his mom used subtle ways of getting what she wanted. So he recognized the signs of wife interference. He'd listened politely to Grant, then said he could take care of himself.

The next thing he did was open up the pantry and get out the plastic bag of herbs that he'd purchased from a grocery store in D.C.'s Chinatown.

About three years ago, he'd written a story on traditional Chinese medicine. By the time he was finished, he'd decided that maybe an herb mixture might be good for him—as insurance that he could avoid the typical werewolf pattern of bonding with a life mate when they reached their thirties.

Of course there were no combinations made specifically for werewolves who wanted to avoid a ball and chain. But based on the properties of various herbs, he'd made up his own concoction. It was a kind of anti-love potion.

So far it looked like it was working. He'd started taking it two years ago, when he was still only twenty-nine.

At thirty-one he was past the age of bonding. And he hadn't met any woman he'd had the slightest urge to sleep next to until death did them part.

He was still enjoying the werewolf charisma that made him attractive as a bed partner—without being saddled with the responsibilities of marriage and children.

He liked his life the way it was. There were plenty of deer in the park to satisfy his hunting urges. And he could stay up until all hours of the night working, if that was what he wanted to do. So he'd secretly found Grant's call disturbing.

What had Antonia been worried about? Deep down in the part of him that cleaved to old superstitions, he wanted to ask her if she saw a life mate in his future. But he was damned if he would acknowledge that his brother's wife had any power over him.

Doggedly, he went back to work. Soon he was deep into his research again, fascinated with the subject of Savannah Carpenter. She'd gone to the University of Pennsylvania, where she'd participated in several student art shows. Those early works had sold to collectors. Now, although she was only in her late twenties, she was already a painter with a considerable reputation in the art world.

So why was she interested in the Eighteen Club? And why hadn't she taken a more direct approach? Too bad that information wasn't in the online material he'd read. Didn't she realize that a woman with her reputation wouldn't have any trouble getting a membership to the Castle?

He finished off the tea in a few quick swallows, then went back to the computer. Ms. Carpenter had never finished her degree at the University of Pennsylvania. But she'd stayed in Philadelphia to begin her career. Apparently, one of her professors had recognized her talent and gone out of his way to introduce her to gallery owners.

She'd taken a brief side trip into marriage. He couldn't get much information on that part of her life, because she didn't talk about it in any of her interviews. But Lance saw that she'd been Mrs. Frank Thompson for less than a year.

He studied a series of her paintings from a gallery Web site. All of them depicted lush gardens, which explained the photos in the camera. But what set her work apart were the people inhabiting the scenes. One in particular showed a woman in a sun-drenched setting that might have been on a Caribbean island. She was lying on a wicker chaise, looking languid and relaxed in a gauzy white dress, with her blond hair spilling down to the side as she tipped her head back.

Was it a portrait of the artist? The picture projected a heated sensuality that made his stomach knot, but could she stand up to Raymond Conrad?

The man played rough, as Ms. Carpenter had discovered last night. If she was going back to Conrad's territory, she needed a bodyguard.

But not him, Lance told himself. If he knew what was good for him, he was going to stay as far away from Savannah Carpenter as possible. She unsettled him. Threw him off balance. And he didn't like that feeling at all.

In the next moment, he changed his mind. Maybe she could be useful to him. What harm would there be in trying to figure out what she was up to?

When he caught himself going down the hall to the closet where he kept his disguises, he made a low sound in this throat, then tore off his clothes, changed to wolf form, and went for a run in the park.


ERICA lay in a comfortable chair, letting the beautician work on her hair, feeling a strange mixture of relaxation and excitement. She could still back out, she told herself. She had that option, right until the last minute.

The Erica Wentworth who played it safe could get up and leave. But she wasn't that woman. Not here. In the depths of this stone castle, she felt a freedom she had never experienced before.

Because Raymond Conrad had given her permission to finally let her fantasies flow freely.

He was so understanding, so willing to fulfill the urges she'd had since she began having sexual feelings but had never had the guts to act upon. Not even with her husband—especially not with stick-in-the-mud Jerome Wentworth—whose male prerogative had dominated their sex life. Jay's idea of a hot time was watching a porn movie, then asking her to go down on him.

She'd done it, because that was part of the package of being married to a powerful man who could give her all the luxuries she'd never had.

She had a mansion in Potomac. A house down at Rehobeth Beach. She could buy any clothes she wanted. And when he'd been alive, her husband had loved to see her wearing the jewelry he bought her.

But she'd paid a price for her lifestyle. Jay spent long hours at the office. He'd had his mistresses. And maybe he would have discarded Erica for a younger wife if he hadn't died of a heart attack before he got the chance.

She could marry again. But now that she was a millionaire many times over, she didn't know if the men she met were after her for the intelligent, sexy woman she was or for her money.

Which was why she'd ended up at the Eighteen Club, where her friend Mildred Dickinson had told her that you didn't have to worry about relationships, only sexual pleasure.

The beautician, a woman named Bonnie, had spoken to her earlier while she worked, telling her what she might do with the slave she selected. The suggestions made her blush, but she had listened with rapt attention.

Bonnie interrupted her thoughts.

"Would you like to see yourself?"

As the woman slowly tipped the chair up, Erica's eyes blinked open. When she stared at herself in the mirror, she was astonished at the transformation.

"Oh!"

"You look lovely."

She had to agree. Her skin had a wonderful glow. And her hair was fixed in a sexy upsweep.

Before Bonnie had started working, Erica had donned a gown that looked like it could have adorned a Roman goddess. It clung softly to her curves, and it was just the right shade of mauve to set off her hair and eyes. She didn't need a bra. The bodice was built to lift and support her breasts, pushing them up so that her cleavage showed to its best advantage.

Leather sandals completed the ensemble.

The door opened and another woman came in. She

was also dressed in a Roman gown, although the fabric was not quite so fine.

"I'm Susanna. I can take you to the slave market now."

Erica felt a little tremor of fear. Was she really going through with this?

If she had been anywhere else, she would have backed out. But this place kept the excitement churning inside her.

Susanna took her arm. "Come along. Let's see which slave you like."

Erica's heart was pounding as she followed the other woman down a corridor, then into a dimly lit viewing area with stone walls and a row of stone archways in front of her.

On the other side of the arches, lights illuminated what might have been a Roman marketplace. There were carts at one side, holding produce and flowers.

But they were hardly the center of attention.

Ten naked men were lined up along the other side of the market facing her. Each was standing with his hands chained above his head to a horizontal beam that stretched the length of the slave area.

A man dressed like a Roman general strode up and down the line of slaves.

When he spoke to one of the men, his voice was gruff.

"You, stand up straighter," he growled, then lashed the slave across the chest with the short whip he carried in his hand.

The man made a sharp sound, and Erica felt an unexpected sexual jolt. The slave master muttered something to another captive, then lashed him as well.

Erica shuddered with excitement. The master strode in back of the men, saying that they were getting what they deserved as he lashed out at random at their backs and buttocks.

Erica heard the sting of leather against flesh. Her knees weakened and she grabbed a pillar next to her.

"They're all so sexy, aren't they?" Susanna whispered.

"Yes," she managed.

"Do you know which one you want to take back to your villa? Or do you want more than one?"

"One," Erica whispered through parched lips. Between her legs, she was very wet. And she knew her nipples must be standing up against the front of her gown.

"Do you want to see them punished again?"

"No." She licked her lips. "Give me a minute."

She contemplated the line of men, looking at each face, each penis, each male body. Some had hair on their chests. Other chests were smooth.

Most of them were circumcised. Two were not.

All of them were in their twenties and thirties. They all looked like they worked out every day.

"Can I go out there?"

"Of course."

She let go of the pillar, waited a moment to make sure she was steady on her feet, then walked through the archway, into the light.

The slaves all watched her, some directly, some more covertly through lowered lashes.

She had turned herself on imagining scenes like this. The reality was even more arousing.

Almost in a daze, she walked among them, breathing in their masculine scent. And as she grew bolder, she touched them, stroking an arm or a thigh or a firm butt.

She stopped by a man with a thick head of brown hair and a nice crinkly rug spreading across his chest. He was one of the older ones. Not her age, but not a baby, either. She saw his penis stir. He was responding to her. And that made her decision.

She cleared her throat and tried to sound commanding. "This one."

The slave master strode over and detached the chain from the overhead beam, allowing the man to lower his arms, but the chain stayed attached to his wrist cuffs. He shook his arms, probably to work the kinks out of his muscles.

"You can take him to your villa." The slave master's voice cut through the fog in her head. He ushered her around the corner to a wooden doorway. "If you wish to uncuff him, the key is on the table by the door."

Trying to keep from trembling, she grasped the chain and led her captive inside.

When she had closed the door, he asked, "How may I serve you?"

The words made her feel powerful. He was hers to use as she wished. She could punish him if she liked. Maybe she would do that later. She was too aroused for that now.

It was impossible to hold her hands steady, so it took several tries to get the key into the lock of his cuffs. She took them off.

"Touch me. Take off my dress," she commanded.

"Is it permitted to kiss you?" he asked in a low voice.

"Yes."

He loosened the tie at the back of her dress and drew it over her head, stroking her and nibbling at her with his lips as he worked. When she was naked, he lifted her breasts in his hands, then plucked at her hardened nipples.

She saw that his penis was erect, and she caressed him lightly, feeling his excitement and her own.

Emotions that she had kept bottled up for a long time bubbled to the surface of her mind. Feeling a kind of feverish excitement, she looked around the room.

She felt like she had stepped into another world. A small but comfortable world suited to her needs. On a rack along one wall, she saw whips, paddles, leather cuffs, and collars. A luxurious bed commanded another wall. And in one corner, she saw a gold and velvet chair that made her think of a throne.

A wicked idea came to her. Maybe something that would only have occurred to her in this room. After walking across the thick Oriental carpet, she sat in the chair.

"What is your name?" she asked.

"Kevin."

She contemplated her slave. "Stroke your penis, Kevin. Let me see what you do to make yourself hot. But don't bring yourself to climax."

He did as she asked, his hand moving up and down his shaft.

"Stop!"

His hand instantly stopped.

"Kneel in front of me," she said in a thick voice as she opened her legs. "Use your mouth to make me come."

# CHAPTER
## SIX

LANCE HELD OUT for three days. Finally he told himself that he had exhausted all other leads, and he needed Savannah Carpenter.

That might be true, but he knew the need had turned into something more personal than a writing assignment.

As he made plans, he dressed in a navy sports jacket, white button-down shirt, and gray slacks. A very conservative outfit. Then he picked up the blindingly blond wig that he sometimes used because he knew that if anyone was asked to describe him, they'd focus on the platinum hair and the total picture of a well-dressed guy in a sports jacket and slacks.

Before he went out, he grabbed a pair of large sunglasses that hid his eyes and distorted the shape of his face. As he checked his appearance in the bedroom mirror, he decided it would do nicely.

The wig made his head feel hot. But that was a small price to pay for a very effective disguise.

His next stop was the garage, where he kept several vehicles, an SUV, a Lexus, and a five-year-old Saturn. For surveillance, he usually used the Saturn. There were a lot of them on the road, which helped make the car invisible, as did its burgundy color.

When he reached Savannah Carpenter's neighborhood, he drove down a few streets, looking at mid-twentieth-century homes, small yards, and lots of neatly tended flower gardens.

Most of the residents seemed to be at work. He had no trouble finding a parking spot fifty yards from the Carpenter house, where he sat in his car trying to look like a real estate agent casing the neighborhood.

Forty minutes later, a woman came out and walked quickly to a green Honda parked in the driveway.

His heart started to pound the moment he saw her. Trying to ignore the reaction, he took in details. She was the same height as the ninja from the Castle. About five seven. Slender. Light eyes. The last time he'd seen her, her head had been covered. Today he saw that she had gloriously long blond hair—like the woman in the painting—and he felt a thrill of recognition.

She was wearing brown pants and a green blouse with a blue and green scarf at the neck. Earth, trees, and sky. Appropriate for a woman who liked to paint garden scenes. But more conservative than her paintings. The contrast between the artist and her work made him think she repressed her sensuality in her personal life but let it blossom in her art.

*Very poetic, Marshall. Where did that come from?*

She climbed into her car and drove toward D.C. Not upper northwest where the Eighteen Club was located but farther downtown.

On the fringes of The George Washington University, she pulled into a parking garage, and he did the same—then stayed well back as he followed her on foot to the entrance.

But they both had to stop to let a couple of cars pass, and she glanced in his direction. He kept his eyes straight ahead, trying not to react to her delicious scent. But it wafted toward him like an airborne love potion.

He swore inwardly, wishing he hadn't chosen those words.

When she started down the block, he seriously considered giving up the surveillance operation. Then he told himself that he'd already gone to a lot of trouble to follow her this far.

Dropping back, he let her get ahead of him, then followed her to the main entrance of the university's hospital.

In the lobby, he stayed out of the way as she checked in at the front desk. But his hearing was much better than most. She was visiting a woman named Charlotte Nichols, in ICU. When he'd talked to people who knew something about the Castle, her name had come up. She'd been a guest there on more than one occasion. And someone had remarked that she was in over her head.

A couple of weeks ago, she'd disappeared from the scene. Now she was in ICU.

He went down a back corridor toward the cafeteria. When a hospital staffer stepped out of a stairwell, he caught the door, then slipped inside and walked to the third floor. As he climbed the stairs, he reached into his knapsack and got out one of the name tags he always carried with him. It said he was Dr. James Martin. It wouldn't fool anyone if they gave it a good look, but to the casual observer, it would help him blend in.

He walked toward the ICU, then stood at the entrance, studying the layout. Like most similar units, it had a monitoring station surrounded by rooms with open sliding glass doors and curtains, to give the staff maximum access to patients.

Savannah had stepped inside the room closest to the door and was leaning over a woman lying on a bed. Her head was wrapped in bandages, her eyes were closed, and her body was connected to various tubes and monitors.

As if Savannah knew she was being observed, she turned her head. He spun on his heel, pretending he'd changed his mind about going into the unit.

Heart thumping, he hurried down the hall, half expecting her to call out and follow him. But apparently she had turned back to the woman on the bed.

Charlotte Nichols.

Savannah Carpenter knew her well enough to visit her in the hospital—which made it a good bet that she was the reason for the late-night invasion of the woods outside the Castle.

SAVANNAH waited several moments, then whipped her head around—staring toward the door of the unit. The man she'd seen didn't reappear.

The feeling of being watched had made her glance over her shoulder in the first place. And she'd caught a glimpse of him looking at her. As soon as she'd spotted him, he'd turned away.

But her work had made her a quick study. He looked like the guy who had been in the garage with her. At least, both men had the same build. The same blond hair and etched facial features. The Roman nose, lips that were just a touch too thin to be called sensual. And, come to think of it, the same navy sports coat.

She'd taken in all those details because the man had interested her. Or—she'd sensed that he was interested in *her*, even when he was pretending otherwise.

Had he followed her from the garage? The question sent a shiver up her spine.

Did his being here have something to do with a few nights ago, at the Eighteen Club? She'd assumed that only the big dog was right behind her when she'd run. Had one of the security men gotten close enough to copy down her license number?

She tried to dismiss the idea as paranoid. But suddenly it was difficult to breathe.

She thought about going to the police. But what was she going to say—that she'd been spying on the Eighteen Club and had gotten caught? That she'd escaped, but now the guards were coming after her?

Oh, sure!

Struggling for calm, she turned back to her sister and reached for her hand. The nurses wouldn't let her stay long, and she'd better make the most of her visit.

"How are you?" she murmured. "You look better."

It was true. The bruises were fading. But that was

only an external improvement. She'd tried every way she knew to connect with Charlotte. Now, once again, she began talking about their childhood. "Remember that time when Dad sent me to my room without any supper, and you sneaked upstairs with some shredded wheat for me? Or that time you cut your leg, and we were afraid to tell anyone so we cleaned it up and bandaged it? We were always there for each other when we were little. Let me help you now."

Charlotte made a sound, and Savannah went very still.

"Yes? What is it? Do you want to tell me something?"

Charlotte's lips moved around the breathing tube, but no sound came out.

Footsteps from the doorway made Savannah whirl. The man was back!

No, it was a nurse. "I'm sorry, but you're disturbing her. Her pulse and breathing are elevated. Perhaps you should come back later."

"Do you think she knows who I am?"

"I can't say." Although the nurse gave her a sympathetic look, her voice remained firm. "I'm sorry, but you can't stay here now."

"Can I come back later?"

"We can see what happens."

Frustrated, Savannah exited the cubicle. Her sister wanted to tell her something. But trying to talk hadn't been good for her.

Savannah stayed at the hospital several more hours, nursing a cup of coffee in the cafeteria and going in to see Charlotte at regular intervals, hoping that her sister would respond to her again. But no luck.

Finally she left, feeling more depressed than when she had arrived. After she exited the building, she looked for signs that someone was following her. As far as she could tell, the coast was clear, so she hurried back to her car and drove home.

# CHAPTER
# SEVEN

SAVANNAH PACED THE length of her living room. She had hoped and prayed that Charlotte would be awake by now so her sister could tell her about the night of the accident. It hadn't happened, but maybe there was another alternative—the clutter all over Charlotte's apartment. Unopened mail. Receipts. Bills. Scraps of paper. She should have looked through them earlier, but she'd kept expecting Charlotte to wake up.

She glanced at her watch. Making a split-second decision, she grabbed her purse—and one more thing. The gun she'd bought after one of her neighbors' houses had been broken into.

She'd never fired the damn thing. She hadn't even had it with her at the Eighteen Club. But maybe she'd better make it a regular part of her accessories, even if she didn't have a permit to carry a concealed weapon.

Outside on the walk, she dragged in a draft of the humid night air and looked around, because she still couldn't shake the notion that someone was out here watching her.

The guy she'd spotted at the hospital?

She hoped not.

Trying not to look like she was spooked in her own driveway, she hurried to her car. Once she was inside with the doors locked, she breathed out a little sigh.

As she started down the street, another car pulled out behind her, and she tensed. When it dropped back several yards, she told herself she was being paranoid.

Stepping on the gas, she watched for a break in the traffic, then plowed onto Wisconsin Avenue.

Two cars honked furiously at her. And one motorist shook his fist in a classic demonstration of road rage, but she pretended she was in the right and kept going.

As she drove, she kept looking in the rearview mirror. If the car had been following her, she'd probably lost him. Still, she turned up several side streets, watching her back. Only when she was sure nobody was tailing her did she head for her sister's apartment.

She felt like she was in the middle of a spy movie. Or maybe whatever had happened to Charlotte had spilled over into her own life.


SAVANNAH stepped inside her sister's apartment and took several deep breaths.

It smelled okay, since she'd emptied the garbage under the sink and washed the pile of dirty dishes on the counter and in the sink.

The decor was still jarring, but she kept her gaze away from the clashing color combinations as she walked through the rooms.

When she came to a stack of bills lying on the dresser, she stopped. She had seen that pile of papers before. But it looked different now—as if somebody had shuffled through it.

She poked at the papers with her finger, then involuntarily glanced over her shoulder. No one was standing in the doorway, and she ordered herself to relax. Still, she made a quick search of the apartment, before hurrying back to the front door and throwing the security bolt.

As she stood in the hallway, she clenched and unclenched her hands, hating herself for feeling so jumpy. But she'd swear someone else had been in here searching through Charlotte's things.

Were they looking for the diary?

She felt a shudder go through her. What if the man in those entries knew about the book and wanted to make sure nobody was clued in to his presence in Charlotte's life? Who was he? She'd like to get a list of the members of the Eighteen Club. Yeah, sure.

If her sister had had a computer, Savannah would have checked her e-mails. But Charlotte had refused to participate in that form of communication. She trusted paper and pen. Like the damn diary. So Savannah collected bills and other junk from around the apartment and dumped the mess beside her on the bright orange couch. First she looked at credit card statements.

Charlotte was using four different credit cards. They all had a hefty balance—many of the charges incurred at expensive clothing shops. She had a standing appointment at the beauty shop that cost her seventy-five dollars every two weeks. And she was having expensive laser treatments to remove the hair from her legs.

Savannah grimaced. Couldn't her sister just shave like everybody else? Or maybe she was still defying their father, who had been so harsh with them any time they'd shown signs of displaying their budding sexuality. Savannah remembered the first time Charlotte had shaved her legs, and Dad had flown into a rage, accused her of turning into a tramp, and beat her. She cut off that memory and went back to business.

The receipts didn't give Savannah any insights into what had happened to her sister. But she did find something that might be a lead, as they said on the detective shows.

Charlotte had thrown five matchbooks onto her dresser. Four were from expensive restaurants. But one was from a club in Hyattsville. Not exactly the D.C. area high-rent district.

She went back to the credit slips. There were no charges for any of the restaurants, which meant Charlotte hadn't gone alone. Someone had taken her—or the matchbooks had been sitting there for months, long before the current credit card bills.

There was also no credit slip for the club, but if Charlotte had gone in and had some drinks, she might have paid cash—or let some guy pick up the bill.

Either way, the matchbooks might lead her to someone who knew her sister.

LANCE turned onto Savannah's street and was startled to see a shadow slip down her driveway and onto the sidewalk.

It was a man, dressed in black. The way Savannah had been dressed at the Castle. The man got into a car parked half a dozen houses down and sped away. Lance's vehicle was pointed in the wrong direction, and the light over the guy's license plate was burned out. Before he could turn his own car around, the vehicle had vanished.

He made a disgusted sound. He'd lost the guy, but at least he was free to do his own snooping.

Finding an unoccupied house, he went into the back-yard and changed to wolf form. Then he trotted back to Savannah's place.

Her car wasn't in the driveway, or on the street, so he assumed she wasn't home.

Where was she at this late hour? Back at the Castle?

Not likely. She'd gotten a good scare the other night. And unless she was an idiot, she wouldn't try to sneak up on the place again.

He caught her scent in the driveway. But the man's scent was more recent and stronger. He followed it to the backyard. When he came to the sliding glass door, the scent was overpowering.

As he poked around in the bushes, he found something interesting half buried in the mulch—a dirt-colored plastic box.

Nobody else would have found it—unless they had a wolf's sense of smell.

Cautiously, he gave it a good sniff. Then he tapped it with his foot. When it didn't explode, he picked it up in his mouth and carried it back to where he'd left his clothing.

# CHAPTER
# EIGHT

**RUSHING THROUGH THE** ritual of transformation, Lance changed to his human form and pulled on his pants. Then he carefully opened the box. Inside was a directional mike attached to a miniature tape recorder. It wasn't running at the moment, so obviously it was voice-activated.

Jesus!

All his protective instincts came surging up from deep inside his being. Savannah was in bad trouble. And he had to warn her.

*Hell.*

He was acting like . . . acting like . . . his life mate was in trouble.

He struggled to drive the unwanted thought from his mind.

*Focus on the facts,* he ordered himself.

He hated to put the damn thing back. But if he didn't, the guy who'd planted it would know someone had found him out. And that would lengthen the odds of finding him.

With a sick feeling in his gut, Lance changed back to wolf form, then replaced the box where he'd found it by the back door and pawed mulch back on top, all the time keeping an eye peeled for Savannah.

As he slunk out of her yard, he wondered if the neighbors paid any attention to what was going on anywhere besides on their own property.

SAVANNAH took the matchbooks with her and drove to Chez Roger, the closest restaurant, where she showed the maitre d' the picture of her sister that she carried in her wallet.

He stared at it, and she thought she saw a spark of recognition in his eyes. Her throat tightened as she waited for him to give her some information.

Then he shook his head, and she wasn't sure what to do next.

"Would twenty dollars help you remember?" she whispered.

He gave her a fierce look, like she'd insulted him.

Discouraged, she decided she'd have better luck at the bar. But not tonight.

LANCE was back at Savannah's before first light.

He had two problems now: making sure he avoided

the woman who lived here and making sure he avoided whoever had put the listening device by her back door.

He waited for twenty minutes, checking to make sure no one was watching the house before getting out his own covert device—a GPS-guided transponder, which he fixed under the front bumper of Savannah's car.

The next time she went out, he wouldn't have to follow on her tail. He could hang back and track her on his portable GPS.

He went home for a few hours of restless sleep, then spent the day researching patrons of the Eighteen Club for the story he was supposed to be writing. Only now he found himself more focused on Savannah Carpenter than the club.

He kept wondering who had set that damn recorder. And finally he couldn't stop himself from driving to her house. Before he got there, the alarm beeped, telling him she was on the move.

SAVANNAH sat in her car looking at the Happy Times Bar in Hyattsville, which was conveniently located next to a public parking lot.

Not exactly a dive. But not the kind of posh place Charlotte favored. So why had she come here? To buy drugs or what?

Savannah closed her eyes, then opened them again. She hated to think the worst of her sister. But Charlotte didn't give her much choice. She'd gotten into something over her head. Either she'd been running away or someone had wanted to make sure she didn't talk about her recent experiences.

Skirting the edge of the lot, Savannah parked several rows away from the bar, then watched two patrons come out and drive away. After another man went in, she knew she was stalling.

The place gave her a bad feeling, and she wanted to turn around and go home, but that would mean she'd wasted her time getting ready and driving over here.

So she got out and smoothed her skirt. Although she usually dressed pretty conservatively, tonight she was wearing one of her sister's outfits—a red sheath cut high in front but with a plunging back that went almost down to her butt.

She'd paired it with strappy high-heeled sandals. As she stood beside her car, she wished she'd worn something a bit more demure.

LANCE was half a mile behind Savannah. By the time he pulled into a public parking lot, she was almost at the door of the Happy Times Bar. What the hell was she doing in a place like this? And dressed like a hooker.

He didn't know what she was up to. But he was pretty sure she was in over her head again. She certainly didn't look very comfortable in the red dress and high heels.

Still, the sexpot outfit had his pulse pounding, even if she looked like she'd put on her makeup with a trowel.

He watched her approach the door of the bar. If she went inside, he'd have to follow her, and that was bad news because smoke and alcohol fumes were poison to a werewolf.

* * *

AS Savannah hesitated outside the bar, a man came out and spotted her. He was wearing jeans, a fancy western shirt, and cowboy boots. He wasn't quite steady on his feet, and she recoiled from the smell of liquor on his breath.

She watched him eyeing her with interest. "Charlotte, baby, where have you been?"

Jackpot!

She swallowed. "Around."

He took a step closer. "You promised to come back and see ol' Warren. What happened?"

"I've been busy."

"We used to have fun. We could do it again."

She shrugged, and his face took on a sharp look.

"So I'm not good enough for you now that you're going to that big fancy club with your new boyfriend? What's it called? Some number, right?"

"The Eighteen Club," she breathed.

"Yeah. That's it."

She took a step back, but he lurched toward her and wrapped a big hand around her arm.

When she tried to pull away, his grip tightened. He tipped his head to one side, studying her more closely in the light from the lamp high up on a pole. "Hey, wait a minute, you're not her."

She swallowed. "I never said I was."

"What the hell game are you playing?" He yanked her toward the shadows at the side of the building, and she felt her stomach drop, amazed at how quickly this charade was going south.

"What are you—a cop?"

"No! I'm Charlotte's sister. I'm trying to find out what happened to her."

"Well, you're asking the wrong guy. 'Cause I haven't seen her in weeks."

He leaned over her, his breath hot and his eyes angry.

She began talking fast. "I—I guess you don't know what happened. Charlotte's in the hospital."

Apparently he wasn't listening. "I don't like girls who play games."

When she tried to wrench away, he held her fast.

Now what the hell was she going to do? Go for the gun in her purse?

Sure. And probably get herself shot when he took the pistol away from her.

LANCE was already out of his car by the time the drunk grabbed Savannah. His first impulse was to rip off his clothing and change to wolf form, since that was his most comfortable fighting mode. But his human intelligence warned him not to do it.

Instead, he sprinted across the parking lot and clamped his hand on the attacker's muscular shoulder.

"Let the lady go," he growled.

From the corner of his eye, he saw Savannah whirl toward him, her eyes wide. He got the guy's attention, too.

The would-be mugger dropped Savannah's arm and turned to face Lance. "Stay out of this, if you know what's good for you."

"All I want is for you to walk away nicely," Lance answered, his own voice dangerously calm.

He wanted to yell at Savannah to get into her car and lock the doors, but he couldn't risk taking his attention away from the angry man facing him.

"You don't want to get into any trouble, do you?" he asked in a conversational tone.

"I wouldn't bet your ass on that," the guy answered, then took a swing at Lance.

But the jerk had telegraphed his move. Lance dodged to the side, and knuckles glanced off his cheek. It hurt, but it didn't do much damage. He swung his own punch, landing a solid blow on an unshaven chin.

The drunk made a wheezing sound.

Lance waited.

He hoped the guy would fold in the face of superior force—and talent. But the stupid bastard didn't have the sense to back off. Instead, he struck out again, this time whacking Lance in the chest.

He grunted.

Savannah's voice cut through the thickening atmosphere. "Stop it! Stop it right now, or I'll shoot!" she shouted.

Lance couldn't believe what he was hearing. Whirling, he saw Savannah facing them with a pistol in her hand.

# CHAPTER
# NINE

**WHILE LANCE'S ATTENTION** was diverted, the guy landed a solid punch to his chin. He saw stars.

When his vision cleared, he watched his attacker slump to the ground.

Savannah was standing over him with the gun.

For a moment, he thought she'd discharged the weapon while his ears had been ringing.

But she was holding it backwards, and apparently she'd brought the butt end down on the jerk's head.

Lance bent over the injured man. He was breathing. And a bleeding gash decorated the top of his skull where the hair was thinning. That was good. Better than caving in his cranium.

Miraculously, they were alone in the parking lot. Nobody else had come out of the bar to witness the assault.

"I . . . I hurt him. We have to call the police. . . . His name is Warren," Savannah whispered.

"Somebody has to call them. Not us." He took the gun from her limp hand and stuffed it into the waistband of his jeans, then led her to his car. "Get in."

She looked dazed and uncertain. "I . . . don't know you. I can't get into your car."

"If you want a formal introduction, my name is Lance Marshall, and I'd like to keep you from getting arrested for assault."

She stared at him wide-eyed. "It was self-defense. I mean—I was defending you."

"Do you have a permit to carry that gun?"

Panic suffused her features. "No. But I can't just run away."

"I understand you want to be a law-abiding citizen, but we're pushing our luck. Get into the car before somebody sees us."

Finally, to his vast relief, she did as he asked, and he got them out of the parking lot.

She looked back over her shoulder. "My car."

"We'll get it later."

His mind was racing as he drove down the block and into the gas station he'd spotted on the corner. He couldn't use his cell phone, because that would put him at the scene.

Pulling up at the pay phone, he got out and dialed 911. When the dispatcher came on, he made his voice low and gravelly to report a fight outside the Happy Times Bar in Hyattsville. "A man is lying on the ground. I think he's unconscious."

"Sir—"

He hung up without giving any more information,

then drove another block to the parking lot of a strip mall. When he turned to Savannah, he saw she was hud-dled in the corner, shaking.

"Oh, God. Oh, God. What have I done?"

"Defended yourself, like you said."

She moaned. That sound of distress and the sick look on her face made his insides tighten.

Before he could stop himself, he reached across the console and gathered her to him.

She stiffened, but he stroked her back, her hair. "It's all right," he murmured. "Everything is going to be all right. Nobody's going to figure out it was you."

He could feel her struggling to get hold of herself. Probably she'd gone from worrying about the man she'd coldcocked to worrying about being in the arms of this stranger.

"Why . . . why did you get involved?"

"Because you were in trouble," he answered, hearing the gritty sound of his own voice.

The words seemed to reassure her, and some of the starch went out of her.

He continued to stroke her, murmur reassurances. She had been frightened both by that Warren guy and by her own actions. And he could help. He was good with women. He knew what to do for them, how to say the right things—to get what he wanted.

This was no different, he told himself as he slid his lips against the tender line where her cheek met her hair while he kept talking to her in a low, reassuring voice.

He wasn't even sure what he was saying. He was too focused on the woman in his arms.

From a distance, he had been entranced by the won-derful female scent of her. It was even better close up.

Her body fit against his so perfectly. And the pressure of her breasts against his chest was the most erotic thing he had ever felt.

He forgot why he was holding her, and why she was clinging to him. Claiming more of her had suddenly become as necessary as breathing. He rubbed his mouth coaxingly against hers. And when she didn't resist, he pressed harder, marveling at the softness of those lips and the rich taste of her.

He had thought he knew what he was doing. He found he had been transported to an undiscovered country filled with treasures beyond his imagining. And she must have taken the same trip. Because she seemed as lost in his embrace as he was in hers.

Later, he was never sure which one of them took the kiss to the next level, which one of them first stroked a tongue along the seam of the other's lips, asking for admittance.

All he knew was that it happened. She opened for him, and he was kissing her deeply, drinking from her essence. The way she responded to him made his head spin—that and the intensity of his own need for her.

His hands moved over her hair, her shoulders. Earlier he had sought to reassure and comfort her. Now he was the one who desperately needed the contact.

She made a sound low in her throat. A sound that he took for invitation.

He eased far enough away to cup his hand around her breast, captivated by the weight of that feminine mound in his hand, by the shape, by the softness, and by the hard button of her nipple straining against his palm. She was aroused by him. He shifted his hand, stroking his fingers across the tip, and she moaned into his mouth.

He was already so hard that thinking had become almost impossible. But he struggled to work out a difficult problem.

Could he make love to her here, in the car? Maybe, if he pulled around to the back of the shopping center where they wouldn't be so conspicuous.

He detached one hand from her, reaching for the ignition key. Before he could turn it, a roaring sound distracted him. It took several seconds to realize he was hearing a siren wail.

SAVANNAH'S body went rigid, and she pushed against the shoulder of the man who held her in his arms as if they were lovers.

"Let me go."

His head came up, his eyes unfocused.

The roaring sound increased, and an ambulance rushed past, then turned the corner. She knew that it had pulled into the parking lot where she and Lance Marshall had fought off Warren.

"We have to see if he's all right," she gasped.

He shook his head. "We can't get involved. I'll find out later."

She stared at him, feeling as if she was seeing him for the first time. She had been kissing him. More than kissing, and she couldn't understand herself. Wild, hot currents had seized her, filling her with an urgency she had never experienced before.

Just as strongly, anguish rose inside of her now. What was he—some kind of wizard? Fighting panic, she gasped out, "Who are you? Really?"

"A guy who wants to help you."

She moved away from him, fumbling with the door lock.

"Wait! Stay."

The deep emotion in his voice made her reconsider. At least for the moment. She longed to assign Lance Marshall all the blame for the wild, erotic kiss. But she knew she had been a full participant.

"Did you slip me some kind of date-rape drug?" she asked, hearing the tremor under the words.

"Oh, come on!" he shot back. "Did I give you anything to eat or drink?"

She conceded the point with a small shake of her head.

He gave her a considering look. "What are you doing—scrambling for an explanation of your own behavior?"

The words hit her with surprising impact. "I guess that's right. Sorry."

She watched him drag in air, then let it out slowly.

When he spoke, his voice was soft and even. "Let's go back to square one, and start again. You don't have to worry about being in my car. I'm not going to hurt you."

"How do I know I can even trust you?"

He sighed. "Because our . . . relationship goes farther back than the last few minutes. I was in the woods at the Eighteen Club the other night."

She stared at him, trying to make sense of the statement.

"I was there," he repeated. "And that was my dog who saved you from the guards."

"How . . . how do I know you're telling the truth?"

He reached into his glove compartment and pulled out a camera, which he handed to her. She turned it in her hands. It was the camera the guard had taken away from her.

As she stared at it, pieces of a puzzle fell into place in her mind. She tipped her head to one side, studying him in the light from the overhead street lamp. "And you've been following me around. You were at the hospital."

He opened his mouth to deny it. But she waved him to silence.

"I don't want to hear any lies from you. I saw you at the hospital yesterday, didn't I?"

He looked doubtful. "How could you have spotted me?"

"I'm an artist. I'm excellent with visual details. You had on a blond wig. You were in the parking garage. Then you followed me up to ICU."

He huffed out a breath. "Okay. Yeah."

"Why were you tailing me? How did you even know who I was?" she demanded.

"One question at a time. I saw your license plate before you drove away from the Eighteen Club, so I was able to get your name and address."

She squeezed her eyes shut. She wanted to block him out, but she knew that wouldn't do her any good. She had to get answers from him, while he was being cooperative. "You'd better tell me what in the name of God is going on. What's your interest in all this?"

Would he tell her the truth? It looked as though he was deciding what to say.

"I'm a freelance journalist."

"And what the hell are you up to?"

"I was staking out the Eighteen Club because I'm going to write a book about the place. As soon as I saw you in the woods that night, I knew you were heading for trouble."

"But you didn't warn me."

"If I had, we would both have ended up in handcuffs. The guard was coming. All I could do was send the dog to get the guy away from you. So . . . what were you doing there?"

"Maybe I'm writing a book, too."

"I don't think so. I think you're trying to find out what happened to Charlotte Nichols."

She winced. "Let's get back to you—to your following me around."

He ran a hand through his dark hair. "You're my best lead so far—if you don't get yourself killed or beaten up or raped because you're in over your head." He flapped his arm in exasperation. "I don't even know why you're taking such enormous chances."

"I didn't think tonight would be such a big risk," she murmured. She closed her eyes, then opened them. "I guess I didn't thank you for stepping in—both times." Before he could read too much into that, she added, "But that doesn't mean I can trust you."

Sirens roared again, reminding her how she'd come to be sitting in this man's car. The ambulance rushed past in the direction from which it had come, presumably on the way to the hospital.

When the noise subsided, he said, "You can Google me. There should be a bunch of information about Lance Marshall. Just like there's a bunch of information about Savannah Carpenter."

"You looked me up?"

"Yeah. I know you're a very talented painter. I've seen your work on the Internet." He gestured toward the camera she still held in her hand. "I guess that's why you have so many garden pictures."

"You looked at the pictures in the camera?"

"I was looking for shots of the patrons at the Eighteen Club. You got a couple of good ones. Particularly of that woman. Someone I recognize—if I can just figure out the context."

*Erica Wentworth.* She knew who it was, but she wasn't going to tell him. "I've had enough of this conversation. Take me back to my car. Unless you're planning to . . ." She stopped, realizing that it wasn't a good idea to give this guy ideas.

His hand tightened on the steering wheel. "I'm not going to hold you captive. But you and I need each other."

She answered with a sharp laugh. "I don't think so."

"You're not making much progress in your investigation, are you? You got into trouble the minute you tried to spy on the Castle. And again tonight. Why are you putting yourself at risk?"

She heard herself say, "I'm overcompensating."

"For what?"

"Being a wimp when I was growing up."

"Care to elaborate?"

"No. Take me back to my car. And give me some time to think about what I want to tell you."

"In a minute." He reached into the door pocket and pulled out the pistol. Holding it by the barrel end, he handed it over, and she winced. She'd forgotten all about the damn thing. "Do you usually carry?"

"Not until recently."

"Did you have a gun at the Eighteen Club?"

"No."

"That's good. Because you can get in trouble with a weapon. Lucky you hit Warren instead of shooting him."

She nodded tightly, then took her property back.

He watched her shove the weapon into her purse. "Have you ever fired a gun?"

"No."

"You should get some target practice. I can take you, if you want."

"I'll think about that," she muttered.

"One more thing."

The way he said it made her head jerk up. "Now what are you going to tell me?"

"Somebody is stalking you."

"You!"

"Not just me."

Her jaw clenched. She wanted to dismiss the frightening statement, but she couldn't deny the feeling of being watched—or the car that had pulled out behind her the night before. Still, she managed to say, "You expect me to believe that?"

"Last night, after you went out, I saw a guy put a small box in the bushes beside your back door. It's half-covered with mulch. It's got a tape recorder and a microphone inside. You can check it out when you get home. Then put it back where you found it, so he doesn't know you're on to him."

She felt physically ill. "How do I know *you* didn't leave the recorder there?"

"Because I'm telling you about it."

"That could be a ploy to get me to trust you."

"I suppose it could. But I'm not that tricky. I'm actually pretty straightforward."

"Oh, sure!"

He started the engine and drove down the block. When they approached the parking lot, they saw a police car sitting in front of the bar.

# CHAPTER
# TEN

AS SHE STARED at the patrol car, Savannah felt her heart start to pound.

"Now what do we do?" she asked, hearing the tremor in her voice.

One cop was standing beside the cruiser. When he disappeared into the bar, Lance Marshall speeded up, entered the parking lot at the other end, and pulled up beside her car.

"I don't think he had time to take down license numbers out here yet. You're probably safe. But don't blow it by rushing home and calling hospitals to find out about Warren. They'll record your number. I can get some information and let you know tomorrow."

"All right. Thanks."

She wanted to leave now. But he was still asking questions. "Does that guy, Warren, know your name?"

"No."

"Does he know why you're interested in Charlotte Nichols?"

"He knows she's my sister." Immediately disgusted with herself, she made a small sound of annoyance. "And now you know, too."

He reached in his pocket and pulled out a card. "Let me give you my number, so you can call me."

As she started to climb out of the car, he put a hand on her arm. "Don't call from home. You don't want whoever left that tape recorder to get my name."

The advice sent her mind zinging back to the microphone he said was outside her door. She felt trapped. Not just here. Her own home wasn't safe.

"Give me your cell phone number," he demanded.

"Why?"

"In case something important comes up."

She rattled off the number.

"Slow down. I'm efficient, but I'm not a robot."

Her lips quirked as she repeated the digits more slowly while he wrote them down in a small notebook.

When she saw him looking over her shoulder, she turned and saw a cop walking toward the parking lot. "I'd better go."

"Yeah."

Quickly she climbed out of his car and into hers, then drove away.

When she reached her home, she tottered inside on unsteady legs, then collapsed on the couch, where she sat trying to will her blood pressure back to normal.

Then she remembered the listening device outside.

Gun in hand, she opened the back door and looked out. When she knelt down, she found the box where Marshall had said it would be.

Her first thought was that she should pull it out of the mulch and call the police. But where would that get her? They weren't going to put a guard on her house. They hadn't even believed her when she'd told them Charlotte hadn't fallen—she'd been pushed.

Her hands felt dirty after touching the box. In the bathroom, she washed with soap and water, thinking that she'd gotten herself into a mess without half trying.

She'd started with the simple goal of finding out who'd put her sister in the hospital. But as Lance Marshall had so kindly pointed out, she wasn't exactly racking up a sterling record as a spy. Three times she'd gone out to collect information. Twice she'd gotten into serious trouble. And the confrontation at the restaurant hadn't been so great, either.

She'd given Marshall a reason why she was doing it—in outline form. Really, she knew she was trying to prove to herself that she wasn't the dim little girl so firmly under the thumb of her father that she wasn't able to go to the library without asking his permission. And forget about the movie theater.

Since her divorce, she'd taken charge of her life, and she knew she had come a long way. But not far enough.

There was another motive driving her, too. She felt that what had happened to Charlotte was her fault, because she hadn't been aggressive enough in making her sister confide about her lifestyle.

But that didn't mean she had to act recklessly. She didn't have to get herself beaten up or killed to prove she would go the extra mile for her sister now.

She'd made a couple of bad judgment calls. She'd better not do it again. And as far as she could see, playing it smart meant keeping clear of Lance Marshall.

The man was dangerous. He might be a journalist, but he appeared to have the instincts of a wolf. And he had forced a physical reaction from her that she wasn't prepared for.

"Stop lying to yourself," she warned, speaking aloud, then clamped her hand over her mouth. The tape recorder must have picked that up. Lord, she couldn't even talk in her own house.

Standing, she paced to the window and drew the drapes. As though that would protect her.

Then she finished the rest of her original thought without speaking. *He didn't force a reaction on you. He drew a reaction from you. There's a difference.*

So what did that mean—on a personal level?

She didn't know. She looked around her house. Her refuge. Her comfort zone. And now it didn't even feel safe. After finding the tape recorder, she couldn't stay here another minute.

In the bedroom, she threw clothing into a suitcase. Then she grabbed toilet articles from the bathroom and her laptop from the small bedroom that she used as an office.

The thought of leaving the painting she'd started made her stomach clench. She needed to lose herself in her work. Now more than ever. She needed to focus on the bright flowers and lush greenery she could create with her skilled hands. But she couldn't take the canvas in the car. It was too big.

Twenty minutes after she'd arrived home, she pulled out of her driveway again. She wasn't even sure where she was going. She darted up and down several side streets, trying to make sure nobody was behind her before heading down Wisconsin Avenue toward the District. The first hotel she saw was a Holiday Inn on the right. Making a snap decision, she pulled into the garage.

She rented a room for the night, wondering what she was going to do in the morning.

Alone in the unfamiliar surroundings, she wrapped her arms around her shoulders and rubbed her chilled skin.

Now that she couldn't paint, there was nothing to do but think. About Charlotte. About herself.

Against her will, memories assaulted her.

Her father had ruled their household with an iron hand, and she'd lived a lot of her life inside her head. He'd realized he could control her actions, and he took a great deal of pleasure in doing it. Probably the only reason he'd let her go away to college was because she'd won a scholarship to the University of Pennsylvania. Getting her education for free had been appealing.

She pictured herself back then—a shy girl who hardly knew how to relate to other kids. But in the way of fate, she'd signed up for an art class with Professor Myerson. He'd recognized her talent and encouraged her to explore the depths of her own imagination. It had been a freeing experience. And she'd found that when she painted, she turned into another person.

She tried to hide the new Savannah from her father, because she knew he wouldn't approve. But he finally caught on, and he ended up storming onto the campus and yanking her out of school. Then he told her that marriage was just what she needed. And he'd put forth a candidate, Frank Thompson.

She shivered, remembering the touch of Frank's hands on her flesh.

He was much older than she. Before their marriage, he'd been respectful. And she'd hoped he'd just let her be. But that had been a foolish hope.

On their wedding night, he made it clear that she belonged to him—and he could do anything he wanted with her.

Maybe he thought she would eventually respond. But she never felt comfortable with him in bed.

In the first months of her marriage, she sank into depression. She even thought of suicide. But fate took over again. Professor Myerson got her number from Charlotte, and he called and asked why she wasn't pursuing her art career.

Somehow she had the guts to meet him for lunch—and he saw at once what a mess she was.

Without his help, she probably wouldn't have gotten out of the marriage. But he must have been convinced that burying her talent was a terrible disservice to herself. He gave her a place to stay, without asking anything of her besides that she start painting again. As she got to know him, she found out that he had mentored a number of young artists—both men and women. As he explained it to her, he was a good judge of talent, even if he couldn't make it as a painter himself. She also discovered he was gay. He had no interest in an intimate relationship with her. But he turned out to be the single most important person in her life. Especially since her parents told her that divorcing her husband meant that she would no longer be their daughter.

So be it. After a couple of years on her own, she

realized that her parents were the last people on earth that she needed.

She squeezed her hands into fists, trying to banish old memories. She had enough problems right now without dredging up the past.

"You should be looking up Lance Marshall on the Internet—like he did with you," she muttered to herself. "So you can figure out whether he's trying to sell you a load of crap about himself."

She hooked her laptop into the hotel's phone system, then Googled Lance Marshall. There were more people than she might have thought with that name. But the man who had come to her rescue tonight was the most prominent.

He'd contributed to the *Washington Post, Washingtonian, Harper's, The Atlantic, The New Yorker.*

Apparently, he was a big deal. She found some of the actual articles online. He'd written on everything from the threat of global warming to an exposé of theft among employees at the Commerce Department.

She could tell from the stories that he'd gotten into some dangerous situations—like when a D.C. drug dealer had put out a contract on him.

On the surface, he looked like a good man to have on her side if she was going up against the Eighteen Club.

In the car he had comforted her. Comfort had turned to passion, and she'd felt something completely unexpected. An intensity that left her whole body tingling and needy.

She'd read a few romance novels where the heroines had strong sexual reactions. She'd thought the authors were just using poetic license.

Then she'd read her sister's diary, and found out that Charlotte had had some shockingly strong sexual experiences with the man who was her lover.

She'd never thought the same could be true for her. But kissing Lance Marshall had been astonishing. He'd kindled sexual feelings that she hadn't been prepared to experience.

If she called him, it wouldn't just be to get his help discovering what had happened to Charlotte. If she got back together with him, she knew her life would never be the same again.

*No—be honest. It's already changed, and you don't know if you can handle it.*

WARREN Buckley heaved himself out of bed and grimaced. Lying down was bad enough. Standing on his feet made his head spin.

On unsteady legs, he staggered to the sink. The doctors at the emergency room had said not to use strong painkillers. To hell with them. He shook a double dose into his hand and washed it down with a couple swallows of water. Then he checked his pupils like he was supposed to and headed for the refrigerator, where he got out a bottle of beer and popped the top.

He carried it back to bed and propped up the pillows, taking a pull on the bottle while he waited for the painkiller to kick in.

A doctor had examined him at the hospital, X-rayed his head, done some other tests, and sent him home with five stitches in his scalp. He was pissed as hell at the bitch who had hit him. And pissed at himself for letting it happen.

The cops had asked for details, and he'd thought about getting the woman for assault charges. Only he didn't know her name. It probably wasn't Nichols, like her sister.

Anyway, it galled him to admit that a dame had gotten the better of him. So he'd made up some story about tripping and hitting his head.

As he considered his options, he started formulating a plan. The owner of the Eighteen Club had put out the word that he would pay for information on anyone who happened to be asking questions about the place. And about Charlotte Nichols.

So he could rat out the sister to Raymond Conrad. That way, he'd end up with some cash in hand. The trouble was, he'd heard some scary stories about the Castle. Like that people went in there and never came out. That could be a load of crap, put out on the street to protect the place.

Or maybe not.

Right now, his head hurt too much to think. When he was feeling better, he'd figure out whether approaching the Castle was a smart move for him or a dangerous one.

LANCE watched the blip on the GPS screen. When the device had first started chirping, he'd stared at it in disbelief.

He'd expected Savannah to go home and stay there. Then he realized that didn't make a lot of sense. He wouldn't stay in the house if he knew somebody was staking out his property.

He'd go out into the woods, turn himself into a wolf,

and wait for the sucker to show himself. So he could maul him enough to scare the living shit out of him.

The fantasy made him grimace. He'd built up a career as a hotshot journalist. But savagery was never far from the surface of his mind.

Keeping that wild streak under control wasn't always easy, but he managed, just like his brothers and his cousins managed.

As he stared at the GPS, it was difficult to stay where he was. He wanted to get in his car and catch up with Savannah.

To his relief, she didn't go far, just down Wisconsin Avenue toward the District. To the Holiday Inn, he discovered when he checked the address on the GPS.

He breathed out a small sigh of relief. She'd be safe there for the night—if she'd been smart enough to make sure nobody was following her.

He had her cell phone number. He could call her. Or better yet, go over there. Then he pictured her reaction if he showed up at her door. Really, if he didn't want to scare her off, it would be a lot better if she was the one to make the next move.

Restless energy surged through his system. She'd become important to him in a very short time.

Because they had the same goal, he told himself, as he went into the kitchen and brewed some more of the Chinese herbs that were supposed to suppress his mating instincts.

While he drank the damn stuff, he went back to the computer and started doing research.

He found out that the ambulance that had picked up a guy named Warren Buckley had come from Prince George's Hospital Center. Then he determined that

Buckley had been treated in the emergency room and released.

That was good. Apparently he hadn't been seriously hurt.

So could he connect Charlotte Nichols with Savannah Carpenter? Lance got on the Internet again and tried. To his relief, he didn't find any link between them. And there were more than fifteen hundred references to the name Charlotte Nichols. That should keep the guy busy for a while.

He stayed on the computer for a couple of hours. But the darkened woods outside the window tugged at him. He wanted to change into a wolf and roam the park. He wanted to take out his frustration on the deer population. But a wolf couldn't answer the phone, and he wanted to be available if Savannah called.

So he pulled on shorts and a T-shirt and went for a jog with his cell phone clipped to his waistband.

When she didn't call, he took a shower with the cell phone sitting on the sink within easy reach. Then he thawed a steak and ate some raw meat with the phone on the table.

At eight in the morning, when recklessness finally overcame good sense, he started to call her cell phone. Then he realized that would be a giveaway that he was still tracking her. So he dialed her phone number and let the answering machine click on. But he didn't leave a message for the tape recorder outside to hear.

Instead, he hung up and called her cell phone.

She picked up on the first ring.

"Hello?"

"This is Lance." He cleared his throat. "You didn't answer your home phone."

"I didn't like thinking someone was lurking around outside stalking me. So I went to a hotel last night."

"Good." So that was out of the way. He rushed ahead. "I found out about that Warren guy. Warren Buckley. He was taken to Prince George's Hospital and released."

He heard her breathe out a small sigh. "Thank God he's okay."

Silence stretched between them. Finally, when he couldn't stand the tension another second, he asked, "Did you decide whether you want to work with me?"

"We should talk again, before I make a decision."

"Where are you? Can I come over there?"

She answered so quickly that he knew she must have been planning what to say. "Why don't we meet at the Botanic Garden down in D.C.? Do you know where I mean?"

"That big Victorian-looking greenhouse next to the Capitol grounds?"

"Yes."

"Why there?"

"I like it. It's a public place. And I can visit my sister on the way down. We can meet at two in the afternoon. In the main room. Right off the lobby."

He wanted to insist that it had to be earlier. But he was in no position to dictate terms.


SAVANNAH put on a sundress, then drove down to the George Washington University Hospital. This time, after leaving the parking garage, she checked several times to make sure nobody was behind her, then made her way to the front desk and the ICU.

When she saw her sister, her heart squeezed. Nothing had changed. Charlotte was still connected to tubes. Still pale and looking lifeless. And she was still breathing with the help of a respirator.

Pulling up a chair, Savannah sat down and pressed her palm over Charlotte's pale hand. The one without an IV.

"How are you, honey?" she murmured.

Her sister stirred on the bed.

"It's Savannah. Do you know it's me? I come to visit you all the time. I wish we'd spent more time together before you had your accident. When you get better, I'll take you down to Florida. We can lie on the beach and just relax."

Charlotte moved restlessly. Then, to Savannah's shock, she pulled the breathing tube out of her mouth.

Her lips fluttered, and she gasped out a word. Or maybe it was just a strange collection of syllables.

Savannah leaned closer. "What is it? What are you trying to tell me?"

"B . . . bor . . . alas."

"What? I don't understand."

"Bor . . . alas."

Savannah couldn't make sense of the collection of syllables. Still, they sent a wave of cold over her skin.

Charlotte's head was thrashing on the pillow now. Obviously the word distressed her.

A nurse—not the one who had kicked Savannah out before—stepped into the room. Savannah steeled herself to be shooed out.

"I'm sorry, but her blood pressure just spiked. I'm afraid you'll have to leave." The nurse looked at Charlotte, then turned her face accusingly toward Savannah. "She's pulled out her air tube. Did she do that while you were here?"

"Yes."

"You should have called me immediately."

Savannah repressed a sigh. "She's trying to talk to me. And I sensed it was important."

"We have to put the tube back." She fussed over the patient, then turned back to Savannah. "Didn't I hear that you upset her the other day?"

"I'm sorry. I didn't mean to."

"Well, you need to let her rest now."

"Can I come back later?"

"In an hour."

She looked at her watch. It was already after one. If she waited an hour, she might miss Lance at the Botanic Garden.

She debated what to do.

Call him?

Stepping out into the waiting area, she dialed his cell phone. But all she got was his voice mail.


LANCE drove the Lexus into D.C. He made good time, and found a parking space not far from the huge greenhouse complex beside the Mall.

After passing through a metal detector, he stepped into the lush, humid atmosphere of the U.S. Botanic Garden.

There were several areas, the main room full of tropical vegetation and some smaller greenhouses with cacti and other specialized plants.

The side rooms afforded no privacy. But he found the

perfect spot where he and Savannah could talk in a secluded corner of the main room, then went back to the
entrance to wait for her.

She was late. Was she going to stand him up? Trying
to ward off the thought, he stared at a cluster of bright
orange flowers hanging from a vine.

Fifteen minutes later, when he finally spotted Savannah, his heart started to pound. She had a purse, and he
watched her hand it over for inspection. As she walked
through the metal detector, she raised her eyes and
saw him.

She stopped short, then strode through and into the
greenhouse. As he followed her progress, he was still
trying to convince himself that there was nothing personal about his feelings for her—or hers for him. She
was just a woman who was going to help him get an important story. His racing pulse told him that was a lie.

# CHAPTER
# ELEVEN

LANCE WATCHED SAVANNAH walk toward him. The real Savannah, fresh and natural in a light green sundress that was perfect with her creamy skin and blond hair.

When their eyes locked, he felt a small thrill along his nerve endings. The thrill he always felt when he knew he wanted a woman, he told himself.

"I see why you like this place," he said, thinking how stilted he must sound.

"I've used it for the background in some of my paintings."

"I'd like to see them."

She turned to face him. "Does that really matter to you?"

"Yes."

"Why?"

"Seeing your work is a way to get to know you better."

She gave a small nod, then hurried down one of the flagstone pathways, and he followed.

They stopped at the edge of a bubbling brook that ran through the building.

"I gather you looked me up, and you found out I really am a journalist."

"Yes."

He cleared his throat. "I'm sorry about your sister. She was playing with a dangerous crowd."

She raised her face toward him. "You know that—specifically?"

"I wasn't there, if that's what you're implying. But I've been doing some research. How did you link her to the Eighteen Club?"

"Her diary."

"A sexual diary."

"Why do you think so?"

"They don't play duck duck goose at the Castle. It's an S&M club."

"Okay—yes, it was a sexual diary."

"Can I see it?"

"No."

He had expected that answer, but he kept the questions coming. "How did your sister get hurt?"

She looked like she wasn't even going to tell him that much. Then she hitched out a breath and said, "The police told me she fell off a cliff in Rock Creek Park. I don't think that's true. I think someone pushed her."

"Are there clues in the diary? Does it give names of people?"

"No. She just talks about the stuff she was doing . . . with her lover."

"One particular man—or woman?"

"Man!" she said quickly.

He tipped his head to one side. "I guess the diary made you uncomfortable?"

"Yes."

"Why do you think she got involved with the Eighteen Club?"

She swallowed. "Charlotte and I had a difficult home life. My dad was pretty rough on us."

"He abused you?"

"Not sexual abuse, if that's what you're thinking. He was strict with us. I tried to stay out of trouble—and please him. Charlotte did just the opposite."

"Like what?"

"By the time she was in middle school, she was doing drugs. Drinking. Hooking school. When she was in high school, my parents ended up throwing her out of the house. Since they basically disowned her, she took the name Nichols."

"Ouch. Was she on the street?"

"She knew how to take care of herself. She moved in with a boyfriend who was five years older. But after my marriage broke up . . ."

"You were married?" he asked, even though he'd already acquired that piece of information.

Her chin jutted up. "Yes, I was married for just under a year. It didn't work out," she said, obviously trying to make it clear by the tone of her voice that she wasn't going to talk about that aspect of her life. "And after I filed for divorce, Charlotte and I started getting together. We'd talk about our childhood. About our lives and what we wanted for the future. Neither one of us had any contact with our parents. That was one of the reasons I moved to the D.C. area, so we could see each other more often. For a while, we did. Then she started pulling away from me."

"And that . . . hurt?" he asked softly.

"Yes," she whispered, and he got the feeling she was telling him things that she had no intention of saying. Of course, that was his job—getting people to spill their guts.

"What else did you notice about her?" he asked.

She probably wanted to tell him her sister's life was none of his business. But she wanted his help, so she said, "She got her GED. But she never had a job that paid a lot. Then she moved to a pretty nice apartment above Dupont Circle." She stopped and swallowed. "I figured she'd found a man to pay her bills. But I didn't act judgmental about it."

"That was when she broke off the contact with you?"

"Not completely. We still talked once every week or so. But she started playing games with me. She acted like she had a big secret. Before I could pry it out of her, the hospital called me. She's been in a coma ever since."

"How long ago did she get hurt?"

"Two weeks. The park police found her. They turned the case over to the D.C. cops."

"Did they investigate?"

"Not much, as far as I can see. They're sticking to the accident theory." She hesitated, then added, "Or somebody is making sure they don't dig too deeply."

"And you want the truth—so you tried getting some answers on your own."

"Yes."

The greenhouse was large, and there weren't many visitors on a weekday afternoon in the summer when the world outside was vibrant with flowers and greenery.

He'd stopped walking—just at the spot he'd scoped out before—where a secluded alcove was formed by a group of trees.

He watched Savannah in the filtered light, thinking she looked as nervous as he felt. "You've already tried some pretty dangerous stunts."

"I . . . yes," she admitted. "So is there some way I can get into the Castle—as a guest?"

His mouth went suddenly dry. Her thinking had gotten pretty close to his.

"There are two kinds of people who get into the Eighteen Club," he said. "In one group are the rich and famous, the influential and the powerful. They can get a membership. Then there are the others—men and women like your sister who are willing to take risks. People who come in as guests and slaves of members."

"Slaves!"

"I said it can be a pretty rough scene. Masters and slaves. And it's not just the paid help who end up as submissives. Some club members want to be . . . disciplined."

She sucked in a sharp breath. "I guess Charlotte was in the slave category. At least from what I read in her diary."

"I wouldn't recommend that."

She took her bottom lip between her teeth. "Can I hire you to go there with me?"

"No."

"I thought you wanted to get inside."

"I don't hire myself out as an escort."

As he took in her disappointment, he tried to ignore the emotions roaring through him. "But I will go there with you."

"Why?"

"I don't have much chance of getting an entrée on my own. For obvious reasons, they're not going to let someone in who might write about them. And if I use some other name, they'll do a background check and find out it's a fake identity. But you're a well-known artist."

"Not that well known."

He shook his head. "Don't be modest. You'd add to the prestige of the club. And if you take me in as your boy toy, they'll only do a cursory check of my credentials."

She snorted. "Who would believe you were anyone's toy?"

"We can figure out how to pull it off."


RAYMOND Conrad walked across the stone floor of the Castle basement and stopped at a heavy wooden door.

Few people had come down here and returned. He was luckier than most.

Or was he?

Three years ago, he'd gotten in over his head.

He forced the thought down.

"Don't lose your nerve," he muttered. "You're the most successful member of your family. When they come to town, they beg to visit this place. And not just them. You're the hottest ticket in D.C."

That thought reassured him. He hadn't been the smartest of the five Coddington siblings. And he hadn't been his parents' favorite, either. He'd seen his mother making sure that Cynthia got a nice outfit to wear on the first day of school. He'd seen her giving Billy extra food in the kitchen after dinner.

He'd been so jealous. As a kid he'd wanted to shout that he was just as good as they were.

As an adult, he'd proved he was better. He squared his shoulders.

"Don't let any doubts get in your way," he said aloud, then took one of the antacid tablets out of his pocket and chewed it to calm his stomach.

When he was ready, he opened the door and walked into a chamber that had been blasted out of the bedrock on which the Castle sat.

His Castle. The club he had built into a powerful force in the nation's capital.

*By yourself? No. With my help.*

Another being's thought echoed in his mind.

He felt a tug at his emotions, and he opened himself to the pull, sharing his satisfaction with the man who sat in a large stone chair at the far end of the room.

The image flickered, as though a movie projector had malfunctioned.

Then the picture became solid again. The man looked to be in his late thirties. A sense of energy hung around him like a golden glow. His hair and eyes were dark. And he was dressed in a dark business suit with a gleaming white shirt and a red tie.

A power tie, Raymond thought fleetingly.

The man didn't ask him to sit down. Raymond stood eight feet away, swaying slightly on his feet.

"Thank you for coming to this meeting," Boralas said.

"I'm sure that if you called me down here, you want to discuss important matters."

"Yes. I sense something coming our way."

"Something good, or something bad?"

"Bad. Initially. But I know we can turn it to our advantage—if we stay on the alert."

"What do you want me to do?"

"If anybody new applies for membership, be thorough about the background check."

"I will," Conrad promised, then cleared his throat. "Can you intervene?"

"My ability to influence actions varies. Getting a person to do something is easier if they are already tipping in that direction. Or if they are very susceptible to me."

"Yes. Okay. Do you need me for anything else?"

"You may go."

He closed the heavy wooden door behind himself, then stood in the hall, his breath shallow.

For a terrible moment, panic threatened to swallow him. He walked rapidly down the corridor, almost running, intent on putting distance between himself and the underground chamber as quickly as possible.

By the time he began to climb the steps, he was feeling better. When he reached the floor with some of the club's private suites, he paused.

To use the rooms on this floor, the guests had to inform one of the attendants, who unlocked the door and made a note of who was inside.

Like all the records at the Castle, the notes were in code. But he knew the code names of all the patrons.

He opened a door in the paneled wall and stepped into a side corridor that gave him access to the rooms on either side. Quietly he looked through a spy hole into one of the chambers. It was set up like a classroom, with about ten desks but only two students—young women wearing blue uniforms and saddle shoes like girls from a private school. "What do you think the punishment for cheating should be?" the teacher asked.

Both girls looked contrite.

"Give me a suggestion," the teacher demanded, slapping a ruler against his desk.

Conrad knew one of the girls had requested the scene. The other two participants were his paid employees. And everything at the Eighteen Club was just as it should be, he told himself.

LANCE'S stomach muscles clenched. "There's one other thing I should point out. The tape recorder outside your house complicates things. If Raymond Conrad is trying to keep you from making trouble for him, then going inside the Castle is dangerous."

"Who is Raymond Conrad?"

So she didn't even know that much. "The owner of the Eighteen Club. You think your sister was pushed off that cliff. If Conrad's involved in what happened to her, he might have figured out who you are."

"Let's assume it's not him."

He looked directly into her eyes. "You need to stop engaging in risky behavior."

He was standing close to her, and when he put his hand on her arm, she froze. "What are you doing?"

"Working on our 'Invaders of the Eighteen Club' act.

I don't want to end up in the hospital in a coma like your sister. If Conrad didn't have anything to do with her 'accident,' then who did? You think it's someone who frequents the Eighteen Club. And we'd better be able to convince them that we're there for fun and games, which means you'll have to convince people that you're completely comfortable with me."

He watched her lick her lips. They were probably dry, like his. Until this moment, he hadn't admitted to himself how much he wanted her.

Somewhere deep in his consciousness, he knew that since the night outside the Castle, he'd been operating as though he'd gone temporarily insane. The insanity had ratcheted up several notches after the heated scene in his car last night.

SAVANNAH felt as though she couldn't draw a full breath into her lungs. She should turn around and walk away from Lance Marshall. Yet something kept her standing there facing him.

Since her disastrous marriage she'd shied away from relationships because she'd been afraid to let herself be vulnerable to any man. But yesterday when Lance had taken her into his arms and kissed her, she'd responded on a deep, intimate level that she hadn't believed was possible for her. She was pretty sure the heated response hadn't been one-sided.

Now the look on his face told her that he wasn't taking this conversation casually. Perhaps that was why she found the courage to say, "What you're suggesting might not be possible. I never did get comfortable with my husband."

"You mean you didn't respond to him sexually?" he asked, putting the question in very basic terms.

She swallowed. "Yes."

"We already know you respond to me."

"What if I can't . . ."

"Then we'll have to think of something else."

"You'll still help me?" she asked, her voice high and thin.

"Yes."

"Why?"

"Because I like you."

She answered with a nervous laugh. "You hardly know me."

"I know enough. You have guts. And determination. You care about your family."

"My sister. The rest of them can go to hell."

"That bad?"

"Yes. I told you, my dad was a tyrant. My mom didn't try to stop him."

"She was probably afraid of him."

"Yes."

"So do you feel responsible for what happened to Charlotte? Is that what this is all about?" he suddenly asked, throwing her off balance.

"No. Okay, yes."

"It sounds like she made her own decisions."

She dug her nails into her palms. "I could have turned out like Charlotte. I mean, with no self-esteem. It was a close thing. But one of my college professors discovered my artistic talent, and that was a life-altering experience for me."

He looked astonished. "No kidding? You really think you could have ended up like her?"

"Yes. And I need to do something for her—even though now it may be too late."

He brought the discussion back to where it had been before they veered off course. "And something for yourself. You want to find out what we can mean to each other."

She couldn't deny it. That thought had been lurking in the back of her mind since last night. She had just met this man. The cautious part of her whispered that she didn't know him well enough to be having this conversation. But he had liberated a passion within her. A passion she had previous expressed only through her art. And she ached to know where it could lead.

They were standing in a secluded nook, partially screened by greenery, and sensuality had been simmering between them during the whole conversation. Now, as he drew her closer, it flared up, bright and hot.

"We should find out if last night was a fluke."

To her surprise, he turned her away from him, so they were both facing in the same direction.

As he pulled her back against himself, she knew instantly that he was turned on.

With her husband, that had always frightened her. She never enjoyed where his arousal led.

Now she felt her nerves stretch taut as she thought about exploring the physical feelings and the emotions Lance Marshall kindled within her.

Well, he couldn't do anything here. She wasn't even facing him.

His hands slid up and down her bare arms, sending tingles of sensation over her skin. Tingles that transmuted themselves to more intimate parts of her body.

Maybe he had deliberately made it safe for her to respond. At least as far as she could respond.

From where he stood, she knew that he could look down her sundress, that he could see the upper swell of her breasts and see the rapid rise and fall of her chest.

His lips moved against the side of her neck, sending more heat through her. And when he nibbled his way to her ear and stiffened his tongue so that he could probe the sensitive inner channel, she made a small needy sound.

All the while, he stroked his fingers over the naked skin of her shoulders, down to the tops of her breasts, sending hot currents through her.

He had turned her away from him, and it would be easy for her to escape if she wanted. Frank never would have done that. And after her experience with him, she hadn't given other men a chance.

Withdrawing his tongue, he nipped at her earlobe, then whispered, "Hunch forward a little."

"Why?"

"To give me a better view."

She could have protested. Instead, she did as he asked, leaning forward so that the bodice of the sundress shifted away from her body.

Her nipples were throbbing now. Probably he could see them tight and hard inside the bra cups of the dress.

He confirmed the assumption by shifting one hand over her shoulder and into the bodice front.

The hand eased down slowly, gliding over the top of her breast, creating a trail of fire. When his finger stroked over the hard point of her nipple, she choked back a moan.

As he stroked back and forth across that crest—then

drew a tight circle around it—she closed her eyes, her whole attention focused on that one part of her body.

His other hand moved downward, pressing over her aching core.

No man's touch had ever kindled this much sensation in her body. Only by herself had she dared to unleash her sexual needs.

"Do you want more than this—with me?"

The sensual web he had drawn around her made it difficult to focus on a coherent answer. But she managed to speak. And she managed not to lie. "Yes."

He was using his mouth again, sliding his lips along her cheek then back to her ear, his teeth and tongue playing with the delicate curl.

The sensation was exquisite. And one thing she had learned about Lance Marshall: he knew how to arouse a woman. She suspected he wouldn't disappoint on the follow-through. Without thinking, she threw her head back, giving him better access. He held her where she was, her body arched, her pulse pounding.

His mouth and his hands were melting her to his will.

She was still fully dressed, but she felt like she was going up in flames.

"Let me turn around," she whispered.

"Don't you like this?"

"You know I do."

He laughed softly. "Oh, yeah."

Two could play at this game. When she pressed her bottom into his crotch, she heard his indrawn breath.

He took a step back, dragging her with him farther into the concealing foliage. Then a sound crackled in the distance, and it took several moments for her to realize what she was hearing.

A loudspeaker.

A man's voice announced, "The Botanic Garden will be closing early for maintenance. Please make your way toward the main exit."

Her eyes blinked open and she came back to reality.

# CHAPTER
# TWELVE

AS SAVANNAH HEADED for the front door, Lance stayed right behind her.

When they stepped into the late-afternoon sunshine, he asked, "So how far do you want to take this?"

"I can't make a decision like this—under the influence of . . . of sexual arousal."

She knew he was struggling to keep his expression neutral as he shoved his hands into his pockets and said, "I don't want to push you into anything that makes you uncomfortable."

"Yes, you do. Is this a game you're playing?"

"No game. Call me when you make a decision," he said in a gritty voice.

"Okay," she whispered. Because she couldn't take his scrutiny, she turned away and walked toward her car.

She had pictured herself driving home. But now she remembered that wasn't an option. Thanks to Lance, she knew that home wasn't a safe place.

She was heading back toward her hotel when she passed a large bookstore on Wisconsin Avenue. After driving by, she circled back and found a parking space. Wishing she had a hat she could pull down over her face, she went inside.

"Can I help you?" a clerk asked.

"No. I'm just browsing," she murmured. But she knew what she was looking for.

Finally, at the back of the store, she found the nonfiction section on sex and began scanning the titles. Lance had said that the Eighteen Club was set up with masters and slaves. She was thinking she should find out more about that—besides what she'd read in Charlotte's diary.

When a man came up beside her and gave her a sidewise glance, she walked away and found herself in the religion section. She took down a couple of volumes, pretending interest in eastern religions and the great spiritual leaders of the world.

After she had the sex books to herself again, she went back and found the bondage and domination titles.

Hoping that nobody was looking over her shoulder, she grabbed a couple of how-to manuals and gave them a quick inspection. Then she strode to the checkout counter.

By the time she stepped outside with her purchases safely hidden in a plastic bag, it was dinnertime. She looked up and down the avenue and, spotting a deli, went in to buy herself a chicken salad sandwich and a bottle of iced tea.

She took the meal and the books back to her hotel room. After hanging the Do Not Disturb sign on the door, she changed from her sundress and sandals into a T-shirt over her panties, then climbed into bed.

As she started reading the books, she nibbled on the sandwich. Her sister's diary had clued her in to what she might find. The books gave her a more dispassionate account of the subject. Yet she found her body responding as she read.

What would it be like to let a man tie you to the bed the way Charlotte had done and do wicked sexual things to you? You'd have to trust him implicitly, wouldn't you?

She kept reading, and when she glanced at the clock, she found that it was after midnight.

Emotionally exhausted, she set the books on the floor and slid down into the bed. She was asleep almost as soon as she closed her eyes.

ERICA Wentworth looked around the private chamber decked out like a Viking lodge. She had started with her Roman fantasy, then moved on to some other historical settings.

When she laughed softly, Kevin turned toward her.

"What?"

"I was a history major. I was thinking that I hadn't done anything with it since college—until now."

He grinned, sharing the joke.

In this fantasy, she was an aristocratic woman. The warriors had come back from a raid and given her the pick of the male captives. And she had taken Kevin to her fur-covered bed.

Since first daring to indulge her secret desires, she had picked several different men to share her private world. But she always came back to Kevin because she loved his body, loved the way he served her, and loved the conversations they had in bed.

This afternoon, she had tied him up and dripped hot candle wax on his body, then let him make love to her.

Sometimes the things that leaped into her mind when she was at the Castle frightened her. It was like they came from outside herself.

But how could that be true?

To reassure herself, she snuggled against Kevin as he stroked her hair and nuzzled his lips against her cheek.

She turned her head toward him. "Is this your only job?"

"No. I work for a tax accountant."

She blinked. "You're an accountant?"

"I'm getting my degree."

"But you've . . . always been available when I come in."

"This is the slow season for taxes." He raised his head and looked at her. "And I was hanging around—hoping you'd call for me again."

She nodded. He seemed to like her. But he was getting paid to like her, she reminded herself. "How did you find you liked painful pleasure?" she asked.

He went very still. "That's private information."

"But I'd like you to share it with me."

"Why?"

"We get along so well. I want to know you better."

He dragged in a breath and let it out. "Yeah, we're good together. Okay. I learned it from a babysitter."

Her eyebrows rose. "You were young?"

"Well . . . I was sexually mature."

Under the covers she reached for his hand and knit her fingers with his. "Can you tell me about it?"

He dragged in a breath and let it out before saying, "My mother's sister was sick. I was in school and my parents needed to leave me with someone while they went to visit Aunt Paula."

"Where did you live?"

"Outside Chicago. The school nurse, Miss Walton, said she could stay with me, and they took her up on it."

"How old were you?"

"Fifteen and a half." His hand tightened on hers. "It makes me hot to think about it."

Lifting the fur cover she looked down at his cock. He was hard.

"Tell me what happened," she said in a throaty voice.

"I was late coming home for dinner because I was shooting baskets with friends. Miss Walton told me she was going to have to punish me, but she made me wait until after we ate. Then she had me help her clear the table and put the dishes in the dishwasher. After that, she said she was going to spank me. She made me pull down my pants and bare my butt to her."

"Were you embarrassed?"

"Terribly. But I had been told to obey her. So I did it. She made me lean on the kitchen counter with my butt sticking out. Then she spanked me. It hurt. But it gave me a warm feeling, too. When she finished, she stroked my bottom, sliding her hands over my stinging skin. Then she slipped her hand to the front of me and found my erection.

"I started to apologize. But she told me to be quiet. She stroked me. Then I heard fabric rustling. She told me to turn around, and she was sitting on the kitchen table with her blouse unbuttoned and her skirt pulled up over her naked twat." His voice had turned thick with the heated memory.

"She wasn't wearing a bra. She took her breasts in her hands and lifted them toward me. She told me to squeeze them and play with the nipples. I'd gotten that far with some girls I dated, but they were always—you know—reluctant to let me touch them. This was different. It was so sexy. Then she lay back on the table with her legs dangling over the edge and told me to put my cock into her. I did it to her right there, standing between her legs while she lay spread for me, fondling her breasts."

"How did you feel afterward?"

"Like I'd lucked into something really good. But I also felt like I'd done something . . . bad."

"I can imagine. That was pretty heavy-duty stuff for a kid your age."

"Right. But that didn't stop me. I mean, I didn't report her to anyone. I could have gotten her arrested. But I didn't."

"She took a chance with you."

"But she must have been pretty sure it would turn out the way she wanted. We had an orgy every night my parents were away."

"You did the same thing every time?"

"No. We did different things. In the kitchen. In the bathroom. Lord, she knew how to top."

Erica wanted to ask if she was as good as Miss Walton. But she knew she couldn't be. She was just learning how to play these games. And Kevin was giving her pointers.

"So what happened after your parents came home?"

He laughed. "They gave her a big bonus for taking such good care of me."

She chuckled with him, then asked, "Did you get together with her again? I mean sexually."

"Sometimes I would go down to the nurse's office at school and we could sneak in a session there. And sometimes I went to her house." He gave her a direct look. "What about your first time?"

"I was a good girl. My first time was on my wedding night."

"How was it?"

"Not great. At least it was fast."

"Did it get better?"

"Not a lot. Sometimes after he'd finish and go to sleep, I'd sneak into the bathroom and make myself come."

He put his arms around her. "Let me help you forget about him."

"You already have." She gave him a considering look. "Do you want to do what you did with Miss Walton?"

"God, yes. It's making me hot just talking about it."

And her, too. The familiar buzzing had started in her brain again, urging her to let her emotions fly free.

"Get up and lean over with your hands against the wall," she said in her slave mistress voice.


BREATHING hard, Lance came back from a run along the road. He had expected Savannah to call him that night. Then the next day. But the phone hadn't rung, and he felt like his insides were tied in knots.

He'd run until his legs were wobbly. But it hadn't accomplished what he needed. His body was hot and tight. He wanted Savannah Carpenter. With an intensity he had never experienced. He didn't want to think about what that meant, so he tried to go back to work.

As he sat in front of the computer, he fought to remember the reason he'd contacted Savannah.

The Castle. He needed to get inside. And if she wouldn't help him get into Raymond Conrad's fortress, then he'd better find someone else. Like the older gal in the picture from Savannah's camera.

But it wouldn't be the same. Not hardly. He wanted Savannah to call him. And if she didn't? He couldn't bear to consider that outcome.

Forcing himself to think about something else, he went to his image file and brought up the picture of the woman Savannah had snapped.

She was in her late forties or early fifties. But she was in excellent shape. Her body could have been that of a woman in her thirties. As she stood beside her car, she looked uncertain. But he was sure that wasn't her usual expression. Her clothing and her car told him she was rich. Probably in most social situations, she was supremely confident.

So who was she? Where had he seen her before?

He went to the Internet, bringing up the Web sites of various charities. Some had held receptions in Washington, D.C. And some had pictures taken at the events.

He started with the Heart Association, then tried the Humane Society Ball and the Potomac Club. None of those gave him the information he needed.

And what the hell did it matter, anyway. He wanted Savannah.

\*   \*   \*

IN the basement of his Castle, Boralas fed. Not on food as a human would understand the term.

On emotions. On sexual arousal. On fear. Pain. Anger. Greed. All the human emotions that his kind craved.

The Castle was the perfect place for his needs. And now he didn't know how he had lived without it.

His own world was on a plane parallel to the one where the Castle sat in Rock Creek Park. For convenience, he called his home Earth Omega. And this time continuum Earth Alpha. They were very different places. In Earth Omega the lucky humans lived inside the high walls of city-states. The rest took their chances in the lawless wilds. Even the slaves were better off inside the enclosures.

He was sure this world—Earth Alpha—was the way life was meant to be. He felt that his own earth had taken a wrong turn—and been cursed by the fates that ruled the universe.

Here they had something called nuclear weapons that they somehow kept in check. In his own world the most fearsome weapons were psychic powers.

And there were powerful beings back in the world he'd come from that didn't exist here. He was one. But there were others. Some of them looked like ordinary people from Earth Alpha, but they had talents that had never developed here.

There were very few of his own brothers and sisters left on earth Omega. Because some of the people there had learned the skills they needed to hunt and kill his kind. Many of his brothers and sisters had gone into hiding in another universe. It was a safer place, but they found little to feed on there. So they had to come back home to eat—where the hunters waited.

One of the best hunters, a woman named Rinna, had sensed his presence, even from the other side of the portal. And that made her very dangerous. But maybe her own people would kill her. She'd gotten herself into trouble in one of the city states on Earth Omega—a place called Sun Acres. As punishment, she'd been sent into the wilderness to track his kind. Many of the elders in Sun Acres hoped she'd get herself killed out here.

But she had one powerful protector. A man who was trying to bring her back. If all went well, she'd get herself killed by some of the thugs outside the city before he found her.

Then Boralas would be safe in this paradise. He had discovered Earth Alpha by accident. And he loved it here. It was the perfect place for one of his people. It was so much like his own earth—yet naïve and trusting.

He had crossed between the worlds and landed in the richest treasure trove he could imagine. Because with the help of Raymond Conrad, he had set up a playground for humans who could afford to pay for anything they wanted.

And when they came here, he fed on the emotional energy they brought with them.

Well, not just what they brought. Because once they came to the castle, he tapped into their brains, encouraging them to act out the fantasies they had imagined but dared not put into words.

And then he pushed them beyond where they might have gone on their own. Compelling the slaves and the masters to come back again and again for the sexual gratification they found here.

It was good. Excellent. Yet now he was finding that he needed more.

SAVANNAH woke, knowing that she had been sexually aroused in her dreams. Because she had kept herself from calling Lance Marshall, she had been dreaming of him.

She had spent most of the day before at the hospital. But each time she'd sat in the cafeteria or lounge, waiting to see Charlotte, she'd thought of Lance.

Glancing at the clock, she saw that it was already ten in the morning—a day and a half since she'd walked away from him at the Botanic Garden.

She climbed out of bed. Showered. Went downstairs to the coffee shop, where she had a quick breakfast. But she knew all along that it was just a matter of time before she pulled out her cell phone.

When she finally dialed his number, he picked up on the first ring.

"Hello."

"This is Savannah."

"And?" In just that one syllable, she could hear the edge of nerves in his voice.

"I can't give up an opportunity to find out what happened to my sister."

Apparently he wanted to be clear on what she meant. "So you're willing to see if we can work together—under the conditions that the Castle would impose?"

"Yes."

"We should meet somewhere memorable." He was silent for a moment. "How about the Watergate Hotel?"

A hotel. Well, they weren't getting together for afternoon tea.

"Okay," she whispered.

"I'll meet you there in a couple of hours."

She caught the warmth in his voice, and she was pretty sure that her agreement meant more to him than he was letting on. Good. At least she wasn't the only one emotionally involved.

"Meeting me doesn't mean you've committed yourself to anything."

"Are you trying to give me the illusion of safety?"

"Yeah. Call me when you get there, and I'll give you my room number."

She paid for her breakfast and stood. The rational part of her mind kept whispering that she didn't know this man well enough to meet him in a hotel room. And she certainly didn't trust him—not completely.

She'd be putting herself at his mercy. The way she had been at her husband's mercy. No. This felt very different. She'd been afraid of Frank. And she was afraid of Lance Marshall. But not because she thought he was going to abuse her or hurt her. She was more afraid of how strongly he affected her.

A couple of hours. He was giving her time to chicken out.

Keeping her mind in neutral, she wandered around the shopping area in Bethesda, looking in store windows. Finally, she headed downtown—then had to hunt for the front door of the damn hotel. Lord, they were in business to rent rooms to people, weren't they? Why did they need to hide the entrance?

# CHAPTER
# THIRTEEN

AFTER PARKING HER car, Savannah dialed Lance's mobile number.

He answered at once.

Five minutes later, she was on the fifth floor. And when he answered the door to his room, she caught her breath.

He was shirtless and wearing only a pair of dark slacks. His chest was wonderful, broad and hard and covered with crinkly dark hair.

He gave her a long, smoldering look that made her heart start to pound.

"I thought you said I could back out," she managed.

"You can. But I decided to stack the deck."

When she stepped inside the room, he lifted her overnight bag out of her hand.

She followed him as he carried it down a short hall, past the bathroom and into a luxurious hotel room.

His naked back was just as sexy as his chest. And now that she had permission to look at him, she was thinking that his butt was pretty good, too.

She stopped walking at the entrance to the one of the largest hotel rooms she'd ever seen.

The bed was at one end, and she saw that he had turned down the spread. Quickly she pivoted toward the other end of the room and saw a sitting area with two large easy chairs and a dark wood wall unit that looked like it could have been in an apartment living room. It had the usual television set and minibar. But the shelves also held hardback books.

Perhaps because she wasn't ready to deal with the bedroom—or with Lance Marshall's naked torso—she turned and looked toward the windows. When she saw the magnificent view, she caught her breath. The room faced the Potomac River and a stretch of trees and greenery on Theodore Roosevelt Island. To her right, on the D.C. side, she saw the Georgetown waterfront and the spires of Georgetown University.

Lance came up behind her, and her heart lurched inside her chest. She was instantly hot and needy, and he probably knew it as well as she did.

Still, she managed to say, "We should talk first."

"Okay."

She didn't have to glance down to know that if he looked over her shoulder at her knit shirt, he would see her nipples standing at attention.

"Thank you for coming," he said in a husky voice.

"The Castle is an important story for you."

"This is about more than a story."

"What, exactly?"

"I think we're about to find out."

He stayed in back of her, the way he had at the Botanic Garden, stroking his palms up and down her arms, soothing away the goose bumps he raised. Just the touch of his big hands on her arms was exquisite.

The need to stay honest with him bubbled up from deep inside her. "I don't have much experience," she heard herself say. "Only with one man. My husband. And I didn't like what we did together."

"What was that?"

"I'd rather not talk about it."

"I promise you'll like what we do." He bent his head and brushed her hair aside, so his lips could find the tender place where her jawline met her neck.

A small sigh of pleasure eased out of her.

His finger moved to her lips, where he touched her with a feather-light stroke.

Without thinking about what she was doing, she arched her neck, giving him better access. He was weaving a sensual web around her again, the way he'd done so easily in the Botanic Garden. What was he, a wizard? Or a man who knew just the right tricks to arouse a woman.

With anyone else, she might have tried to keep the conversation going. Instead, she opened her mouth so he could stroke the sensitive tissue of her inner lips. Then, with a little grin, she took his finger between her teeth, biting then stroking with her tongue.

Behind her, he caught his breath, then moved back far enough so that he could pull up her knit top.

He eased it over her head and off, along with her bra.

The cool air of the room hit her breasts, tightening her nipples even more.

As she stood in front of the window, naked to the waist, he pressed her backward, moving her shoulders against his hair-roughened chest, sending currents of sensation through her.

"Someone will see us," she protested.

He laughed softly. "Not unless they're a helicopter pilot."

He held her where she was, catching her breasts in his hands, teasing her nipples with his fingers, making her cry out with the pleasure of it.

He kept one hand on her breasts. With the other, he worked the snap at the top of her pants and the zipper so he could push the garment down to pool around her feet. Then he pushed her panties down and out of the way.

Part of her was standing somewhere else in the room, watching in amazement.

Was she really letting this man undress her? Was she really so aroused that she wouldn't have been able to stand without leaning against him?

Her breath hissed in and out of her lungs as she felt the pressure of his erection against her bottom.

His lips played with her cheek, her neck, her jawline while he built her need higher—then higher.

One hand moved back and forth, teasing one breast and then the other. His other hand moved between her legs, slipping into her folds.

He made a hungry sound when he found her wet and swollen for him. He bent his head, nipping at her shoulder, then soothing her with his tongue.

Hot currents surged through her. As he played with her breasts, he stroked her most sensitive flesh, gliding two fingers from her clit to just inside her vagina and back again.

Her hips moved frantically against him, trying to direct the pressure where she needed it. Finally, with a moan, she covered his hand with hers, holding his fingers in place as she surged against him.

Unbearable tension tightened every muscle in her body. He kissed her neck, teasing one nipple, while she slid the fingers of his other hand against her clit until she came—crying out and falling back against him.

He cradled her in his arms, kissing her cheek as she dragged air into her lungs.

"Well, we know you respond to me," he murmured, his lips playing with her ear.

"Are you teasing me?"

"No. I'm relieved the heat exchange goes both ways."

He let her rest against himself for a moment, then swung her into his arms and carried her across the room, where he laid her on the bed and stood looking down at her.

Still feeling dazed, she watched through slitted eyes as he unzipped his slacks and pulled them off, along with his undershorts, before coming down beside her on the bed.

His erection stood out, hard and red. She thought he would cover her body with his and plunge into her. Instead he kissed her cheek.

"Don't you want to . . ."

"Mm-hm. But not yet. I want you hot and needy again before I come inside you."

"I . . . think that will be a while."

"I hope not. Because intercourse won't be much fun for me unless you enjoy it, too."

She struggled to absorb that. In her experience, men didn't give a damn about making sure they weren't the only one having fun. Of course, she was relying on a sample of one.

Lance reached to smooth back a damp lock of her hair, combing his fingers through the blond strands.

She closed her eyes, drifting on the sensation of his light touch.

He stroked her hair, her face, the top of her chest, her arms. Bypassing her breasts, he dropped his hand to her midsection, then her thighs.

By the time he reached her knees, she was moving her legs restlessly.

He hadn't touched any of the spots she would have expected. Yet those were precisely the places where her nerve endings had begun to tingle.

"Lance, please," she whispered.

"What do you want?"

"You know."

"Tell me."

She managed a laugh. "It's hard to say it in words."

"Maybe. But unless you tell me, we're not going any further."

She swallowed around the tightness in her throat. He was forcing her to ask for something she'd never talked about. "Touch . . . my breasts."

"Oh, yeah." He drifted his fingers over the soft mounds, avoiding the taut centers.

"My nipples," she gasped.

"What about them?"

"Play with them."

As he did, they tightened even more.

"Oh!" His touch was incredible, and she arched into the caress. He bent to take one distended bud into his mouth, sucking, then using his teeth to gently clamp down on her, all the while playing with the other nipple.

"Lance. Oh, God, Lance."

He raised his head to ask, "What else do you want?"

"I . . ."

"Tell me."

"I . . . touch me. Between my legs."

He pressed his fingers over her mound, playing with the crinkly hair.

"Here?"

"Damn you." She was too far gone to play games with him. "My clit. Between my lips."

His hand slid lower, into her most sensitive flesh, teasing and stroking and driving her insane.

Her hips rose and fell, pressing against his hand. When he took it away, she cried out in disappointment— until he moved between her legs.

"Now," he growled as he slid into her, stretching her. Filling her.

"Oh, God, Savannah!"

He drove into her, and she felt his need for release. But he only moved at a slow, steady pace, waiting.

"Press your fingers against your clit."

She was beyond refusing him anything.

She slid her hand between them, wedging her finger against that sensitive spot.

Her need surged. And when he plunged deep into her vagina, her inner muscles clenched around him.

He let himself go then, shouting his satisfaction as he poured himself into her—while her own orgasm swept over her, through her.

He collapsed on top of her, holding her close, then rolled to his side, taking her with him.

She looked into his face, shocked to see that he seemed as dazed as she felt.

"I didn't know sex could be like that," she whispered.

"Neither did I."

Was he lying? She wanted to know exactly what he'd felt, but she couldn't ask.

He held her for long moments, and she snuggled against him, looking around at their luxurious surroundings. She hadn't planned this, but here she was. With a man she hardly knew.

And now that they had made love, she wanted to get to know him a lot better. But she didn't want to give away too much. So she only whispered, "I'll remember today for the rest of my life."

"So will I."

It was late afternoon. But anyplace outside these four walls might have been situated in another universe. Her world had contracted to the confines of this luxurious room.

They could have been long-familiar lovers who'd arranged a special night together. She closed her eyes and burrowed into Lance's warmth.

He held her close, stroking her shoulder, her hair.

Then he spoke—and reminded her that the romantic atmosphere was only her illusion.

"Did you bring your sister's diary?"


LANCE waited for Savannah's answer. They'd just had mind-blowing sex. But that didn't mean she trusted him completely. Lord, he didn't even know if he could trust himself.

Things were probably moving too fast for her. For him, too. But at least he could pretend he was focused on the job they'd agreed to do together.

She swallowed, hesitating several heartbeats before saying, "Yes. I brought the diary. It's in my bag."

He kept his voice even as he said, "Can I get it?"

"Okay."

She started to sit up, then apparently changed her mind when she realized she was naked. "Would you bring me a T-shirt from my bag? And some panties."

He couldn't hold back a grin. "You're modest—now?"

"Yes."

Because he was perfectly comfortable with his own nudity, he climbed out of bed and closed the curtains before turning on one of the bedside lamps. Then he grabbed a luggage rack from the closet, and set down the overnight bag.

After opening the zipper, he handed her a mint green T-shirt and panties.

While she was getting dressed, he picked up the diary. The cover showed *Starry Night*. An odd choice for personal reminiscences.

Maybe Charlotte was an artistic type like her sister.

That stopped him, and his gaze flicked to the woman watching him. Maybe it wasn't that Charlotte was artistic. Maybe this was a message to Savannah.

Her gaze on him was intent. Suddenly feeling like he was on display, he looked at the clothing he'd thrown onto the floor. But he wasn't going to pull his pants on just because he was feeling a little bit uncomfortable. Instead, he bent his head and began skimming the diary. The contents made him draw in a quick breath.

The passages were very explicit. Very kinky. And very hot.

He whistled through his teeth. "This is pretty potent stuff."

"Quite."

He felt his cock stir. He'd just made love with Savannah, but her sister's descriptions were turning him on again.

Feigning a casual air, he returned to the bed, plumped up the pillows, and slid under the covers, pulling the sheet across his lap.

After getting settled, he opened to another section of the book and read some more.

When he glanced at Savannah, she shut her eyes.

He found her hand, twining his fingers with hers as he turned pages.

After about twenty minutes, he said, "These scenes disturb you."

"Yes."

"Why?"

She opened her eyes and looked at him. "It's not about a normal relationship. He's enjoying dominating her—and hurting her. And she likes what he's doing."

"Yes. It's obvious that it turned them both on. Which means that they agreed on the rules of the game."

"And she ended up in the hospital."

He searched her face. "You think that was part of their . . . sexual play? That things got out of hand?"

"I don't know!"

"Okay. We don't know what happened. So let's stick with the diary. Which scene disturbed you the most?" he asked, wondering if she would tell him.

Instead of answering, she said, "That's a pretty personal question."

"Yeah. But the two of us need to understand each other if we're going into the Castle. Because once we get in there, we're not going to be able to explain anything."

"Then what was your reaction to the diary?" she shot back.

"Your sister is a very vivid writer."

"Does reading that book turn you on?"

"Hm, let's see." Hoping to lighten the mood, he pulled up the sheet and looked down at his erection, an expression of mock surprise on his face. "I guess it does."

She laughed, then sobered. "Be serious."

"You don't always have to be serious about sex. You're allowed to have fun. Didn't you have fun a while ago?"

She gave a small nod.

"So I know what works with you physically. I'd like to know which of those scenes bothered you the most."

"Why?"

"So I'll know how far you think you can go, when we get inside the Castle."

She shivered. "Okay. I hated the scene that's set in medieval times. She's a witch. And he's her jailer. He's dressed all in black, wearing a hood and a cape. He's bare-chested and has on tights. He shaves her . . . her pubic hair."

"Back in the bad old days, they really did that, you know. So they could look for witch marks."

"Yuck." She made a face, then went back to the scenario. "Then he punishes her for her sins. At least he doesn't burn her at the stake."

"But he ties her to one."

"Yes—until he unties her and throws her on a pile of straw, where he screws her, and she comes in a great roiling orgasm."

"Yeah, that one's a little rough. But not outside the bounds for the Eighteen Club."

"That's what they do in there?"

"They play whatever games the participants agree to. Sometimes pretending to be reluctant is part of the fun."

"Are you saying that if we go inside I have to do stuff like that? My sister and that man were in a private room. How would anyone know what they were doing?"

"Probably they have peepholes—and cameras. Because there are people who like to watch. And then there's the blackmail consideration. If Raymond Conrad needs to keep anyone in line, he can pull out the videos and show them. So I wouldn't consider anything we do there really private."

She blanched. "You know for sure that he films the people who come to the club?"

"I don't know anything for sure. That's why I need to get inside. If I find evidence of criminal activity, it makes a better book."

"Oh, right. And meanwhile, we might find out what happened to my sister."

"I'm betting the Eighteen Club creates an atmosphere of lawlessness. If you're into sexual activities that are considered . . . extreme . . . then you could get carried away and go too far. That could have happened with Charlotte. Or she could have found out about something illegal, and threatened to spill the beans unless they paid her off."

She was watching him with unnerving intensity, taking it in. "How do you know all that?"

"I've talked to people who have been there as guests. And as slaves."

She sighed. "Yes. I got some books on the way home from the Botanic Garden and read about slaves."

"Your sister obviously got a lot of sexual gratification by putting herself into her lover's power. Some people enjoy that. Some people enjoy playing the role of the master." He kept his gaze on her. "You've never done anything like that yourself?"

"No." She looked down at her hands, then up again. "Have you?"

"I've played some mild bondage games," he admitted.

"Do, uh, normal people go to the Eighteen Club?"

"There'd be no point in going if they didn't want something unusual. I suppose some people just like to soak up the wicked atmosphere. Others are looking for group sex. Or someone who will act out fantasies with them—fantasies they might not be able to share with a husband or wife. But none of that is outside of 'normal' bounds—if nobody gets hurt."

"Oh, great," she muttered.

"We don't have to get into anything heavy there."

"So why can't we just have a drink in the bar?"

"Because if we look like we're enthusiastic new members, people will think we're just regular folks—at least by Castle standards. They'll make friends. They'll talk to us."

"And ask us to join in group 'games'? Like that scene where he . . . he put Charlotte into a slave market and let some other guy buy her, then went along to watch the other guy . . . do stuff to her."

"Again, you're picking an extreme example. Are you saying there's nothing in your sister's diary that you can relate to?" He gave her a considering look. "What about the scene where he handcuffs her to the head-board?"

She dragged in a sharp breath. "Are you planning to do that to me?"

"I don't have any handcuffs. But we can pretend."

Lance moved quickly, watching her eyes widen as he pulled the covers to the foot of the bed and tossed all but one pillow onto the floor.

Lord, was he using this whole Castle thing as an ex-cuse for mind-blowing sex? He didn't know. And he didn't really care. Not at the moment.

"Take off those panties you just put on, and lie down, with your hands above your head. Hold on to the edge of the headboard with your fingers," he said in a voice that had turned gritty.

His heart pounded as he watched her hesitate. He let out a breath when she did as he asked. As she stared up at him, he saw the raw nerves in her eyes.

"Raise your hips."

When she did, he slipped the pillow underneath.

"Now spread your legs, like I've tied your ankles."

She licked her lips, and he wondered if her mouth was as dry as his.

Still, she did as he asked. He stood beside the bed, staring down at her.

When she closed her eyes and turned her head away, he made his voice harsh. "This is a lesson in obedience. I want you to start by looking at me."

She did, and he felt a surge of satisfaction. "You're so open to me. So vulnerable," he murmured, echoing what she must be thinking. "And I love the way that pil-low brings your pussy closer to me."

She hissed out a breath as she looked up at him. He made her wait for almost a minute before he touched her.

As he had before, he started with her extremities, playing with her knees, then her thighs, before stroking his hands along her ribs, over her stomach, making the muscles quiver.

He and Savannah had satisfied each other completely not long ago. But he was as hot as he'd been when she first walked into the room.

He played with the front of her T-shirt, then rolled it up, exposing her breasts. Her nipples were already tight buds. He watched them stiffen even more as he rolled them between his fingers, then he reached toward the bedside table, where he picked up a ballpoint pen.

"What are you going to do?"

"In this scene we're playing, I'm in charge of you. So I think we'll put an imaginary gag in your mouth, too. You're not allowed to speak."

She swallowed, watching him as he sawed the pen back and forth between two fingers, then flicked the shaft against one hardened nipple. Not too hard, but hard enough to create the effect he wanted.

She drew in a quick breath.

"Did I hurt you?" he asked at once.

"No."

He used the pen a while longer, then put it down. With deliberate movements, he leaned over her, using his fingers to spread open the lips of her sex so he could look at her.

He could see she was embarrassed.

When she closed her eyes, he growled, "Don't hide from me."

She opened her eyes again, fixing her gaze some-where in the vicinity of his shoulder.

But he was thrilled by the intensity he saw on her face.

He watched what he was doing carefully as he stroked the valley between her legs, then slipped two fingers inside her, sliding them in and out, feeling her slippery heat. She was ready to come. More than ready. So was he. But not yet.

Angling his hand, he pressed against her clit at the top of each stroke.

She made a low, needy sound that almost undid him.

When she moved her hips, he stopped the motion with a hand on her thigh. "Lie still," he said in a harsh voice.

She obeyed, quivering with heat as he bent to use his tongue and lips on her, increasing her need for release but stopping short of satisfying her.

She struggled to keep her hips still. He raised his head and saw she had pressed her lips together to keep from . . . what? Begging. He hoped she wanted to beg.

Part of him watched Lance Marshall with surprise. He had never done anything like this before. But he was enjoying himself very much. In fact, he was so hard that he wondered how long he could keep from doing what they both wanted.

He bent to her again, loving the taste of her. The silky feel of her against his lips and tongue.

Her whole body quivered. And when she couldn't hold back a moan, he took pity on her—and himself.

Covering her body with his, he plunged his cock into her. And she surged upward.

Her hands dug into the edge of the headboard as he rode her, his harsh breathing and his rhythmic movements echoing the frantic need that he had built inside them both.

He looked down at her, watching her face, holding himself back until he felt her inner muscles clench. As she came, he followed her over the edge, satisfaction roaring through him.

He moved off of her and dragged the pillow out of the way, then came down beside her, gathering her close as he kissed her cheek, her eyelids, her lips.

Her breath was still coming in gasps. The first thing she said was, "Why did that make me so hot?"

# CHAPTER
# FOURTEEN

"BECAUSE THE ELEMENT of power adds to the sexual excitement. One partner agrees to give up power. The other wields it."

"What if . . . the power went the other way? What if you put yourself at my mercy?" she asked.

She watched him considering it and watched his breath turn shallow.

"Being the one in charge is important to you," she guessed.

"Yeah. It's part of my background."

"Care to elaborate?"

"I come from a family where the big bad father is solidly in charge. And the sons avoid crossing him."

"What about your sisters?"

"There were only brothers."

"Oh."

He stroked her cheek. "I guess I have something in common with you. I went off to college to get away from Dad. And I never wanted to come home to live again."

She studied his taut features. "Do you see your family?"

"Not often." His gaze had turned inward. "Back to the previous subject—you and me. If you can submit to things that make you . . . nervous, so can I. If you want to be the one in charge—I can handle it."

She couldn't stop herself from saying, "You're sure you're not afraid? As you pointed out, it can get out of hand."

"Not with us."

"How do you know?"

His gaze locked with hers. "Because I would never do anything to hurt you. And I'm willing to bet that's true for you, too. You might like the power games. But you wouldn't go too far."

"You know that—just from a few days' association with me?"

"Yeah."

The honest emotion in his voice spoke to something deep inside her. In the space of a few hours, he had taken her into completely unknown territory. And she was still trying to figure out how she felt about it.

"The books you bought—are they in your luggage?"

"Yes."

"We could look through them for some more ideas," he murmured. "But first, we both need some fuel."

He got out of bed, pulled on his undershorts, and opened the closet. To her astonishment, he brought out a

picnic cooler. After straightening the bedclothes, he laid
out a red and white cloth on the bed and set the basket
on it.

"What's this?"

"Very personalized room service."

She gestured toward the cooler. "Is that why you
wanted some time before we met?"

"Yeah."

Taking off the lid, she saw that he'd bought gourmet
crackers and cheese, paté, slices of sausage, roast
beef, pickles, potato salad, designer sparkling water,
and other goodies.

"No wine?"

"I don't drink. But you can get some from the minibar."

"Not if you aren't." She got out plastic plates and cut-
lery, then helped herself to crackers, cheese, paté, and
potato salad. He took paté and some sliced sausage and
roast beef.

"No crackers?"

"I stay away from carbs."

"Oh." She nibbled on a cracker topped with something called Cotswold cheese. "This is delicious."

"Yeah. I tried to get things you'd like."

"Who are these for?" she asked, pulling out a bag of
gourmet chocolate chip cookies.

"Both of us."

He rolled up a slice of roast beef and ate it. She dug
into the potato salad, thinking it was endearing that he'd
shopped for her.

"Are you trying to make an impression on me?"

"Yeah." Getting up, he brought over two glasses,

filled them with ice from the ice bucket, and poured sparkling water.

"Does the real Lance Marshall go grocery shopping?"

"Of course—I'm a bachelor."

"Good point."

He finished the food on his plate and opened the bag of cookies. As he munched on a cookie he gave her a considering look. "Are you . . . tired?"

"A little."

"We could get some sleep."

"Sure."

He was being so accommodating that she felt overwhelmed.

"Is this the genuine Lance Marshall?" she asked.

"When I'm with you," he answered in a low voice.

She finished a cookie, then helped him clean up the meal and put the food away.

Then she settled down beside him under the covers, liking the feel of his large, warm body occupying the space next to hers.

He reached for her hand, and she drifted off to sleep. Some time later, a chirping noise woke her.

Disoriented, she looked around the room. Lance climbed out of bed and brought her purse over. "It's your cell phone," he said.

Alarm shot through her. "Who would be calling me?"

"Maybe you'd better find out."

"Hello?" Savannah said, hearing the tension in her own voice.

"Ms. Carpenter?"

"Yes."

"This is Dr. Singh."

Her breath caught in her throat as she felt Lance's arm slip around her. "What's happened?"

"I'm sorry. There's no easy way to say this. Your sister has died."

"No," she gasped.

"I'm sorry," the doctor said again. "It happened very fast. Her heart stopped. We tried to resuscitate her. But we couldn't get the heart beating again."

"I . . . I'll be right down."

"All right."

Lance was already getting into his clothing. "I'll take you."

"No." She gave him a fierce look. "I want to go alone." With jerky motions, she began gathering up her clothing. "While you and I were in bed having a wonderful time playing all the nice little games you suggested, Charlotte was dying."

"Neither one of us knew that," he said in a calm voice that set her teeth on edge.

"I know it now!"

"Savannah, this has to be rough for you. Let me help you through it."

"I don't want your help."

He pulled a T-shirt over his head, then focused on her again. "You shouldn't have to go over to the hospital alone."

Tears stung the backs of her eyes. She pulled on her own shirt, fighting to keep the moisture from spilling down her cheeks. Not now. She wouldn't cry now. Not in front of Lance Marshall.

Without looking at him, she said, "In case you can't

figure it out, I don't feel very good about myself right now. And I don't want you with me at the hospital."

"Okay," he answered, his voice low and tight.

"In fact, I don't want your help with anything."

She saw his hands clench at his sides. "You're upset. Don't throw away our relationship because—"

She snorted. "Relationship! I don't think so. You're damn right I'm upset. I could have stayed with her the day we went to the Botanic Garden. Instead, I went to meet you. Then I came here—with you again. Because I was being selfish." She could barely speak. She knew if she raised her voice, it would be impossible to hold back the tears. "I think she knew she was dying, and I chose to be with you instead of her."

When she started to say more, he stopped her. "I understand why you're reacting this way. You feel guilty. But you have to be careful. So don't do anything reckless. I think you'd better have a private funeral. You don't want to call attention to yourself. And you don't want to be in your house, either. Not when somebody's watching you."

"Thanks for reminding me about that." She moved around the room like a robot, stuffing the diary and the rest of her clothing back into the carry bag.

She didn't look at Lance. But she could feel his eyes on her as she grabbed her belongings and marched out of the room, then took the elevator to the lobby, where she gave her parking ticket to the valet attendant.

At least there was one good thing about being downtown. She was close to the hospital. Twenty minutes later, she was at the door of the ICU.

Dr. Singh wasn't there. But a nurse met her at the ICU station.

"How was . . . her death?" Savannah whispered.

"Peaceful."

Savannah hoped it was true, hoped they weren't just saying what she wanted to hear.

The nurse ushered her into the cubicle, where her sister lay pale and lifeless. But she did look peaceful, at last. Savannah pressed her hand over Charlotte's.

"I'm sorry," she whispered. "I should have been here with you."

Her sister didn't answer. She would never speak again. Or do anything else. She would never dance around the bedroom giggling because she'd just faked out her history teacher with a report she'd copied from an older student. And she would never slip out of the house at night to meet her friends down by the pizza parlor.

"You never knew how to have fun and keep yourself safe, did you?" Savannah whispered.

The tears she had struggled to hold back finally leaked from her eyes. As she stood by her sister's bed, she made a vow. "It's not your fault things turned out the way they did for you. It's Dad's fault, for trying to make you into what he wanted. I'll tell him what happened. I'll find out who did this to you. And I'll make sure they're punished."

She could feel someone hovering in the doorway and turned to find a tall, thin man wearing a dark suit.

"Ms. Carpenter?"

"Yes."

"I'm Reverend Samuels. I'm one of the hospital chaplains. I'm here for you in any way you need me."

Savannah hadn't been to church in a long time, and she wasn't sure what to say.

"Why don't we go out in the waiting room, while the staff takes care of your sister," he advised gently.

"Yes."

She let him lead her outside. She might have asked him about funeral homes. But she remembered Lance's advice. She needed somewhere out of the area.

"Thank you for being here," she murmured.

"If you need me, just call."

She nodded, then walked down the hall, where she used her cell phone to call her parents' number.

Her throat tightened when her father answered. "Dad, this is Savannah."

"I don't have a daughter named Savannah," he answered immediately.

She realized she should have expected that response. "Wait. Don't hang up! I have to tell you—Charlotte just died."

"I don't have a daughter named Charlotte, either," he snapped, and she heard the phone click.

"Thank you, Daddy dearest," she whispered, then pushed the end button. Clutching the phone, she struggled to cope with her outrage—and her sadness. She had known her father's wrath. She hadn't known it would outlast death. But why was she surprised?

At the nurses' station, she got a Maryland phone book and picked a funeral home in Baltimore County. For an extra charge, they would transport Charlotte's body.

She was immediately assigned a counselor, a Mrs. Graves, of all names. But the woman turned out to be very helpful. And when Savannah said that she wanted her sister cremated, Mrs. Graves didn't try to argue—or try to sell her a fiendishly expensive urn.

Savannah kept the whole process low-key. She opted for a minister saying a few words after the cremation. Then she told the funeral home she was in the process of moving and asked if it would be all right if she came back in a few weeks for Charlotte's ashes. To her vast relief, they agreed, and she wouldn't have to cart an urn back to her present hotel room in Columbia.

ERICA Wentworth stood in her closet, trying to decide what to wear. Which made no sense. What did it matter what she wore to the Castle, as Kevin called the place?

After she walked in the front entrance, she was going directly to the floor below, where she'd tell them what scene she wanted to step into today. Then they'd ready a room for her and get the appropriate clothing.

She could even call ahead and have everything set up before she got there. But she rarely did that, because on the drive down, she savored the delicious anticipation of deciding what she was actually going to do when she arrived.

Initially, she'd debated about what partner she wanted. But since that intimate talk with Kevin about his background, she had never considered anyone else.

They seemed so well suited to each other. Once again, she reminded herself sternly, he was getting paid to like her.

At first she'd been so thrilled to act out her secret fantasies. Now when she went back, she felt like something in the atmosphere was messing with her head.

She'd get an idea—and she'd know that it had come from outside her own mind. That was frightening. It made her want to stay away. But she didn't want to stay away from Kevin.

Could they meet outside the club? Could she suggest that to him? It was against the rules. And she'd always been the type of person who never broke rules. But she was starting to think about it more and more.

AN unaccustomed feeling of restlessness gripped Savannah. She made one quick visit to her house to get clean clothing and her mail. But all the time she was in her own home, she felt spooked. When she found herself wishing Lance was with her, she quickly shut off the thought. She had made a mistake getting involved with him. He had kept her from being with Charlotte in her last hours.

In her rational moments, she realized it wasn't fair to blame her feelings of guilt on him. But during the first few days after Charlotte's death, she wasn't always rational. It helped a little to call Chad Myerson and talk. Really, he was the only person close to family that she had now.

Because she simply couldn't deal with sorting through Charlotte's possessions—not yet, anyway—she paid the next month's rent on her sister's apartment. She'd go back there when she wasn't so emotionally fragile, she told herself.

Partly because it helped her channel her grief, she spent a lot of time writing and rewriting a letter to her parents about Charlotte. When she was finally satisfied with the results, she sealed it in an envelope and posted it, thinking that if her mother got to the mail before her father did, her mother might even read it. The letter didn't accuse her parents of anything. It simply told about Charlotte falling off a cliff in Rock Creek Park, her two and a half weeks in the hospital, and her death.

After Savannah mailed the letter, she felt empty. Working might have helped her, but she couldn't do that in a hotel room. And as she sat in front of the television set, mindlessly watching one of the all-news cable channels, she began thinking again about avenging Charlotte.

Every time she considered her alternatives, she came back to Lance Marshall. Not because there was any-thing special between them, she kept telling herself. Even when she knew she was lying.

Something important had happened in that posh hotel room at the Watergate. Something very personal. It wasn't just great sex. It was a whole lot more.

She wanted to see him again. She wanted to feel his arms around her. And not just because she needed comfort.

Finally, she dug his business card out of her wallet. She could have called him on the phone.

But she wanted to drive out to his house. Because she had sensed all along that he wasn't telling her the whole truth about himself. And maybe if she could surprise him, she could catch him in the act.

Of what?

She didn't know, but if it was very bad, perhaps it would give her an excuse to get him out of her life for good.


RINNA'S eyes fluttered open and she looked around the cave, struggling to remember where she was. She had been sent to track Boralas, one of the Suckers, and she had sensed him nearby. Then she had lost him.

"You look like Corfolian hell," Haig muttered.

"Thanks, old man." She sat up on her pallet of animal skins and propped her shoulders against the cold rock wall. She was exhausted from her quest, but she struggled to keep her voice steady. "I felt Boralas. Strongly. Now he's gone again."

Haig hobbled to her side, unscrewed the top from a water bottle, and handed it to her. She drank deeply, gratefully.

"What did you feel?"

She ran shaky fingers through her wavy brown hair. "He was hiding in one of these caves, sucking the life force out of his victims. In my mind, I was circling the place where he fed. Getting closer. Then . . . he was gone. I couldn't sense him anymore."

"He can't just vanish. If he was feeding, he has to be somewhere close by. Maybe in another cave."

She looked up at Haig, seeing her frustration mirrored in his wrinkled visage. "Do you believe in the myths of the portals?" she murmured.

He gave her a sharp look. "The portals to another universe?"

She nodded.

"No. That's just a story people invented because they're so desperate to get out of this grunge hole. Wouldn't you like to escape to a place where you don't have to watch your back every moment?"

"But people have vanished."

"Of course. Slaves vanish."

She gave him a direct look. "I could have been one of them."

"Falcone wouldn't kill you."

"When he was finished with me, he might. But it's not just slaves. The monsters can suck the life out of people like us, then throw away the husks into deep cracks in the earth where nobody can find them." She shuddered. "I'd rather believe in . . . escape. You think this is the way people should live? There has to be something better."

She turned away from him. He had saved her life. And she had saved his as well. But sometimes his attitude exasperated her.


LANCE couldn't stay in the house. He felt strung out on fine wires of frustration. He needed to know how Savannah was doing.

Did she still blame him for taking her to bed when her sister was dying? Would she let him back into her life?

He had told himself he would be different from the other men in his family. He would never bond with one woman, never lust after his life mate.

He had thought his Chinese herbs would save him. But he had been wrong.

He reached for the phone, to talk to Grant or Ross. They could tell him the rest of it. Was it just the werewolf who went crazy when he met his life mate and then they were separated? Or was it the woman, too? Would she come back because she had to?

He wanted to ask that question and a lot of others, but he didn't want his brother or cousin to know how bad off he was.

So all he could do was follow Savannah's movements around town. Apparently she had taken his advice and had a quiet burial for Charlotte. Away from D.C.

He'd thought of driving over to where she was staying and paying his respects. But, of course, then he'd have given away that he had tracked her down.

He had given up on thinking she might call him. When he couldn't get her out of his mind, he changed into wolf form and headed for the park. He was feeling reckless, yet he still had enough sense to stay away from park rangers and hikers. If someone spotted a wolf, his life would turn into a living hell.

So he trotted deep into the forest, but he couldn't even take satisfaction from hunting. He was too wound up with thoughts of Savannah.

Finally, when there was no alternative, he decided he would drive to her motel. Maybe she wouldn't talk to him. But he had to try.

When he reached the patch of woods that bordered the park, he stopped short. A car was in the driveway. Savannah's car.

# CHAPTER
# FIFTEEN

LANCE'S HEART STARTED to pound as he circled the house and found Savannah peering in his back window. Probably she'd knocked and hadn't gotten an answer. But if she'd looked in the garage, she'd have seen his cars.

She hadn't spotted the wolf, so he faded back into the underbrush, wondering what the hell he was going to do now.

She stood for several minutes looking at his home. Her shoulders slumped, and she started walking back to her car.

God, she was leaving. And the thought of her disappearing again drove him over the edge.

Plunging farther into the woods, he found a spot that was totally obscured by greenery, then rushed through the process of transformation, feeling his muscles and internal organs contort as his body changed from wolf to man.

SAVANNAH reached for the door handle of her car. She'd felt compelled to come to Lance's place. And all the way over here, she had been thinking about what she would say to him. But he hadn't even been home when she arrived.

After she'd pounded on the front door, she had walked all the way around his house. It was beautiful, a perfect combination of natural wood and stone sheltered by a small hill.

You couldn't even see the structure until you were almost on top of it because it fit so well into the woodsy location.

She hadn't thought of Lance Marshall as poetic. Now she knew that he was. Or at least he appreciated the aesthetics of his environment.

So they had something in common that she hadn't realized.

Like her, he loved nature. And he'd found a place to live that was right next to the Patuxent State Park.

She'd seen three cars in his garage. She couldn't imagine that he needed any more than that, so probably he hadn't driven anywhere. Had he gone for a long walk in the park?

She glanced at the sky. It was going to rain. If he was out in the river valley, he was going to get soaked.

And so would she if she didn't climb back in her car.

And drive away? Or hope the rain would bring him home?

She had just opened the car door, when she heard someone shout her name.

Whirling, she looked toward the park—and saw Lance running toward her, buck naked.

THE expression on Savannah's face stopped Lance in his tracks.

Jesus! What was he thinking?

He had hurried through the change from wolf to man because he'd been sick with fear that Savannah would leave. But in his haste to prevent her escape, he hadn't even considered a minor detail.

He was naked as a jaybird.

He came to an abrupt halt, feeling his face heat. "Uh, sorry," was the best he could manage.

She tipped her head to the side, staring at him.

"I was walking in the park," he said lamely.

"Naked?"

"I guess I should have grabbed a fig leaf on the way here."

That earned a small grin from her.

"But I was afraid you'd leave."

"Do you always ramble around au naturel?"

"No. But one thing I like about this neck of the woods is the privacy."

She answered with a little nod, just as raindrops began to fall through the leaves above them. Perfect timing!

He gestured toward the house. "Come on in. The key is under one of those fake rocks." He turned toward the door and started to bend down, then thought better of mooning her. Instead, he squatted to retrieve the key.

"You can have a cup of tea while I get dressed."

"You drink tea?"

He opened the door and stepped inside, acting as if he thought she was going to follow. "Yeah. My tea collection and mugs are in the overhead cabinet to the right of the stove."

He didn't let out the breath he was holding until he heard her follow him inside and close the door.

Glad to escape, he hurried down the hall and started to grab the shirt he'd left on the bedroom chair. But he'd worn it for the past few days. Instead he took the fastest shower on record, then dried off, scraped a razor over his face, and pulled on clean clothes.

All the time he kept listening for the front door to open and close. But Savannah was still in his house—and he wasn't prepared for visitors.

He stepped back into the kitchen, seeing that she had taken down two of his mugs. In her right hand was his plastic bag full of Chinese herbs.

As he watched, she opened the seal and lifted the jar to her nose.

"This smells awful," she said as he stepped into the room. "Don't tell me it's your favorite tea."

"It's Chinese medicine—to settle my stomach. When I need it."

"Oh."

"Cranberry sounds better today."

"You only have herbal tea?"

"Yeah. Caffeine and I never got along."

She took down two cranberry tea bags and poured hot water over them in two pottery mugs.

"It has to steep."

"I know."

The conversation ground to a halt, and she walked

into the living room, taking her mug with her as she looked at his sparse modern furnishings, then turned to the window wall and stared out into the rain.

When he couldn't stand his own tension, he asked, "Why did you come here?"

"Because you were right about my bumbling attempts to play private detective. I only got myself into trouble." She kept her back to him, and he saw the rigid set of her shoulders. "But I want to find out what happened to Charlotte. Now, more than ever."

"And you think I can help you?"

"Yes."

He wanted to ask, And what happens after we find out about your sister? But he couldn't get the words out. Instead he said, "If I help you, you have to follow my rules."

She whirled to face him. "Like we did at the Watergate?"

"You regret the time we spent there?"

He watched her lower lip quiver.

"I should," she answered in a barely audible voice.

"But?"

"Don't force me to say anything personal."

He clenched his hands around his mug of tea. "Okay."

"How soon can we get into the Eighteen Club?"

He had been thinking about their options. "Maybe going in isn't such a good idea."

Her eyes turned fierce. "That was your plan. What changed your mind?"

He wanted to shout out his fear for the safety of his mate. Instead he said, "If Raymond Conrad knows Charlotte is dead, he could be looking for you."

She raised her chin. "He doesn't know about me."

"Who left that recorder outside your house?" he countered.

She drew in a sharp breath. "Maybe you and your dog better find out."

For a moment he didn't know what she was talking about. Then it clicked in his brain—his dog.

"Where is he, by the way?"

"I let him roam in the park."

"Is that safe?"

"It works for him."

To his relief she changed topics—although he didn't love the new subject.

"I'd like to see your research notes."

He might have objected; instead, he turned and led the way down the hall to his office.

It was a small room with a large desk area. The computer was in the center. He kept much of his research on the hard drive. But he also had a folder with his notes and articles about some of the people who he knew had visited the Castle.

When she reached for the folder, he tensed. He'd collected this stuff for his own use, and he honestly couldn't remember if they gave away anything about the wolf.

Savannah sat down at the desk and thumbed through the material.

Looking up, she said, "You have some names of patrons."

"Nobody I'd trust."

"You wouldn't trust the deputy D.C. police chief?"

"Of course not. If I told him I knew he was a regular at the Eighteen Club, he'd probably figure out a way to get me eliminated."

"Charming."

"And don't think about approaching any senators or congressmen. They'd be just as hostile."

"Doesn't your status as a reporter buy you anything?"

"More likely they'd start figuring out how to scuttle my career. I can't write about the Castle until I have more solid information."

She came to a color photograph that he'd enlarged to eight by ten. "That's my picture of Erica?"

He went very still. "You know that woman?"

"Erica Wentworth?"

She hadn't told him the name when he'd given her back the camera. Now he struggled to keep his voice casual. He'd spent hours trying to identify the woman, and Savannah had just given him her name.

"How do you know her?"

"She bought one of my paintings at a gallery show."

He was suddenly breathing a little easier. Just a little. "I wonder if she'd like to invite you to the Eighteen Club. That would be a safer way to get in than calling up Raymond Conrad and applying for membership."

"Why?"

"Because the focus wouldn't be on you."

"Maybe she was only there that one time. I should ask her."

"Not until I do a background check on her—to make sure she's not one of Raymond Conrad's favorite informants."

THE man drove slowly down Savannah's street.

He didn't usually resort to vile language. But when

he saw her car still wasn't in the driveway, his frustration boiled over.

"Damn it!"

She hadn't been there for over a week. And he had no idea where she had gone.

He'd kept track of Charlotte's status. He'd thought he could figure out where Savannah had taken her body. But the hospital wouldn't give him that information.

So he'd gotten out a phone book and called every funeral home in the city to inquire about Charlotte Nichols. She wasn't at any of them.

What had Savannah done? Shipped her out of town? If so, she could be anywhere. So he was reduced to coming back here, hoping Savannah would show up.

He found a parking place fifty yards down the block and pulled in. Then settled down to wait.


"AND there's something else we need to do," Lance said. "Before you go to the Eighteen Club, you have to change the way you look."

"Why?"

"If that Warren character could figure out you were related to Charlotte, so could other people."

Lance reached to touch her hair, watching her face, knowing she was very aware of the contact. "I love your hair. But I'm afraid you need to cut it and change the color."

"I . . ." She started to grab his hand to move it away—then stopped.

"You need to look different," he said. "We can give you a haircut, to chin length. Then darken the color."

"I can get all that done at a hair salon."

"I'd rather not have people see you altering your appearance."

"Nobody knows me around here!"

"Let's not take a chance," he said, keeping his voice firm. It was a reasonable suggestion, but it wasn't his only reason. His senses were filled with her. And he needed the excuse to touch her.

"You have much experience cutting women's hair?" she asked.

"Are you afraid I'll make a mess of it?"

"Uh-huh."

"I've cut wigs when I needed them for a disguise."

"Don't tell me you've disguised yourself as a woman!"

"Actually, I have."

"You must have made a damn ugly female."

He laughed. "Yeah. Worse than Dustin Hoffman in *Tootsie*. But it's a good ploy for sitting in my car, watching someone's house. I look so ugly that people turn away, embarrassed to stare."

"And you have hair color around the house?"

"Yes."

"Why?"

"I bought it for you."

Outrage crept into her voice as she said, "That was damn nervy of you. You might never have seen me again!"

"I was hoping I would," he answered. "Maybe I was using it as a way to nudge destiny along."

"You believe in destiny?" she challenged.

# CHAPTER
# SIXTEEN

LANCE WONDERED HOW to respond. She'd given him the perfect opportunity to talk about the werewolf and his mate. But it was too soon to bring any of that up. So he said, "You're here, aren't you? Let's do the haircut."

"Before I regain my right mind?"

"If you say so."

"If you make a mess, I'll have to go to a salon and get it fixed."

He wanted to lead her into the bathroom and suggest that she get undressed so she didn't get hair on her clothing. But he figured he'd better not press his luck.

Instead he said, "The house is built into a hill, so there's a lower floor. We can do it downstairs."

Before she could object, he went to gather up a sheet to drape over her shoulders, another sheet for the floor, his haircutting scissors, and a comb, which he carried down along with the step stool from the kitchen.

She sat down, then looked uncertain when he settled the sheet over her shoulders. Tension radiated from her as he picked up a lock of hair at the back of her head.

"Relax," he murmured, making a cut, then another. There was nothing sexual about cutting hair. Yet he felt his cock swell as he touched her.

His whole body felt hot. Couldn't she feel the heat rolling off of him?

It was all he could do to keep working, because all sorts of more interesting ideas were playing through his head like scenes from an erotic movie.

"You're not going to try anything fancy, like layers?" she asked.

Layers? What kind of sexual activity was that? When he realized she was talking about her hair, he struggled to bring his mind back where it belonged.

"No. Just straight across," he managed to say, hearing the husky quality of his voice.

He looked at the adorable curl of her right ear. He had kissed her there. Stroked inside with his tongue. He remembered the wonderful taste of her. The texture. He dragged in a breath, taking in the essence of her scent.

He had stopped, with the scissors raised.

"Lance?"

"Just checking to see if the line is even."

He forced himself to focus on the job because he'd hate to make a mess of her appearance. Her hair was thick, which meant that he had to go back after every cut and make sure it was straight.

He worked from back to front on one side, then the other, getting more and more turned on and running his hands through her hair at every opportunity.

He finished, then stood back to inspect his work.

"How do I look?" she asked anxiously.

"Sexy. And beautiful," he added. Laying down the scissors on a nearby table, he stepped forward and pushed the sheet off her shoulders. It was a surprise to find her wearing a knit top and pants, since he had been imagining her naked under the covering.

"What?" she asked in alarm, searching his face. "Were you lying to me? Do I look horrible?"

"No." He had reached the limits of his endurance. Gathering her into his arms, he prayed she wouldn't push him away.


RAYMOND Conrad was in his working office—the one with the desk and computer—when someone knocked at the door.

He glanced at his watch. It was still early afternoon, and the staff understood that he wasn't to be disturbed unless there was something important.

Greg Dalton, one of the receptionists, stepped into the room looking pleased with himself. "There's a man waiting in the main entrance hall. He says he has some important information for you."

"What's his name?"

"Warren Buckley."

"Never heard of him."

"He says it's vital that he talk to you."

"About what?"

"He won't tell me. He just says you'll want to talk to him."

Conrad thought about it. So what could this Buckley guy want? Did he have some kind of blackmail he thought he could get away with? Or what?

"Maybe I'd better see him. Escort him back here."

"Yes, sir."

Conrad got up and walked to the narrow window that looked out over the park. He'd always thought it was a damn shame he could only see a little sliver of the view. But he knew that putting in a larger window would make the Castle less secure.

A knock sounded at the door and he called out, "Come in."

He saw Dalton step aside and usher in another man. Then the receptionist withdrew and closed the door.

"Come in. Sit down," he said to the man standing awkwardly near the doorway. "Mr. Buckley?"

"Right."

Conrad crossed the room and they shook hands as he sized up the other man. He was about five nine, with a lanky build, brown hair, brown eyes. He was wearing a cheap sports jacket, slacks, and a western string tie.

"What can I do for you?" Conrad asked.

The man shifted his weight from one foot to the other. "It's what I can do for you."

"Such as?"

"You wanted to know if anyone was asking about the Eighteen Club."

"What makes you think so?"

"I hear things." He cleared his throat. "There was a woman asking about Charlotte Nichols."

Conrad kept his expression neutral. "Where?"

"At a bar where Charlotte used to go. But she hasn't been there in a long time."

"So what do you know about the woman asking questions?"

"She was aggressive."

"In what way?"

"She hit me over the head when I wouldn't tell her anything."

Probably there was more to the story than that.

"Did you get her name?"

"No. But she said she was Charlotte Nichols's sister."

That got his attention.

"She knew Charlotte came here. She said Charlotte was in the hospital."

Conrad's gaze sharpened. "When did you talk to her?"

Buckley licked his lips. "Uh . . . about ten days ago."

"And you waited this long?" Conrad asked. So it was before Charlotte had passed. Did Buckley know she was dead? He'd like to ask, but he decided it was better not to bring up that detail.

"I didn't know whether I should come or not," the man said, his excuse sounding lame.

He looked lame. And he looked like he might be holding something back.

*He could be dangerous to us.* The thought echoed in his head. It was Boralas. His silent partner. He listened some more to the inner voice, then asked, "You know what kind of entertainment we offer here?"

A smirk flickered around Buckley's lips. "I've got ideas about that. I know why you like to keep this place private."

*He came here with information, and he wants a reward. Why not give it to him?*

"I appreciate your coming to talk to me," Conrad said. "Would you like to relax with one of the slaves? Or do you enjoy playing a more submissive role?"

"I'd like a slave," the man said immediately.

*Yes. In one of the downstairs rooms. Near me. Let me feed off his emotions. And the substance of his mind.*

The substance of his mind. That last part echoed in Conrad's consciousness. The blatant hunger of it shocked him. Boralas was getting bolder. There had been more unfortunate incidents lately. And that was disturbing.

*Don't worry. Everything's fine. I have control of the situation.*

Conrad felt his tension go down several notches. "Come downstairs. Let me show you our facilities," he said to Buckley.


SAVANNAH stood tautly in Lance's arms, and he thought she would pull away. To his relief, she sighed and let her head drop to his shoulder. "What are we going to do?" she whispered.

"What do you want to do?"

"I don't know!"

"Let's start with the basics. Does being close to me feel good?" As he waited for her answer, he held his breath.

"Yes," she whispered.

"Thank God." He hadn't meant to say that. He hadn't meant to give so much away.

His words and maybe the emotion in his voice seemed to reassure her, because he felt her relax into his embrace. Nothing was settled between them, but it seemed they had made a good start.

He tipped her head up so that he could take her mouth in a deep, hungry kiss.

When he finally lifted his head, they were both breathing hard.

Still, the first words she spoke tore at him.

"Charlotte's dead, and I'm . . ."

"You're alive," he finished for her. "And you're with a man who makes you feel things you thought you would never experience."

"Does that make you proud of yourself?"

"It makes me feel good, yes. But I suspect you're having trouble getting past your guilt."

When he felt her push against his chest, he groaned. "Don't."

"You're overwhelming me—again," she said in a small, pleading voice. Then she ducked under his arm. "Let me look at my hair."

He waited until she was facing in the other direction before gritting his teeth.

"Where's your bathroom?"

"Down the hall, on the right." He stayed with her, followed her inside, standing back as she inspected his handiwork.

"You did a good job."

He felt a little of the tension ease out of his chest. "Thank you."

"I don't think I need to dye it brown. Maybe we can

get some spray hair paint and do a few streaks of blue or purple."

"You're kidding, right?"

"I'm not sure. I already look considerably different. That would finish the job."

"Let's make a judgment about that later." He stepped up behind her, the way he'd first done in the Botanic Garden, and later at the Watergate. Only this time she could watch in the mirror as he bent to stroke his tongue around the curl of her ear, then take the lobe delicately in his teeth. He could watch her in the mirror, too— watch her nipples straining against the fabric of her knit top.

They drew his hand like a magnet, and he brushed his fingers against her.

She moaned and threw her head back. Just when he thought he had won the battle, she reached for his hand and moved it.

"You want me," he growled.

"Is that all there is between us—sex?"

"You don't really think that, do you?" he asked gently.

"I'm . . . confused. I don't know what I'm feeling— or what you're feeling."

"Would you believe me if I told you I had fallen wildly, desperately in love with you?" he asked.

In the mirror her eyes widened. "No."

"So much for honesty."

"You hardly know me."

"I know enough."

"I don't."

He dropped his hands to his sides, clenching his fists. "All right."

"Every time we're together, you sweep me away with sexual . . ." She let the sentence trail off.

"What?"

"Magnetism," she said in a barely audible voice.

"That's bad?"

"It is when I can't think. When I get pushed into things that make me uncomfortable."

"Better here than at the Eighteen Club."

"You keep holding that place over me."

"Because you have to take it seriously."

She glared at him in the mirror. "Right. And what do you want me to do—practice being your slave again?"

He kept his gaze steady on her. "We can try it the other way around. I can be *your* slave."

"You'd do that?"

"I made that offer before, if you remember." He stopped abruptly. He'd made the offer when they'd spent the night at the Watergate. And before they'd done anything about it, her sister had died.

But she nodded, then met his gaze in the mirror. "Why did you agree to that?"

"Because we have to learn to rely on each other. And submission is a shortcut to trust."

He watched her expression turn from serious to wicked. "Well, maybe we should put that statement to the test."

"You've been thinking about it?"

"Yes."

"I wouldn't want to interfere with your fun."

"But I'm making you nervous?"

"Yes."

"Good."

He wondered what had happened to her guilty feelings. Maybe she was working hard to push past them by focusing on whatever game she'd decided to play. Or maybe it was the same for her as it was for him. She needed to forge that intimate contact again. But she couldn't just come out and say it. She had to pretend that the game was the important part.

She looked out the sliding glass door. "You can go sit on the patio. I'll search around the house for some equipment, and call you when I'm ready."

He stood very still, wondering what he should do now. Maybe he'd made a mistake putting ideas into her head.

# CHAPTER
# SEVENTEEN

"GO OUTSIDE," SHE urged, opening the door.

He had gotten himself into this, thinking she was going to be shy about assuming a dominant role. Now he couldn't very well refuse to play, not after she was making it a kind of test.

So he walked outside onto the patio under the deck and sat in one of the Adirondack chairs facing the park. When she closed the door behind him, the sound vibrated along his nerve endings.

He sat staring out at the rain, watching it hit the leaves of the trees. When he glanced at his watch, ten minutes had passed.

He lasted another eight minutes before looking again. Probably making him wait like this was part of her plan. If she was trying to up his tension level, she was doing a good job.

She kept him on the deck for twenty-five minutes. He was about to get up and find out where she was, when she came to the door.

"I'm ready for you," she said in a stern voice.

He stood. "Okay."

"I will be your master, and you will be my slave. You agree to those rules?"

He swallowed. "Yes. What are you planning to do?"

"Slaves get punished for asking questions."

"Did you get that out of a book?"

"Don't you give me credit for any imagination? Or are you too chicken to play?"

"No," he snapped, giving away more than he liked with his reaction.

She slid her gaze over him, making it difficult for him to simply stand with his arms at his sides. "You're the one who said we had to be comfortable with our roles before we went into the Eighteen Club."

He answered with a tight nod.

"This is where you find out if you can let me take control, give directions, . . ." She hesitated for a moment, then added, "And inflict strong sensation."

That last part gave him pause. But he followed her into his exercise room and looked around. One of his pieces of equipment was a stand with a bar where he could chin himself. She had moved the bar as high as it would go.

"Take off your shoes and socks and jeans. Leave on your T-shirt and underwear."

He hadn't known exactly what to expect from her—or from himself. But following her directions was strangely arousing. And embarrassing, too. Because he couldn't hide the erection bulging at the front of his boxers.

She had brought a small table into the room and covered it with a towel. Reaching under the covering, she produced one of his old ties.

"This is hideous."

"Thanks."

"No comments from you, if you please." She held up the tie, her lip curling as she inspected it. "About all it's good for is tying your hands. Stand between the parallel uprights and raise your arms, so I can tie you to the top bar."

He complied, watching her bring over the step stool so she could easily reach over her head.

"Why don't you grip the bar? That's probably the most comfortable position for you."

He did, and she used the tie to secure his wrists. Then she stepped back to inspect her handiwork.

"I have the feeling you could get loose if you wanted. But I assume you'll honor the agreement and stay where I put you."

He wanted to say, Unless you go too far. But he kept the observation to himself.

She turned away and pulled something else from under the towel. An Ace bandage.

He swallowed hard as she started winding it around his head, covering his eyes. The bandage was stretchy and conformed to the shape of his face, making a very effective blindfold when she had secured it in place.

He couldn't repress a dart of alarm. Not being able to see when he was in this position was decidedly unnerving.

"Very nice," she murmured, stroking her hand across his chest, then down to his shorts, pressing against his erection for just a moment before taking her hand away. "I think we're ready to play now."

Lifting up his shirt, she ran her fingernails along his ribs and into his armpits, twisting her fingers into the hair there and tugging. Not hard, but enough to get a reaction from him. It shouldn't feel arousing, but somehow it did.

Her hand slid lower, over his ribs again and across his belly.

He gave an involuntary start, then waited in the darkness behind the bandage, feeling his stomach knot.

He heard her step away from him and did a double take when he heard a metallic click. He knew it came from the boom box he kept in the exercise room. She had gotten one of the CDs from his classical collection, and he fought to hold back a grin when he recognized the beginning of Tchaikovsky's 1812 Overture.

Music to torture by? Lord, what was she planning for the grand finale when the cannons boomed out?

His mood shifted immediately when she pulled up his shirt. He felt something cold and hard against his side and couldn't hold back a gasp.

"Is that a knife?" he growled.

"Quiet. Or I'll have to gag you."

It took all his resolve not to jerk at the knots in the tie. But he stayed where he was because he had said he trusted her.

She began to cut his shirt away, and he realized it wasn't a knife but a pair of scissors.

His hands clenched around the bar while she cut off his shirt.

When she started on his boxers, he cringed again. But he managed to hold his emotions together as she cut off the last of his clothing so that his erection could spring free.

"So this is turning you on. Good," she murmured as she lightly stroked him, then withdrew her hand.

He pictured himself standing there naked and blindfolded with his cock sticking out like a pole in front of him.

He wanted to beg her to touch him again. And she did—but only his hip, before sliding her hand around the back of him, dragging her nails across his ass, then to the front, up and down his thighs.

He ached to shout at her to do it to his cock, but he kept his lips pressed together, then gasped as she found his nipples, lightly scratching across them, her nails intensifying the sensation.

He strained his ears, but the Ace bandage covering the top half of his head muffled sound as well as sight. So did the classical music she was playing. His strongest sense was that of touch. The metal bar clasped in his hands. Savannah's fingers on him.

She moved in close to him, pressing her body to his, and he knew in that instant that she had taken off her clothing and was as naked as he.

He longed to pull her close and end the charade, but he kept his arms where they were, gripping the bar for all he was worth.

She moved away and walked behind him, caressing his butt for long moments, making a production of it. Then he felt something strike him there. Hard enough for him to feel the sting of a coat hanger.

"This is for following me around, without letting me

know what you were doing," she murmured. Then she gave him five more strokes, each one a little harder than the last.

When she quit, he was left with a tingling sensation.

He wanted to tell her he'd had his reasons for following her. But he kept the observation locked behind his lips.

Her hand went to his front again, dancing over his belly, making his muscles jump before touching the base of his cock, right where it joined his body.

He wanted to beg her to move down the shaft. Up and down. At the Watergate, he had been the one in charge, and it had turned him on. He found this equally arousing.

Her next words got his attention. "I read in one of those books how to bind a guy's cock," she murmured, caressing him again with maddeningly light strokes that sent fire licking through his body.

Still, the image of genital bondage wrung a strangled exclamation from him. "Jesus!"

She stepped away. Then she was back, and he felt her wind something slick and flexible around his balls, then circle his cock close to his body.

"What the hell?"

"No talking."

He focused on the sensation, then he realized she was using goddamn plastic wrap that she'd compressed into a ropelike length.

"Christ."

"Does that hurt?" she whispered.

"No."

"Good. Because it looks very, very erotic to see your penis and testicles bound to my will."

She leaned in, finding his mouth with hers, giving him a long, smoldering kiss, which he returned with greedy urgency.

When she broke the kiss, he had to clench the bar to stay silent.

Slowly she began to move her body against his, dragging her breasts back and forth against his chest, then pressing his cock down so she could slide the top side into the folds of her pussy.

She moaned, and he did too, as she rubbed against him, slowly at first and then more frantically as her need built.

He hung on to the bar, clamping his hands tight, panting as he heard her small exclamations of pleasure.

She cried out, and he felt her climax against him.

As she clung to him, he knew he couldn't take another second of sexual torment. If she kept doing this to him, he was going to come right here tied to this damn bar, shooting his wad out into the air.

"Enough torture!"

The tie she'd used on his wrists had just been a polite contrivance—for both of them.

Tearing his hands loose, he clawed at the blindfold, then blinked in the sudden light.

Savannah's eyes went wide as he scooped her up in his arms and carried her to the exercise mat on the floor. On the way, he turned off the music.

In the sudden silence, she lay staring up at him while he unwound the damn plastic wrap. Then he came down beside her, kissing her, playing with her nipples, stroking his hand between her legs, plunging two fingers into her wet heat while he angled the base of his thumb toward her clit, pressing and stroking.

She gasped, moving against him. And he took that for a good sign, because she had made him so hot with her inventive little games that he knew he was about to go up in flames.

Covering her body with his, he plunged into her. Then watched her face as he moved in and out, trying not to push immediately for climax. But he was too far gone for anything slow.

He came in a great roiling wave of release and kept moving inside her, feeling her inner muscles begin to contract.

She joined him in a long, shattering climax.

When he rolled to his side, she sprawled against him.

"Jesus, where did you learn that stuff?" he managed to say.

She raised up, looking down at him. "Bedtime reading."

"You're a quick learner."

"So it was good for you?" she whispered.

"Oh, yeah. But, uh, when were you planning to let me come?"

"Right about when you did. I was going to untie your hands and order you to make love to me."

He laughed. "Sorry I ruined the end of your performance."

"It worked out." She grinned, then sobered again. "So, do you think I'm ready for the Eighteen Club?"

"Is that what you were trying to prove just now?"

"Partly."

"What was the other part?"

"I was trying to see if I had the guts to do a . . . scene like that. And then I found out I was enjoying it."

"Another way to prove to yourself that you've changed?"

"Yes."

He kept his gaze fixed on her. "You went further than I would have gone with you."

"Yes."

He felt a smile flickering at the corners of his lips. "But you've given me some interesting ideas. Turnabout is fair play, don't you think?"

She swallowed hard. "I was sure you would say that."

"But first things first. Where have you been staying?" he asked, already knowing the answer but wanting to preserve the fiction that he hadn't been checking up on her.

She blinked at the change of subject. "Motels."

"Would you stay here?" he asked, struggling to sound a hell of a lot more casual than he felt.

"Why?"

"So I can protect you."

Savannah huffed out a breath. "If I agree to stay, is there somewhere I can paint?"

"Down here. I can move the exercise equipment to the side."

"I don't want to . . . make you change your lifestyle."

He considered that statement. He wanted to tell her that having her in his house felt like the most natural thing in the world. But he said only, "I think we can manage."

"Okay."

"Then let's go get some of your clothing—and your painting paraphernalia."

"I haven't agreed yet."

He wanted to shake some sense into her. Instead, he made himself grin. "Let me try some sexual persuasion."

"Like what I did to you?"

"Give me a few minutes to think about what I want to do."


RAYMOND Conrad sat at the computer in his office. He didn't usually do background checks himself. But he didn't want to talk to any of his staff about Charlotte Nichols's sister. Not when that was the only thing he knew about her.

Well, he knew that she had encountered Warren Buckley. Or maybe that wasn't even true. He paged through Nichols's file, looking for something that would indicate family relationships. She'd left the space for "next of kin" empty.

Which had been good, because having an employee with no family ties was always a plus.

As he looked at the application, he saw she'd been careful to keep herself anonymous—except for her recent activities in the nation's capital.

Where was she from? What had she done before coming here? Did she have a criminal record?

He couldn't believe that one of his managers had hired her with so little personal information.

He thought about calling the man in, then he decided against drawing attention to Charlotte Nichols.

Instead he went to the Internet and looked her up. There were over a thousand search results. He sighed and began paging through them. None seemed to refer to the Charlotte Nichols who had worked here.

But he did have contacts in the D.C. police department. He'd get someone to run her prints, to see if she had a record.

He thought for a moment. He had another option. He could contact the man she'd been seeing.

He reached for his card file and dialed a number. There was no one at home, and when the answering machine clicked on, he hung up. Since he didn't want to leave a message, he'd try later.


SAVANNAH'S eyes blinked open. After the games Lance initiated, they had both fallen into an exhausted sleep. She looked toward the window. Earlier, light had seeped in along the edge of the shade.

Now it was dark outside, and Lance had left the bed. She could hear him moving quietly around. Then she heard the sound of a car starting.

Glancing at the clock, she saw it was around eleven in the evening, although it seemed later.

She was pretty sure she knew what he was doing— going to her house to get some of her clothing and perhaps her paint supplies. Alone.

Well, he wasn't going to get away with that. She wanted to be there herself.

Quickly she got out of bed and pulled on her clothing. Then she dashed upstairs. Of course, if she was right, she didn't have to follow right behind him because she knew where he was going.

She scrabbled in her purse for her keys.

Oh, shit! He'd taken them.

To keep her from following in case she figured out what he was planning?

Maybe. But, to be fair, he also needed the keys to get into her house.

Whatever his motives, her anger at his preemptive strike boiled over. Fists clenched, she paced back and forth, thinking it would be easy to punch a hole in one of his walls.

So now what? She couldn't use her own car to follow Lance. But what about his cars?

Surely he had spare keys somewhere.

With her jaw set in a grim line, she marched into the kitchen and looked around. The drawer under the phone was a likely place. But she found no keys in it. So she hurried down the hall to his office.

She lucked out. Spare car keys were in the upper left-hand drawer. Triumphantly, she brought them to the garage and inspected her choices.

Lance had taken the SUV, probably because it had the biggest hauling capacity. But the Saturn and the Lexus were still available.

After trying several keys, she found the one that fit the Saturn. The automatic garage door opener lifted the door, but she didn't want to leave his house open and vulnerable. So she paused to close the door, then headed for Bethesda, hoping that she'd find Lance at her house.


LANCE stopped short before he reached Savannah's house. From down the block he saw a man get out of a car. Then he saw a shadow flit across her driveway. It looked like the guy he'd seen before.

He found a parking space at the curb and pulled in while he debated his next move. He could confront the bastard here and now—which could lead to a messy situation if they got into a wrangle and disturbed the neighbors. Better to wait and follow him. Then Lance would know where he lived. Or where he was reporting to.

He waited in the darkness. As the minutes ticked by he felt his chest tighten. What if the guy was doing more than checking his spy box?

Just as Lance was about to get out of the SUV and go investigate, the stalker came back, climbed into his own car, and drove away. Lance pulled out. Keeping his lights off, he followed.

SAVANNAH turned onto her block just as she saw an SUV pull away from the curb with its lights off. In the illumination from a street lamp, she saw it was Lance's car. Could he have finished at her house already? And if he'd gone inside, why had he parked down the block? It didn't make sense.

Then she realized what was happening. He was following another car.

Did that mean he'd gotten here and discovered the person who had been trying to keep tabs on her?

Hoping she wasn't screwing this whole thing up, she followed the SUV. Like Lance, she kept her lights off.

He switched them on when he reached Wisconsin Avenue. She did, too, then kept Lance in sight as they headed toward Rockville, then onto I-270. There was enough traffic so that Lance was able to keep the other driver in sight. And she stayed behind him, because he wouldn't be expecting anyone to follow *him*.

They ended up in a development off Falls Road in Potomac. The other car pulled into a driveway and then into the garage. Lance hung back. When the garage door had closed, he drove past, then turned the corner and stopped.

Now what?

Was he going to accost the other guy? Or just spy on him?

The lots in the neighborhood were large. Lance had stopped at a driveway where Savannah could see several wrapped newspapers lying on the ground. Apparently nobody was home. On the other side of the house was a large park, further isolating the property.

So what was Lance up to?

She watched him stride up the driveway. When he stopped and looked over his shoulder, she was glad that she had scrunched down low in her seat.

Then he disappeared into the backyard.

She sat in his car for several seconds, trying to figure out what Lance might be doing. Setting up his own listening device? That didn't make sense. Had he come here to meet someone? That seemed unlikely, since he'd gotten here by following the other car. Of course, he could have made a phone call on the way.

She could wait for him to come back and see what he did next. But she was too worked up for that. She'd driven here from his house, and she wanted to know what was going on.

Climbing out of the Saturn, she followed the same route that Lance had taken up the driveway then around to the backyard, the moon lighting her way.

When she reached the side of the house, she heard his voice. He was saying something in a low, singsong tone. She couldn't understand any of the words, but they made the hairs stand up on her head.

What the hell was he doing? Meeting someone who spoke a foreign language?

But no other voice joined his. She had the feeling she should get out of there. Instead, some horrible fascination made her walk rapidly toward the backyard.

When she stepped around the corner, she wasn't even sure what she was seeing. Lance's clothing lay in a pile on the ground and next to it stood . . .

A . . . what?

The moon gave her only dim light, but it looked as if the form of the creature beside the clothing was fluid, as though changing from one shape to another.

Finally it resolved itself into . . . an animal. It came down on all fours, then raised its head, staring at her. And she looked into the eyes of a wolf.

# CHAPTER
# EIGHTEEN

SAVANNAH STOOD GASPING, staring at the animal, trying to make sense of what she'd seen moments ago—and what she was seeing now.

Her eyes flicked to the knapsack and the pile of clothing on the ground, then back to the wolf.

He remained very still in the moonlight, unmoving, his sharp gaze focused on her face. The intelligence in his eyes sent shivers down her spine.

It looked like he wanted to say, What the hell are you doing here? But apparently he couldn't talk.

She might have turned and run. But her legs felt about as substantial as shafts of wheat, and she had to reach out and steady herself against the side of the house, where she stood, feeling sick and disoriented.

She kept her gaze fixed on the wolf. When he moved,

she tensed. But he only took a slow step back. Then another and another, as though he knew that coming forward would be far too threatening a gesture.

He disappeared into the shadows of the shrubbery, then around the side of the house.

The sane part of her brain screamed at her to run for her life. Instead, she waited with her heart pounding to find out what would happen next.

Long seconds ticked by. When Lance walked into the backyard again—naked the way he had been when she'd arrived unannounced at his house—she wasn't really surprised.

His first words were the line she'd given to the wolf. "What the hell are you doing here?"

"I could ask you the same question."

He reached to pick up his sweatpants and pulled them on. Naked to the waist, he faced her.

She stared at his magnificent chest. She had caressed that broad expanse. Winnowed her fingers through the dark hair. Felt the taut muscles under his skin. Now the fingers that had touched him tingled. But not because she was aroused. She had thought she was caressing a man.

"What are you doing here?" he repeated.

"I came to help you get some of my things. Then you took off after that other car, and I followed you." She felt her chin jutting toward him. "That was a load of baloney about your dog saving me, that first night outside the Castle."

"Yeah, but the operative word is *saved*."

"I think the operative word is *werewolf*," she shot back. She made a harsh sound in her throat. "Lord, I punished you for following me around. You must have been really laughing at me."

"I never laughed at you. Never."

"What are you going to do now that I've found you out? Eat me?"

"Hardly. You're not Little Red Riding Hood, and I'm not the Big Bad Wolf."

"Let's stop playing games. And I don't mean bondage games. You are the wolf I saw outside the Castle. And yesterday when I came to your house, you saw me and had time to . . . to get . . . human. But you forgot you were naked."

"Yeah."

She should feel sick. She should feel horrified. But maybe she was too numb for any of those emotions.

"Don't you think you should have told me—before you made love with me?"

"If I went around talking about it with every woman I took to bed, I'd be in big trouble," he answered.

"Oh—there are a lot of them?"

"There have been. Now there's only one," he said slowly and deliberately.

She answered with a little nod. Yet she couldn't stop feeling betrayed by him.

Probably he had figured that out, because he asked, "So—are you still going to the Eighteen Club with me?"

"I don't know."

"You don't trust me enough?"

"We were playing trust games. You didn't tell me there was a whole bigger issue."

"Like I said, I couldn't."

"When were you planning to come clean with me?"

"When I had to."

"Oh, great."

He looked over her shoulder, toward the street behind her. "Let's worry about that later. Maybe I should find out about the guy who was lurking around your house."

"You know it was a man?"

"Yes."

Well, that narrowed it down to half the U.S. population. She sent Lance an inquiring look. "The wolf was going to check him out?"

"Yeah," he answered, clipping off the syllable. "It's safer for the wolf to do it."

"Well, you don't have that option now. We're going back to his house together. And I don't mean I'm going to be taking my wolf for a walk," she added hastily.

"I don't want you anywhere near the man I followed here! He's certainly dangerous—maybe armed."

"And maybe I'll recognize him."

He gestured toward the knapsack. "You don't have to go in person. I have a camera. I can take a picture of him."

She found herself continuing the argument—perhaps because it was easier than dealing with the wolf issue. "I'm not going to wait here while you slink over to his house," she informed him, her tone leaving no room for argument.

He grimaced. "Now why did I think you'd insist?"

As she pictured them walking down the street in the middle of the night, an inconvenient detail occurred to her. "What if we run into somebody? What are we doing casing the neighborhood at midnight?"

"Looking for our lost dog. And we're going to set some ground rules before we start."

"Now why did I think you'd have ground rules?" she shot back.

"Because somebody has to play it smart."

"Oh, thanks."

"I don't want both our cars parked around here. So we're going to drive up to the other side of that park back there and leave your car."

"The guy could . . ."

"Get away? Not likely. He lives there. And even if he's not home, we can match a name to that address."

She gave him a considering look. "You're not trying to trick me into leaving?"

"I've given up on being tricky," he said with a resigned sigh. "We'll leave your car at the other side of the park and go in mine."

They had to drive around several streets to get to the location. As she followed Lance, Savannah had time to consider what she'd discovered a few minutes ago. Now that she wasn't standing face-to-face with him, she could give some thought to his life. And she was surprised that she could be fairly dispassionate.

She'd caught him changing from man to wolf. Hiding that kind of secret must be a considerable strain.

On the surface he seemed like a tough, aggressive guy. And when she'd driven out to his house without calling, she'd been thinking that she might catch him at something.

Tonight she understood why she'd sensed that he had a major secret. After learning it, she wanted more information.

He could change from man to wolf, and back again, apparently at will. But did he change to a wolf at the full of the moon and roam the woods? Or was that just a myth?

\* \* \*

WARREN Buckley leaned over the young woman. He had tied her up so that she was on her knees with her head resting on the bed. Her arms were pulled back toward her ankles, and her bottom was in the air, facing him.

She was very cooperative. She had suggested the pose. Suggested that he blindfold her, so she didn't know what would happen next.

Unspeakable excitement surged inside him. He had thought of scenes like this. He had even tied a few women spread eagle to a bed. But he had never done anything like this. Never gone so far. Never felt the exhilaration of total control.

It was intoxicating. Beyond his wildest imaginings. He had dripped hot wax onto her bottom, then followed it with ice.

While her scream was still ringing in his ears, he slathered lubricant on his cock, then jammed himself into her ass, fucking her until he came in a powerful orgasm.

The sexual climax set off a buzzing in his head so that he could barely think. He flopped down beside her on the bed, breathing hard.

"Untie," she whispered.

"What?"

"My muscles are starting to cramp. Untie me."

"I'm not through with you."

"We can do more later. But I need to change my position now."

He closed his eyes, listening to her words, hearing the pain in her voice and liking it.

The feeling of power crested. Yet incredibly, the wave did not break. It only carried him higher.

He felt like some outside force was controlling him. Egging him on to try new things, dare new experiences.

*Yes. Tell me what you can imagine. Anything you want can be yours in this room.*

He had seen a knife on the wall rack of toys that came with the room. He picked it up and turned it in his hand.

He could use it to untie her. Or . . .

Lust sizzled through him. Through his body. Through his brain. What was it that he had thought of doing?

He couldn't even remember now.

It was hard to focus around the swimming sensation in his mind. Thoughts floated past, and he tried to hang on to them, but they only drifted away in an endless sea of excitement.

The door opened, and two burly men came in. He blinked owlishly at them.

One bent over the girl and removed her blindfold. "Are you all right?" he asked her.

"Barely. He was pretty rough."

"Sorry." One man untied her, while the other one helped Warren put his clothing on, then held him up until his legs were steady.

"Let's go."

He struggled to form thoughts, words. Finally he was able to ask, "Where . . . ?"

"Out of here. You've overstayed your welcome."


AS Lance pulled the SUV to the curb, Savannah considered her options. She could keep on driving right past him. Maybe that was what she should do—and get as far away from him as she could.

Instead she got out and walked to his SUV, then slipped into the passenger seat.

Apparently he'd had time to think, too, because she saw the tension in his shoulders as he sat gripping the wheel.

"We have to talk," he said.

Maybe she was showing her old yellow streak when she answered, "Yes. But not until we take care of our present business."

"Okay."

He drove back the way they'd come, past the house where the guy lived. There were still lights on downstairs. And the upper floor was dark.

"I guess he hasn't gone to bed yet," she whispered.

"Or he has, and he's left lights on downstairs."

Lance continued down the block and stopped several houses from where the man lived.

Reaching into the backseat, he grabbed his knapsack and took out the camera and a gun.

"I'll take his picture. You carry the gun," she said.

"You're still dictating your terms?" he asked.

She shrugged. "As you pointed out before, I don't have any weapons training. But I'm good with a camera."

He shoved the gun into the waistband of his pants and covered it with his untucked shirt, then handed her the camera. "It's automatic. You just click off the safety catch and shoot. If he's in the light, you should be able to get a shot."

"Okay."

"Stay in back of me."

They made their way up the walk and into the side yard of the house.

Lance stepped toward one of the lighted windows. At

first it seemed as if no one was inside, but then he gestured toward a plush burgundy couch.

They were seeing it from the side. She looked at an arm, then saw a man's shoulder and shirtsleeve. He was leaning over to pick up something from the floor.

When he straightened, she got a look at his face. With a low moan, she clamped her hand onto Lance's shoulder to keep herself from falling over.

For a moment she couldn't move. Then her legs unlocked and she turned and ran back the way they'd come, her breath wheezing in and out of her lungs.

She heard Lance follow her, but she didn't turn.

Climbing into his car, she sat with her head thrown back against the seat, gasping, trying to cope with her second nasty shock of the evening.

# CHAPTER
# NINETEEN

LANCE SLID INTO the driver's seat and turned to Savannah, watching her struggle to catch her breath. She looked like she'd just been hit by a truck.

"You know him?" he asked, his voice low and urgent.

She opened her mouth and gasped in air, her face contorted with anguish. "Oh, God, oh, God."

"Just take it easy." He turned her toward him and stroked her arm, feeling the goose bumps peppering her flesh. "Tell me who he is."

She swallowed convulsively, started to speak, then closed her eyes. Frustrated, he clamped his hands over her shoulders.

"Savannah!"

Her lips began to move. Finally, words came out. "He's . . . he's Frank Thompson . . . my ex-husband."

That was the last thing he'd expected to hear. "Jesus! Why would he be stalking you?"

She shook her head, looking helplessly at him. "I don't know."

He took her icy cold hand between his, rubbing her skin to warm her. Slowly, giving her time to pull away, he drew her toward him, then folded her into his arms.

She leaned into his warmth, and despite the circumstances, he counted that a good sign. She'd seen the wolf. More than that—she'd seen him in the middle of a transformation. And she was letting him hold her instead of running screaming in the other direction. Or maybe this Frank Thompson guy had driven thoughts of the wolf out of her mind.

"Tell me about him," he said, hearing the gritty quality of his own voice. "Did you love him? Does he want you back?"

Her whole body stiffened. "I hated him."

"Why did you marry him?"

She gulped in air, then expelled a breath. "Well, I didn't hate him before we were married. I didn't know him well. My parents wanted me to marry him. They thought he would . . . would settle me down."

"This isn't the Middle Ages," he muttered.

"No. But I've told you about my family. About what a . . . wimp I was. My father was very strict with us. And he didn't like the influence of . . . of a university on my thinking. He pulled me out of college and brought me home. Then he looked around for a suitable husband for me."

"Jesus!"

She raised her head, looking into his eyes. "Maybe

you thought I was exaggerating when I talked about the old me. It was all true. I was terrified of my father. I did what he demanded of me because I was afraid of his wrath."

Lance had wanted to know more about her background. Now he had the perfect excuse, although he fervently wished the circumstances were different. Still, he wasn't going to lose this chance. "He used physical punishment?"

"Yes. But the verbal stuff was worse. Telling us we were worthless. That we'd never amount to a hill of beans. That we were no good at anything."

"He sounds like a real bastard."

"Now I realize he must have had low self-esteem. So he had to make everybody else feel worse."

Lance took it in, letting her talk.

"When he proposed Frank as a suitor, I didn't feel any love for the man. But he seemed to respect me. And I saw being someone's wife as a way to get out of my father's house. I realize that's not a great motivation for marriage, but I felt trapped where I was. So I agreed. After a few months, I was like one of those battered women you hear about."

"He beat you?"

She swallowed. "Yes. I found out he was a lot like my father." She laughed hollowly. "Maybe they met at some abusers club. But the main point is that I was so afraid. And I had no skills. I didn't know how to support myself. I felt trapped. But I was thinking that anything would be better than staying in the marriage. I was trying to save up some of the grocery money to use as an escape fund. Then Professor Myerson found me and told me it was a shame I'd given up my art career. He invited me out for lunch. I guess he could see I was a mess, because he got me to talk about my life. He helped me escape. I mean—he gave me a place to live, a place to paint."

"Was he your lover?"

She laughed again. "No. He's gay. He didn't want anything sexual from me. He just wanted me to develop my talent. That was such a strange experience for me. Someone who was so committed to me, but who didn't want anything personal. Just the satisfaction of seeing me reach my potential."

He nodded.

"I was dependent on him for a while until I started selling. I'd spend all day painting. It was such a relief to lose myself in my work. I'd go into the studio, and hours later he'd come in and remind me to eat. It was incredible to be so caught up in something I loved."

"And now you support yourself as an artist. You beat the odds. Do you know how fantastic that is? How fantastic you are?"

"I used to be so damn dependent."

His gaze burned into hers. "Stop dwelling on the past. Just focus on what you made yourself into."

"I can't help remembering what I was. That's why I take chances. Because I'm afraid of turning back into that woman who was under the thumb of the men in her life—and afraid of her shadow."

"Impossible," he said, meaning it. Still, what she'd just told him explained a lot about her recklessness. She had something to prove—over and over. He hoped he could change her mind about that. He suspected it wouldn't be easy.

He saw her eyes glistening with tears. "Thank you," she whispered.

He pulled her back into his arms, stroking his hands over her hair, her shoulders, her back. "I understand why you push yourself to take chances. But I need to understand something else. You were inhibited sexually?"

He felt her stiffen, but she answered, "Yes."

"Sex with Thompson was—what?"

"I hate even thinking about it."

He waited because he wasn't going to force it out of her.

Finally, in a low voice, she continued, "It was brutish. Quick. He did it fast. He didn't care if I responded to him. He just acted like it was something dirty. Something he wanted to do—but in the dark and as quickly as he could."

"Christ."

"I think he actually didn't want me to respond. So I just turned myself off when I was in bed with him. I went away." She gave a harsh laugh. "Lost in a beautiful flower garden where I could bask in the sun, away from him."

"Like the gardens you paint," he murmured.

"Yes."

"And when you started painting, you poured your sensuality into your work."

"Yes."

He stroked her, feeling her tension.

"What does he want from me now? Why is he spying on me?" she whispered. "I didn't even know he was living in the D.C. area."

"I'll find out."

"With you, I know that's not an idle boast."

"Yes." He could do something for her, but what would happen when the crisis was over? Would she walk away from him? He tried not to think about that.

CONRAD ushered Richard Dixon into the quiet elegance of his private sanctuary. The forty-five-year-old man had separated from his wife three months ago. A friend had recommended the Eighteen Club, and Dixon had been coming here for the past two weeks, spending his time in the nightclub, absorbing the atmosphere. Tonight Conrad had invited him downstairs for the kind of private chat that he loved.

He waited while Dixon looked around at the opulent surroundings.

"I see you like your comfort."

"Yes. Can I offer you a drink?"

"I was drinking champagne."

"I have a very fine vintage. Let me get you a glass."

He walked into the pantry area, where he opened the refrigerator and got out a bottle of Louis Roederer Brut, 1990. Bringing it back, he showed it to Dixon. "What do you think about this?"

"An excellent choice."

Conrad twisted off the wires, then put a white cloth over the cork as he carefully worked it out of the bottle, before pouring the sparkling white wine into two flutes.

He and Dixon both took comfortable chairs, both sipping the wine and enjoying a comfortable silence.

"So I take it you've been enjoying your visits with us," Conrad finally said.

Dixon turned his glass in his hand, betraying that he wasn't quite as relaxed as he looked. "I'm very impressed."

"But you know there are more private pleasures we can provide you with."

The man shifted in his seat. "Such as what?"

"Anything you can imagine."

"That's pretty wide open."

"We're noted for that. If you could step into any sexual fantasy you chose, what would it be?"

"Well, I've always been attracted to the Old South."

"To a plantation scenario?" Conrad guessed.

"Mm."

"You like the idea of the master-slave relationship?"

Dixon swallowed. "Yes. With black women slaves."

"Ah . . . You like the idea of them being at your mercy?"

Dixon licked his lips. "Yes."

"And they exist to serve your pleasure."

"Yes."

Conrad definitely got the picture. But before he could pursue the subject any further with Dixon, the phone rang.

Conrad's eyes narrowed as he stared at the instrument. Who the hell was that? His staff knew that when he was in this office in the evening, he was not to be disturbed—unless there was an emergency.

"Excuse me," he said to Dixon, picking up the phone and walking into the pantry. Instead of hello, he said, "I'm with one of our guests." The implication was, *This better be good.*

Ivan Jergenson, one of his most trusted managers, was on the other end of the line. "I'm sorry, sir," Jergenson said, his voice high and shaky. "But we have a situation in room 15."

Conrad glanced over his shoulder and lowered his voice. "What kind of situation?"

"Kevin Amsterdam is . . . is . . . in bad shape."

"On my way." He strode back into the office and looked toward Dixon. "I'm sorry. There's an immediate problem I must take care of. I'm not sure when I'll be back. Perhaps you'll be more comfortable back in the nightclub."

"Is something wrong?"

"It's under control. But the staff needs me."

Dixon set down his drink. Conrad hurriedly ushered him out, then walked rapidly to the stairs at the end of the hall.

In one of the fantasy rooms, he found Kevin Amsterdam lying on a low bed covered with furs. His eyes were closed, and blood trickled from the corner of his mouth. Erica Wentworth was sitting on a chair in the corner, her eyes round with fear.

"What happened here?" Conrad demanded.

Erica made a moaning sound and shook her head.

Conrad strode toward her and tipped her chin up. "Tell me exactly what happened," he demanded.


LANCE tipped his head toward Savannah. "I come from a screwed-up family. It sounds like yours was worse."

"Your werewolf family," she said.

Instantly, he wished he'd just kept that observation to himself. He didn't want to talk about his parents. He just wanted things to drift along the way they had, even when he knew that was impossible. Even when drifting was hardly the correct term. It was more like riding the rapids. But when he thought about their raft smashing into an enormous rock that was smack in their path, he felt an aching pain in his gut.

Savannah was speaking again, and he fought to focus on the words, not his own emotions.

"All of you can change into wolves?" she asked.

"No." He sighed. "It's hard for me to talk about it. But I know it wasn't easy for you to open up with me."

"That's right."

He closed his eyes for a moment, wanting to plead that the only important thing was keeping her with him. Fighting to prevent her from seeing his vulnerability, he said, "I don't know about other werewolves. There may be others on the planet. Some different genetic group. In my family, it's a sex-linked trait. The only were-wolves are males."

Her tone matched his. They might have been at a college lecture, where the bright student was asking the professor questions. "The girls don't get . . . the trait?"

He heaved in a breath and blew it out. "Up until this generation, the girls died at birth. But my cousin Ross married a woman who's a genetics specialist. They have a little girl. It's a big event in our family."

"And will she be . . . a werewolf?"

"We can't know for sure. But we don't think so."

Unwilling to volunteer any more information, he waited for her next question.

"You said your family was screwed up. Did you mean just the wolf traits?"

He kept from shifting in his seat. "It's all related. In a wolf pack, there's one dominant male, and the others are all subservient to him. There's a pecking order. But in our family, all the men are alpha males. So we don't exactly get along real well. We all leave home in our teens, to avoid fighting with our fathers."

"Your father kicked you out?"

"He sent me away to college. It was understood that I'd make myself scarce if I was home for vacation."

"What did your father do?"

"He's a lawyer. Very fierce in the courtroom, I've been told."

She looked like she was hanging on his words. Was that a good sign?

"Werewolf social relations leave a lot to be desired. But Ross is trying to change that, too. He's gotten his brothers and his cousins together." He laughed. "Well, not in big groups. But he's coaching us to cooperate." He stopped and ran his hand lightly up her arm. "Ross is a private detective. And he's got a good friend in the Montgomery County police department. I asked him to run your license plate that first night. That's how I found you—with his help."

"Oh." He watched her hands clench in her lap. "So, do you have to . . . howl at the full moon?"

"No. That's just a myth as far as I know. We change when we want to."

"When did it start for you?"

"When I became sexually mature." He closed his eyes for a moment, remembering that first terrible time. "In my generation, half the boys died trying to get through that first change."

She made a strangled sound. "That must be hard on the parents."

"Yeah. And terrifying for the kids facing it," he

admitted. "But Ross's wife, Megan, is working on that, too. She thinks that by monitoring the hormone levels of the boys, she can make sure they all survive the change."

He should own up to the rest—that a werewolf mates for life. And he was sure he had found his mate the night he had saved her outside the Castle, maybe *because* of those damn herbs. He'd pushed himself past the point when he should have bonded. And his emotional reaction to Savannah in trouble had tipped the balance. But he didn't want to tell her they were already bound together. Maybe they weren't. Maybe he'd screwed things up and he was the only one who felt the tie. His heart clenched when he considered that possibility.

So what should he do now? Remind her how good they were in bed together? Keep his damn mouth shut? Or shift the focus of the conversation.

He settled for saying, "We need to find out what happened to your sister."

"You're changing the subject."

"Yeah. Like I said, the wolf stuff is hard to talk about."

"Have you ever told anyone else?"

"Nobody outside the family. Never. And I want to drop the subject now. So let's get back to our other problems—like your ex-husband. And your sister."

"Those are my problems."

"I've made them mine," he said, then wondered if he should have been so blatant.

"Why?"

"I already told you how I feel about you."

She answered with a small nod. He wanted more, but he wouldn't press her. Not yet.

"How will you investigate Frank?"

"I'll start with the Internet. Maybe I'll ask Ross to help."

"And we're still going to the Eighteen Club—to find out about Charlotte?"

"You trust me enough for that?"

"What better guard than a werewolf?" she said, tossing off the observation with bravado.

"I guess you're back in your danger-defying mode."

# CHAPTER
# TWENTY

OVERCOME BY THE horror of what she had done, Erica had been the one to step into the hall and use one of the house phones.

As she watched Conrad kneel beside Kevin, she whispered, "Is he breathing?"

"Yes."

As Conrad pressed his fingers to the carotid artery, Kevin's eyes fluttered open.

"Thank God," Erica gasped, instantly going down on her knees beside the bed. "Are you all right?" she asked. She half expected him to cringe away from her, but he stayed where he was.

"Yes," he whispered.

"What happened in here?" Conrad demanded.

Before Erica could speak, Kevin answered. "We got a little hot and heavy into the scene."

"I . . . I . . . ," Erica stammered.

Kevin reached for her hand. "Shush. I'll be fine."

"Your mouth is bleeding."

His tongue flicked out and tasted the blood. "I must have bitten my lip."

"He needs to rest," Conrad said, as though he was getting ready to kick her out.

But she wasn't going to let him control this situation. "At my house," she answered, never taking her gaze off Kevin. "I can take good care of him there."

"Our rules—" Conrad started to say.

"Screw the rules," Kevin answered. "I think she can make me comfortable."

"Get my car," Erica said to Conrad.

He hesitated for a moment, then got up. "Okay."

As he left the room, relief flooded through her. She wanted to get out of this place. And take Kevin with her. And she was profoundly grateful that he wasn't afraid of her.

He sat up and winced. When she saw the bruises on his chest, she made a strangled sound.

He looked down, then at her. "I'm okay. I just fainted."

"I hurt you."

"It's nothing. I've had worse."

Rushing to the stand in the corner, she filled a cup with water from the pitcher and brought it back to him. He took a sip, then another.

He was naked. And she was dressed like a Mayan queen. "How are we going to get you out of here?" she murmured.

"Not a problem." He felt along the edge of the wall, then opened a panel she hadn't known was there. Moments after he'd pressed a hidden button, a burly man walked through the door.

"My clothes are down in my locker. And Mrs. Wentworth's are in the guest dressing area. Can you bring them, please."

The man looked at Erica for authorization.

"Please get our clothes and my purse," she confirmed.

When the guy had departed, she asked, "How did you call him?"

"There's a panic button."

"Why didn't I know about it?"

"Because you're the guest and I'm the employee."

"Oh, right."

Moments later, a slave girl walked in carrying two plastic bags. One had Erica's clothing and her purse. The other had Kevin's clothes.

Erica helped him dress, wincing again when she saw how gingerly he moved.

"You're not afraid to go home with me?" she asked.

His eyes met hers. "No."

When she started to speak again, he shook his head. "Not yet," he said in a low voice.

They walked together to the front entrance, where her car was waiting. Kevin climbed into the passenger seat. She slid behind the wheel. As they pulled out of the circular drive, he breathed out a sigh. "I wasn't sure he'd let us go."

"Conrad?"

"Yeah."

"He can't keep me here."

"If he thought you were a danger to the Castle, he would. He records conversations between guests and employees."

Her eyes widened. "Are you serious?"

He sighed. "Yes. There are a lot of things here you don't know about."

She felt her heart leap into her throat. "I thought this was a safe place to . . . to explore my fantasies."

Kevin shrugged, then winced. "Don't count on it. And it's not just the security precautions. A lot of strange stuff has been going on there lately."

"What?" she demanded.

"Didn't you feel it?"

"I don't know," she answered haltingly.

"We got into a pretty wild scene back there. I should have stopped you when I knew it was getting too rough for me."

"That should be my responsibility."

He shook his head. "No. Mine. I'm more experienced at S&M than you are."

"S and M," she repeated slowly. "Sadism and masochism. Not very nice words."

He laughed. "Would you prefer calling it kinky sex?"

Her hands tightened on the wheel. "I don't like any of those names."

He reached out and covered her hand with his. "It's okay. You're a sweet, giving woman."

She snorted. "Sweet? I wouldn't call what I did to you sweet."

"Were your sexual fantasies always about"—he stopped, then apparently decided on—"being a top?"

"Yes," she whispered.

"And all your life you wished you could really try it?"

"Yes."

"Well, it's good you finally decided it was okay to explore your sexuality."

"It's more like, worked up the courage."

"But you did. And that's the important thing."

"And I got involved with Raymond Conrad."

"Yeah. But you met me, too."

"Oh, Lord, Kevin." She turned her hand down, clasping his fingers. "And I hurt you."

"Because, like I said, I couldn't stop myself when I knew I should."

"Why not?"

"I . . . was too into it. So were you."

She clung to him more tightly. "Kevin, I'm so sorry. I don't know what came over me. It was like I went into a frenzy, and I wanted more and more."

"Did you feel something in your mind? Some outside force—egging you on?"

"Yes," she whispered.

"Probably lucky for both of us that I fainted and scared the shit out of you," he said in an offhand manner. Then his gaze flew to her. "Sorry for the language."

"Nothing I haven't heard before," she murmured.

She wanted to ask him what he pictured for the two of them now. Would he stay with her? Or what?

And how would she explain Kevin Amsterdam to her friends?

Screw her friends.

She felt like herself again. But Kevin was right. Something had happened to her back there. Something dark and frightening. And she was never setting foot inside the Eighteen Club again.

\*   \*   \*

LANCE and Savannah drove back to his house in separate cars. He worried all the way home that she'd change her mind and go back to her motel. But she was behind him when he turned into the driveway around two in the morning. When she asked to sleep in the guest room, he didn't argue. He should have been wrung out enough to sleep. But instead he tossed in his bed, thinking about striding down the hall and taking her in his arms. Then he reminded himself that fucking her eyeballs out was not the civilized way to cement their relationship.

Finally, at four thirty, he got up and staggered to the computer. Now that he knew Erica Wentworth's name, it was easy to find information about her.

She had been at a recent Kennedy Center Honors gala, and he studied her picture.

To collect more information, he went back to Google. She was the widow of Jerome Wentworth, who had made his fortune with a chain of drugstores that he had later sold to an out-of-town conglomerate. Then he'd bought a women's clothing chain and various real estate around the city.

Wentworth had died a few years ago, leaving his widow with millions. Now she was apparently spending some of that money at the Eighteen Club.

How did she feel about the place? If they told her about Charlotte, would she be sympathetic—and help them get inside?

While he was at the computer, he also sent a message to Ross, asking if his cousin could take over the investigation of Frank Thompson and giving a little background on the man.

When he realized he didn't know much more about Thompson than his address, he did some more poking around.

The guy had originally lived in Philadelphia, but he'd moved to D.C. three years ago.

Lance's eyes widened when he saw that the man had started a small publishing company called Gold Standard. And many of his titles were S&M-oriented.

*Whip Hand*, *The Total Submissive*, *Turning Your Fantasies into Reality*, *Setting the Scene for S&M Fun* were some of the titles.

At seven in the morning, he knocked off his research. He might have gone hunting in the park, but he figured that Savannah had had enough werewolf stuff for now.

So he showered, shaved, and changed into clean clothing.

He thought he'd sneak in some steak before she got up. But she came into the kitchen just after the thaw cycle finished on the microwave.

He'd been going to eat the meat raw, the way he usually did. Instead he put it into the refrigerator.

She was wearing a T-shirt and jeans, but her hair was tousled from the night, and her eyes betrayed her tension. He shoved his hands into his pockets.

"Are you all right?" he asked.

"I didn't sleep well."

"That's a relief."

She gave him a narrow-eyed look. "That's not exactly a comforting remark."

"I'm just glad I wasn't the only one tossing and turning." He couldn't stop himself from going to her and folding her close. After several heartbeats, when she relaxed against him, he let out the breath he'd been holding. He wanted to press her with questions about their relationship. But he only held her for a few moments before saying, "I looked up Frank Thompson on the Internet."

Immediately she went rigid in his arms.

"What kind of job did he have when you were married to him?"

"He was an investment banker."

"Christ! He's made some changes since then."

She tipped her head up, looking at him inquiringly. "Like what?"

"He started a publishing company. And a lot of his books are of the S&M variety."

She looked stunned. "I can't believe it."

"Well, I can show you his Web page."

"I want to see it."

He led the way to his office, where he brought up the Gold Standard listing.

Savannah sat down and scrolled through some of the books. After several minutes, she looked at Lance and shook her head. "This seems like the project of someone interested in fantasy games. He never did anything like that."

"Maybe something changed his mind."

"I guess," she said reluctantly.

"This could tie him back to the Eighteen Club."

"Yes," she breathed.

"Maybe he ran into Erica Wentworth there."

"We need to talk to her." She looked toward the clock on the wall. It was before eight. "It's too early."

When Savannah got up and paced across the room, then back, he said, "Let me show you the park. It's beautiful early in the morning. There are some scenes you might want to paint. Some real hidden jewels," he said, then felt embarrassed.

She stopped short. "You've thought about bringing me there?"

"Yeah," he answered, hearing the thickness in his voice.

He led her down one of the trails into the woods.

"We should call Erica when we get back," she said.

"Or just go over there. Surprise might be our best option. That way she won't have time to prepare a bogus story."

He took her into the river valley, showing her some of his favorite places near the house. As they walked, he asked questions about Frank Thompson. She talked about his rigid personality. His subtle and not so subtle ways of controlling her. Then she changed the subject and asked more questions about the Marshall family.

"How did your mom meet your dad?" she asked.

"She was in college. He was in law school."

"And when did he tell her he was a werewolf?"

"After she had already agreed to marry him," he answered honestly.

"And she didn't back out?"

"No." Savannah had given him another opportunity to come clean about the lifetime bond between the werewolf and his mate. But he couldn't force the words out. Knowing he was a chicken, he turned toward home. When they came back inside, he suggested that she take a shower while he fixed breakfast.

"To show me you can not only buy groceries, but cook as well?"

"Mm-hm." When she was safely out of the kitchen, he wolfed down some of the raw steak, then put the rest back into the refrigerator, before making them both some tea and scrambled eggs.

After cooking the simple meal, he went up the driveway to retrieve the *Washington Post*.

He handed Savannah the front page while he grabbed the Metro section to check the local weather forecast. But an article in the front of the section made him do a double take.

"Jesus!" he exclaimed.

"What?"

"Warren Buckley."

She cringed. "What about him?"

He held up the paper and pointed to an article below the fold. The headline said LOCAL MAN KILLED IN HIT-AND-RUN ACCIDENT.

She sucked in a sharp breath. "He's dead?"

"Apparently." He read the text aloud.

"Warren Buckley, a resident of Hyattsville, was killed when he tried to cross the Washington Beltway near Silver Spring early Friday morning. Eyewitnesses said that Buckley dashed into the flow of traffic. Several drivers swerved to avoid him. But he was struck by a white van, which sped away, leaving Buckley on the roadway—where he was struck by another driver."

She stared at him in disbelief. "Oh, my God. He sounds like he was wigged out. Do you think that it has something to do with my hitting him on the head? And that turned him wacky?"

"I doubt it," he shot back. "The incident at that night-club was over a week ago. And they discharged him from the hospital."

"They could have made a mistake. He could have had . . . I don't know, bleeding in the brain that finally built up and . . . and . . ." She flapped her hand.

"They would have done an MRI on him and seen any bleeding. If you want to jump to conclusions—think about how this is similar to your sister."

"How?"

"An accident. After you asked him about Charlotte."

She gave a small nod.

"What if somebody found out you had a conversation about her?"

"How?"

"Maybe he *told* the wrong people . . . like Thompson."

"But how . . . would he know him?"

"I don't know. Which is why I'm glad you're out here rather than in your house."

"Yes," she whispered.

"You told me Erica Wentworth bought one of your paintings. What else do you know about her?" he asked.

"You think she could be involved?"

"No. I'm trying to change the subject."

"Okay." She sighed. "I don't know anything about her, except that she was very well dressed. She was friendly in a reserved sort of way. And she obviously liked my work enough to buy a large canvas."

"I looked her up on the Web."

"When?"

"Early in the morning—when I couldn't sleep. Eat some breakfast, and I'll tell you about her."

While she took small bites of her food, he filled her in on his research.

"So what's she doing at the Eighteen Club?" Savannah asked.

"Indulging her tastes for the exotic?"

"Maybe she doesn't want to talk to us about that."

"If you tell her about Charlotte, that might help."

"Yes."

Savannah played with her eggs. Finally, Lance took mercy on her. "You can stop pushing your food around. Let's go."


RINNA had gone outside the cave to hunt for food. Now she huddled behind a rock, watching uniformed men move through the landscape. Falcone's private army. They had spread out to search, and she was sure they were looking for her.

She'd been sent out here as punishment for a small transgression. Really she knew the members of the council were afraid of her powers. And they'd been hoping she wouldn't survive.

Now men were looking for her. Falcone's men.

He was worse than the council. More dangerous. She'd rather take her chances out here than with him.

But maybe there was a way out. In her search for the suckers, she had come to believe that she might escape Sun Acres, the council. Falcone. Through a portal into another world.

Haig didn't believe her about the portals. But she had focused her future on them.

If the Sucker could get out of this world that was strangling itself to death, maybe she could, too.

Could she make a life for herself in the other place? Was that too much to ask?

The patrol passed, and she made her way cautiously through the outcroppings of rock, heading for another one of the caves. Not the one she'd been in with Haig. A deeper cavern. Maybe where Boralas was lurking.

SAVANNAH and Lance drove back toward Montgomery County.

"Tract mansions," she murmured when they entered the Wentworth neighborhood.

"You mean big houses on lots that are too small for them?"

"Right."

They found the address and pulled up in front. Lance looked over at Savannah, seeing her hands clutched in her lap. He pulled her gently toward himself, wrapping her in his arms.

"Okay?" he asked.

"No. But I'll pretend I am."

They got out and walked to the front door, where Lance rang the bell.

Half a minute later it was opened by a man with brown hair and broad shoulders. He looked to be in his mid thirties, and Lance recognized him as one of the men he'd seen entering the Castle through the employee entrance. He wondered if he'd made a bad mistake by coming here. Had Conrad sent someone to guard her? And why?

Erica Wentworth appeared in back of the man. "Who is it, Kevin?" she asked—then spotted Savannah. Looking puzzled, she asked, "Ms. Carpenter?"

"Yes. Call me Savannah."

"Erica," the other woman supplied. "I hope you're not here to tell me you didn't intend to sell that picture to me."

"Oh, no. Nothing like that. Can we come in and talk to you? It's about something important," she added. "We won't take up much of your time." Gesturing toward Lance, she said, "This is my friend Lance Marshall."

Erica Wentworth looked at him nervously. "Where have I heard your name?"

"I'm a journalist."

"Oh, yes. I guess I've read some of your articles."

The Kevin guy slipped his arm protectively around her shoulder. They looked like there were at least ten years between them in age.

If Conrad had sent him here to guard her, then they had cozied up pretty quickly.

"Come in," she said, glancing at her companion and then back at him and Savannah. "Would you like to see where I hung the painting?"

"Of course."

She led them down a hall to a large sunroom that spanned the back of the house. One of Savannah's beautiful garden canvases had a place of honor on an end wall.

"It looks lovely there," she commented.

"Well, it's a lovely painting. And perfect for this room." Her hands fluttered nervously. "Please sit down. Can I get you anything?"

"No, we're fine."

There were two white wicker love seats in the room. Lance and Savannah took one, and he reached for her hand, feeling her icy skin.

Kevin and the lady of the house took the other love seat, and Lance noted that the man eased himself down—as though he'd been injured and was moving carefully.

When he was seated, he slung his arm protectively around Erica's shoulder again. They looked as nervous as Savannah. He wanted to ask what they were worried about, but he let Savannah open the subject.

"I'm hoping you might be able to give us some information about my sister, Charlotte Nichols," she said.

"I don't know your sister," Erica said immediately.

Savannah looked disappointed.

After several seconds of silence, Kevin cleared his throat and said, "I do."

Erica looked at him, startled. "How?"

"From the Eighteen Club."

The woman made a small sound, then glanced toward Savannah. "Did you come here because you know Kevin works at the club?"

"No, we came here because we know you're a member."

"How?"

Lance cleared his throat. "We've done some checking around. And your name came up," he said, hoping that the bold statement might get her to cooperate.

Her open expression turned closed. "I really can't help you," she said stiffly.

Lance watched Savannah's face take on a look of desperation. "Please, my sister is dead."

"I'm so sorry," Erica murmured.

"Did she die at the club?" Kevin asked, making Lance wonder what he'd heard or knew about problems at the Castle.

"No," Savannah answered. "The police told me she fell off an outcropping of rock in Rock Creek Park. But I don't think that's true. I don't think she fell—on her own. I think she was running away from someone. Or she was pushed."

Keeping his gaze fixed on Savannah, Kevin pressed his hand against Erica's shoulder. "We should help them," he said.

"I don't want to get involved."

"Maybe they can help *us*."

She looked at him, obviously torn.

Kevin turned toward Savannah. "I met your sister. She started off as one of the part-time employees. She'd come in some evenings and be available to guests."

"As a slave?" Savannah asked.

"Yeah."

Erica had gone gray.

But Kevin kept talking. "After a few months, she started palling around with an older man. I don't remember his name. I did see him in the nightclub recently. But he was alone."

"Charlotte was in the hospital for a few weeks . . . before she died."

"Can you tell me anything more about Charlotte—or the man with her?" Lance asked.

"He was the dominant. She was the submissive. Sometimes when he brought her in, he had a collar around her neck, with a leash."

Savannah winced.

"He was in his forties. Dark hair turning gray at the temples. A trim figure. Obviously he worked out." He stopped and thought. "He was about five ten or eleven.

Dark eyes. I saw him talking with Raymond Conrad a time or two."

"Like they were friends?" Lance asked.

"Colleagues. The guy was a publisher. Apparently a lot of his books were S&M-oriented."

Savannah sucked in a strangled breath. "Could his name have been Frank Thompson?" she asked in a thin voice.

# CHAPTER
# TWENTY-ONE

"FRANK THOMPSON. YEAH, that sounds right," Kevin answered.

The color had drained from Savannah's face, and Lance pulled her close.

"What's he to you?" Kevin asked.

"I was married to him."

Erica looked shocked.

"Sorry to hear it," Kevin murmured.

Savannah swallowed hard. "I thought I would never see him again, hear about him again. And now he's popped back into my life."

"You don't like him?" Lance asked Kevin.

"Not much."

"Why?"

"He liked to assert his importance by pushing people around—especially the staff."

"Nice guy," Lance answered.

Kevin gave him an assessing look. "Ms. Carpenter told us about her sister. What's your interest in the Eighteen Club—specifically?"

"I heard about it, and I realized the owner, Raymond Conrad, wanted to keep his business secret. So I started doing some investigating, with the idea of writing a book. Then I met Savannah, and the interest became more personal."

Kevin swung his gaze toward Erica. "I think we should help them."

"You're too trusting. We barely know them!" she objected. "Conrad could have sent them, for all we know."

"I'm not here to help him cover up my sister's death! I want to find out what happened to her."

Kevin kept his gaze on Erica. "I'd like to tell them about last night."

She sat rigidly beside him, saying nothing.

He pressed his hand over hers. "You felt bad about what happened. But more people could get hurt if we don't speak up."

She answered with a tiny nod.

Lance felt his heart pounding as he watched the small drama. He longed to probe for information. Instead he waited for Kevin to speak again.

The man cleared his throat. "What do you know about the club?"

Lance answered, "People go to relax in the nightclub. Then they get into more intimate activities in the private rooms—which are set up to act out fantasies."

"Yeah. That's how Erica and I met."

He seemed to choose his words carefully as he said, "Last night, we got really involved in a scene. She was a Mayan queen, and I was her slave."

"A pretty violent period," Lance murmured.

"Yes. And like I said, we got into it. The role-playing went further than either of us expected." He looked at the woman sitting beside him. Her face was a study in tension. "This may sound crazy. But when we talked about it later, we both felt like some outside influence had been egging us on."

"Can you explain that?" Lance asked.

Kevin shrugged. "The best I can tell you is that something lowered our inhibitions."

"A drug? A drink?"

"Not something we took on purpose," Erica said. "I don't take drugs. And I never indulge in more than a couple of drinks."

"Something piped into the air-conditioning ducts?" Lance asked.

"I don't know," she answered. "But what would be the motive?"

"To addict you?"

She made a sound of distress.

"I don't think so," Kevin answered. "During the tax season, I'm away for a couple of months. And I don't feel any physical withdrawal."

"What about blackmail?" Lance suggested. "If a drug got you to do things you wouldn't ordinarily try, perhaps someone did a videotape."

She winced. "I hope not."

"But it's possible," Kevin said in a low voice.

She glanced at him, then looked away.

"I was wondering about that. You know for a fact that there's recording equipment in the club?" Lance asked Kevin.

"Yeah. But they don't tape every room all the time."

They were silent for several seconds. Then Savannah turned to Erica. "We need to get inside so we can explore the club. Can you take us in there as guests?"

She made a helpless gesture with her free hand. "I'm sorry. No."

"Don't you want to know what happened to you last night?" Lance pressed. "Don't you want to make sure it doesn't happen to anyone else? If there were covert drugs involved, someone else might not walk away."

The woman looked torn, and Kevin squeezed her hand. "Let's talk about it a little more," he said, then looked at Lance. "If the two of you come as Erica's guests, you'd have to convince the management that you fit in."

"I've been explaining that to Savannah. I've told her that the safest arrangement would be for us to be a couple—so no one would hit on her. One of us would act as the dominant and one as the submissive."

"Act?" Kevin asked, his voice turning sharp.

"I didn't mean as in fake it. She and I enjoy playing those roles," Lance snapped.

"She'd be the submissive?" the other man pressed.

"No. I think it would be safer for her to be the top."

Kevin tipped his head to the side, staring at him. "You don't exactly look like the submissive type. You're comfortable with that?"

He weighed his answer and decided that the closer he could get to the truth, the more likely Kevin and Erica were to trust them.

"We've discovered that we can both swing either way. But if we invade the club, I don't want to put her in a position where someone could ask me to borrow her."

"I . . . still don't want to go back," Erica said.

She kept her gaze away from him and Savannah. He wondered if he could get her to tell him any more.

"What happened after . . . the scene that got too heavy?" he asked gently.

"We left—pretty abruptly," Kevin supplied. "I was afraid Conrad might not let us go."

"Oh, yeah?"

Kevin didn't elaborate.

Erica sat across from them with a closed expression on her face. And Lance was pretty sure that trying to change her mind would only waste time. "Okay. Thanks for the information," he said. "We'll stop badgering you."

Erica looked relieved.

Savannah looked like she wanted to object. But he kept her hand tightly in his, pulling her up with him when he stood.

"Let me give you my card, in case you change your mind," he said, then laid a business card on the wicker and glass coffee table.

Savannah followed him out, not speaking until they had climbed into his SUV and closed the doors. "I thought you would keep working on her. Why did you give up like that?" she asked.

"Because we can't force them to cooperate. Or if we did force them, then they'd be unreliable if the situation deteriorated. Unless they really want to help us, going into the Castle with them would be dangerous. What if someone started interrogating Erica, and she blurted out who we were?"

Savannah sighed. "I guess you're right."

As they pulled out of the driveway, she asked, "They never were very explicit about last night. What do you think happened?"

"Maybe one of them was disciplining the other and got too enthusiastic."

She winced. "And which one of them gets disciplined?"

"Kevin was moving a little stiffly. I'd bet it was him."

"Like he said about you—he doesn't look like the submissive type."

"Does she look like a top?" he countered.

"You have a point." She clasped her hands in her lap. "So I guess we're back to plan A."

"I've changed my mind about plan A," he said in a grim voice.

"Why?"

He swallowed. "Because I love you, and I want to protect you." He wanted to hear her tell him she felt the same way.

But she only said, "My applying for a membership may be our only option for getting inside."

He hated to admit that was true. Maybe if he hadn't been staring at her, he would have missed the expression that flickered across her face.

"What?" he demanded.

"Nothing."

"Something. Don't hide information from me."

She was silent for several moments, and he was afraid she was going to keep her thoughts to herself, but finally she said, "I was thinking about what Kevin said. About something affecting him and Erica last night."

"What about it?"

"Do you think they might have used it in the woods outside the building?"

"Why would Conrad do that? What are you getting at, exactly?"

She clenched her hands in her lap. "We've talked about my acting reckless because of the way I toed the line when I was younger. But at the Eighteen Club that night, there was something more."

"Like what?"

"I was in a kind of . . . hyperdrive or something," she said slowly. "I felt a compulsion to push myself into dangerous territory."

"Not unusual for you," he murmured.

"Yes, but this was . . . more. That's why I went close to the front door with my camera. If I'd stayed back in the woods, maybe the guards wouldn't have gotten me."

"Maybe," he conceded. "Maybe not. But I want to hear more about that compulsion."

She thought for several moments, then murmured, "I can't describe it. Kevin said something was egging him on. And that's as good a way to put it as any. I wanted to do more—dare more. Feel more?" She turned her head toward him. "You didn't experience anything like that?"

He considered the question. "I don't think so. And usually the wolf is affected more strongly by drugs than, uh, normal people. My cousin Adam was hired to supervise a private nature preserve in Georgia and found himself investigating a murder. It turned out there was a bunch of people with psychic powers using the park for secret ceremonies. They burned some kind of mind-altering herbs to enhance their powers. The smoke made them high. But it made Adam crazed. He could barely function. So if there was something hanging in the air around the Castle, I'd expect it to drive me bonkers. Only it didn't."

"Maybe it was something that didn't affect you."

"Maybe," he said, hearing the doubtful quality of his own voice.

"So where does that leave us?"

"I don't know."


RAYMOND Conrad stared at the newspaper headline: LOCAL MAN KILLED IN HIT-AND-RUN ACCIDENT.

It was Warren Buckley. And Boralas had tipped him over the edge. The guards had kicked him out of the club when he'd gotten too rough with one of the girls. And he'd gone to play in traffic. Too bad for him. The man had tried to use a chance encounter to get something from the Eighteen Club. And he'd gotten more than he'd bargained for.

Buckley had come to him with information about a woman asking questions about Charlotte Nichols. He'd said she was Nichols's sister. But he could have been lying. What if he'd held back information—or hyped it up—so he could get himself another visit?

He crossed the room to his desk and pulled out the Nichols file again.

His police contact had come up with a few facts. At the age of eighteen, she'd been convicted for shoplifting in Baltimore. After that, she'd stayed out of trouble—at least as far as the law was concerned.

He sat at his desk, breathing deeply, struggling for calm.

Charlotte Nichols wasn't the problem. It was Boralas.

His partner. The creature from another—what? A world parallel to this one? It was a strange concept. But Boralas had dropped enough hints to make Conrad believe it was true. He came from a place where war or disease or something had wiped out a lot of the human population. And his kind, too.

But he had found a door into this world. And he had taken refuge here.

Boralas had said he wanted only to feed off the emotions of the people who came to the Eighteen Club. For over three years he'd resided in the basement, quietly doing his thing.

Now he was getting out of control. Not all the time. But too often. Like last night. Conrad was sure it was Boralas who had pushed Erica Wentworth over the edge.

He stood up, pacing the length of his office, wondering what he should do. Was there anything he could do to get himself out of this mess? When he thought of Dave O'Hare, he felt a sudden flash of fear that made his stomach roil. He took an antacid out of his desk drawer and chewed it, then swallowed. He had worked so hard to get what he wanted out of life. Suddenly he felt like he was on a collision course with disaster. Not because of anything he'd done. He was running the club exactly as it should be run. Bringing in rich and famous patrons who loved the services he provided. Hiring slaves who loved to bottom, but who could top if that was what a patron wanted.

And Boralas was going to ruin it all.

Conrad's fear flared . . . then receded, replaced by a soothing calm wafting into his brain from outside his own consciousness.

He knew that the feelings weren't his own. But it didn't matter. He felt better again.

*Everything is all right. You have nothing to worry about. Come downstairs and we'll have one of our nice chats.*

He wanted to resist. He wanted to stay up here in his office and work through the problem. He'd handled it wrong. He was sure of that now.

Instead, he left his office and walked down the stone stairs to the basement. And as he descended the stairs, his mood elevated.

He had wanted to argue with his partner. He had wanted to tell Boralas that they were making trouble for themselves, and they had to be circumspect if they didn't want the authorities swooping down on the Castle and—what?

Arresting them for murder?

No. Charlotte Nichols had died in the hospital, after an accident in the park. And there was nothing to tie Warren Buckley to the Castle.

Still, they had to be more careful if they wanted this happy partnership to last.

He tried to hang on to that thought, but it floated out of his mind. And he drifted downstairs on a wave of contentment.

He had everything he had struggled so hard to attain. A satisfying business. A sense of purpose. Power. Money.

And Boralas would take care of any problems. Just like he always had.

# CHAPTER
# TWENTY-TWO

LANCE FELT HIS tension grow as they sped toward home. He slid Savannah a quick glance. She was still sitting with her hands clasped in her lap. But a look of determination had replaced the defeat on her face.

He was pretty sure he knew what she was thinking. When they got to his house, she was going to insist on calling Conrad and asking for a membership in the club. But too much had happened for that to work. Conrad would do a background check on her. He would find out that Savannah had been married to Frank Thompson. Then he could connect her to Thompson's lover, Charlotte Nichols.

He had to get her to change her mind. But he knew that giving her orders was the absolute wrong approach.

"So what do you think happened to change Thompson from the guy you were married to into someone else?" he asked.

Savannah shook her head. "Maybe he met Conrad, and the man convinced him to let go of his inhibitions—like he did with Erica. She said he was very persuasive."

"Yeah. And then he could have run into your sister at the Castle and decided that if he couldn't have you, he could have her," Lance theorized.

She nodded. "I guess that makes sense—in a screwed-up kind of way."

"Why would she agree?"

Savannah sighed. "Knowing Charlotte, maybe she twisted it around in her mind and decided to prove she was better than me."

"I'm not following your logic."

"I'm just fishing for answers here. But . . . she knew that I'd felt used and humiliated by Frank. She could have taken that as a challenge. She could have hooked up with him . . . to show him he'd have a much better time with her."

"That's pretty twisted."

"Some of the things she did would curl your hair. In high school she took several girls' boyfriends away. As soon as she knew she had them, she dropped them."

"Why?"

"She enjoyed playing with people."

"If Thompson is the man in the diary, he was the top and she was the bottom."

"He was always dominating. He just didn't have much imagination. But maybe he read some books."

"Or got into S&M videos."

Savannah grimaced. "Or maybe Charlotte used what I'd told her about him to come up with ideas he'd like. Then she found out she enjoyed it."

He touched her cheek. "You put a lot of energy and emotion into feeling like you let your sister down. It sounds like she never was a very nice person."

"A damaged person. Yes," she whispered; then more strongly she said, "and in case you're going to make another argument for my staying out of the Eighteen Club, forget it."

He heard his voice turn hard as granite. "Even though she knew you'd be devastated if you found out she was playing sex games with your former husband?"

Savannah shook her head. "Maybe it's what Erica said—about the drugged air inside the Eighteen Club. And in that case, it's not her fault."

"Maybe," he conceded. He wanted to argue the point, but he knew he'd be wasting his breath. She had invested too much emotional energy in Charlotte to have her mind changed easily. Instead he switched the subject. "There's still Thompson. We don't know why he's been stalking you."

"Probably he knows that I'd want to find out what happened to Charlotte. And he wants to make sure that I haven't figured out he was involved with her."

Lance nodded, but he was still wondering if there might be more to it.

They were almost to the Beltway when his cell phone rang.

He reached for the instrument, flipped it open, and pressed the speaker so he could still drive with two hands.

"Hello?"

"This is Erica Wentworth."

Lance and Savannah exchanged a quick look. "Yes?" he asked.

He heard her drag in a breath and huff it out before saying, "I've changed my mind."

"About taking us into the Eighteen Club as guests?" he clarified.

"Yes."

"What made you reconsider?" Lance asked.

"I keep thinking about innocent people wandering into that place. If somebody else gets hurt, and I didn't do anything, then I'm responsible. Can you come back here, and we'll talk about it?"

"We're on our way."

Lance headed back to the Wentworth mansion. He still didn't like the idea of going to the Eighteen Club with Savannah, especially now that he had to worry about happy gas—or whatever it was—being pumped into the ventilation system. But he wanted to hear what Erica and Kevin had to say.

Once again they parked in the driveway, but this time Erica had the front door open before they reached the porch.

"Thank you for calling us," Savannah said.

Erica led them into the breakfast room. "It's lunchtime. I can fix something to eat while we talk."

Lance ached to get right to business, but he sensed that she wanted to keep busy during the conversation.

"Is salmon with a tossed salad all right?" she asked.

"Fine," Lance answered, thinking he didn't have to eat much.

When they were all seated, the guests helped themselves to salad, with Lance taking what he hoped looked like a polite amount.

Erica bent to her food, and he wondered if she'd changed her mind again.

Finally, he couldn't wait any longer. "If we're going to do this, the sooner you go back to the Eighteen Club, the better for you."

"Why?" Kevin demanded.

"Because Conrad may be worried about your leaving abruptly last night. He'll be relieved to see you again. And he'll be happy that you feel comfortable enough to bring guests."

"Or he may think we've come in with a team of private detectives," Kevin countered.

Erica sucked in a sharp breath.

"Thanks," Lance muttered, then lightened his tone. "What will we see when we get inside?"

"The ground floor has two nightclubs," Kevin said. "One's a bit tamer than the other. Upstairs and downstairs are rooms where guests can act out fantasies with other guests or with employees. There's also a beauty salon for the female guests and changing areas with lockers. The Castle is built into a hill. The changing areas for the staff are in the lower level in back. We come in through a staff entrance at the rear."

"And what about cameras?"

"There are a lot of them. I never mapped the specific locations," Kevin said. "I never had any reason to."

"But you think that if we were in a private room, we wouldn't be able to slip out without being seen?"

"You'd be taking a chance if you did."

Lance thought about that for a while. "Are they infrared?"

Kevin laughed. "I'm not that technical."

"Can you draw me some floor plans?" Lance asked.

"I can draw what I've seen, yes."

"Would guests of a member be able to use the private rooms?"

"Sometimes yes. Sometimes no. It would probably depend on whether Conrad wanted to do a favor for the member—or if he thought you might become repeat customers."

Lance set down his fork and looked around the table. "Since we're going with Erica, we can use false names."

"What names?" Savannah asked.

"Ones we can remember." He thought for a moment. "What about Samantha Carter for you. And Larry Marsh for me."

"Okay." She looked at Erica. "Thank you for doing this."

Their hostess poked at a piece of lettuce on her plate. "I guess I should call the club."

"Why don't you say that an artist from out of town is visiting you with her boyfriend, and they'd love to come to the Eighteen Club," Lance suggested.

"I'll sit next to you when you make the call," Kevin said.

"Yeah, and then I want some advice about what to wear," Lance said to him.

"A dark T-shirt and jeans would be fine. And a collar around your neck would add a very convincing master/slave touch."

Lance swallowed. "Is that necessary?"

"Not necessary. But it sets the tone you want to convey." A wicked grin spread across Kevin's face. "And you could add a leash and come in on all fours."

"I don't think we need to go that far," Savannah murmured, glancing at him.

Lance wondered if she was picturing him as her guard dog. "Let's get back to problems at the club. Are there any other incidents that you know of, where things got out of hand?"

Kevin shifted in his seat. "The staff would hear rumors."

"Like what?"

"A . . . uh . . . member was found hanged to death in one of the play rooms."

Savannah and Erica both gasped.

"Was he using asphyxiation as a way to increase the intensity of orgasm?" Lance asked.

"Probably. But his partner should have made sure he was okay."

"And the police weren't called?"

"Not as far as I know. A lot of things happen that are . . . irregular," Kevin clipped out.

"Nice. Anything else we should know about?"

"From time to time slaves get beaten unconscious." He said it casually as he cut Erica a quick glance, then looked away. "It's always taken care of in-house," he added.

"Except last night, when I brought you home," Erica broke in, pain evident on her face.

Savannah gave her a startled look. "That's what happened last night—to Kevin?"

"Yes."

Kevin reached for her hand. "It wasn't your fault. And you don't have to talk about it."

"I know. But I want them to understand that things happen in the Eighteen Club that you're not expecting."

RAYMOND Conrad was in his office when he heard police sirens in the distance. He expected them to pass by, but instead they got closer.

Every muscle in his body tensed as he waited for patrol cars to pull up at the door. Mercifully, they ended up passing the Castle. But from the way the sirens cut off abruptly, he knew they had stopped nearby.

He walked to a window at the back of the building and looked out, but he could see nothing.

*It's not anything you have to worry about,* a voice answered in his head.

"Boralas?"

*Yes.*

"Do you know what's going on?"

*Yes.*

"Tell me."

*A woman on the other side of the trees was very, very sad. She was thinking of killing herself. And she finally took her own life. She went into her bathroom and hanged herself from the shower rod. Her little boy found her a few minutes ago and called 911.*

"Jesus! How do you know?"

*I was with her when she died, helping her focus on the sensations. Death is always very stimulating to me. A good meal. And I can feel the boy's grief now. That is also very rewarding to me. He is young. Different from any of the people who come to this place. His emotions have quite a different flavor. It's good to have different flavors, don't you think?*

Conrad went very still. "You were outside the walls of the Castle?" he asked carefully.

*Well, not physically, of course. But every day now, I find I can send my mind farther into your world. There is so much for me to discover beyond these walls.*

Conrad swore again, struggling to mask his disquiet.

*Are you no longer satisfied with our arrangements?*

He gulped. "Of course I'm satisfied."

*Then calm yourself. Everything is fine. I find that I can extend my feeding radius. That is all. Nothing to worry about. Everything is fine.*

The words echoed in his head. Soothing words. And as he listened to the voice of his silent partner, his sense of dread receded.

RINNA'S whole body was shaking. She felt Haig's hands on her shoulders, trying to rouse her. But she couldn't wake. The horror held her fast.

The horror of Boralas.

"Rinna, come back. Rinna!"

Haig's voice and the power he wielded penetrated the fog of her mind. Her eyes blinked open, and she stared at him.

"What happened?" he demanded.

"Boralas was . . . feeding again . . . pushing people to the edge. A woman . . ." Her voice trailed off in a shudder. She looked up at Haig. "He knew she was depressed. And he tipped her over the edge. He made her kill herself. Then he sent the son to find her body."

Haig's face turned hard. "Can you locate him?"

"I'm trying. I told you, I think he's gone through one of the portals."

He made an exasperated sound. "I don't believe in portals. They're a fairy tale for people who want to imagine a different life."

"If they're just a story, how else do you explain that most of the Suckers have disappeared? They only come back when they're hungry."

"They're hiding in deep caves, where we can't find them."

She pressed her lips together. Haig had been one of her teachers. When she had needed someone to be a substitute parent, he had fill that role. She had depended on him for emotional support, and she had spent hours learning the lessons he had to teach. He was wise in so many ways. And when she had been sent out from the city, he had risked his life to sneak out and come with her.

He had helped keep her live out here in this lawless world. For a long time, she had put her absolute trust in him. But living with him like this on the run, she had come to realize that he had his blind spots.

Now she spoke softly. "Don't dismiss the idea."

"You want me to change my view of the universe?" he asked.

"Just keep an open mind."

# CHAPTER
# TWENTY-THREE

SINCE NOBODY SEEMED very hungry, Savannah helped Erica clear the table while the men went into the den to discuss the club in more detail.

"How dressed up should I get?" Savannah asked.

Erica stacked another plate in the dishwasher. "I can show you some of the outfits I've worn there," the older woman said.

Savannah couldn't imagine that her taste and Erica's were anything alike. And she was about to say she didn't need a fashion show. But the look in the other woman's eyes told her there was something she wanted to say.

"I'd love some pointers," she murmured.

They went upstairs to Erica's gigantic closet, where she brought out some of the dresses she'd worn to the Castle.

They were all quite expensive and exquisitely tasteful.

"Very nice," Savannah complimented her.

Erica fiddled with the sleeve of a blue dress. "So am I crazy for thinking that Kevin and I could make a go of it?" she asked.

"How long have you known him?"

"Just a few weeks."

"He seems to care about you."

"And I care about him. That's why I was so ashamed last night when I hurt him."

"Apparently he took it in stride," Savannah answered, hoping to reassure the other woman.

But Erica still had doubts, and not just about her own behavior. "When you're wealthy—and in your fifties—it's hard to know a lover's motives. Especially when he's ten years younger."

"I imagine."

Erica gave her an assessing look and switched the subject abruptly away from herself. "What about you and Lance; do you really play S&M roles with each other?"

Savannah felt her face heat. "We have."

"But it's not the basis for your relationship?"

She struggled for honesty, even as she wondered how much to say. "We were sexually attracted from the first. Lance told me that if we were going into the Castle, we had to conform to the standards there. He suggested we try some dominance and submission games to make sure we were comfortable with that." She swallowed. "It turned both of us on."

"So you don't think someone who enjoys those things is . . . a deviant."

Savannah strove for objectivity. "Not unless you get into something that's nonconsensual. And I take it you and Kevin kept meeting at the Castle because you both liked what you were doing."

Erica breathed out a sigh. "I always had fantasies about dominating a man. I never acted on those fantasies with my husband. He would have been horrified. It took Raymond Conrad to get me to admit what I wanted."

"He must be very persuasive."

"He's a smooth talker. He knows how to get people to reveal their secret desires." She stopped for a moment, then continued. "But maybe it's more than that. Maybe he pipes some of that drugged smoke into his office—to get his clients to forget their inhibitions."

Savannah nodded.

Erica switched the subject abruptly. "Was S&M part of your secret fantasy life?"

"No. I grew up in a very repressive household. I was very conservative . . . even in what I dared to imagine."

Erica looked down at her hands. "So knowing about my . . . proclivities doesn't make you think less of me?"

"It might have, before I became involved with Lance," she answered honestly. "Until I found I enjoyed that kind of play. And, of course, I'm grateful that you're willing to take us to the Castle."

"Let's hope it goes the way you want."


THEY joined the men in the den, where Savannah looked at some of the drawings Kevin had made of the Castle floor plan.

"How about if we come back at eight," Lance asked, "and leave from here together?"

"Yes," Erica agreed.

As they drove out of the development, Savannah asked, "Should we stop at my house to get evening clothes?"

He answered with a clipped reminder of why going home wasn't such a great idea. "If Thompson is lurking around, I don't want him to see you with your haircut. If you're really determined to do this, let's go shopping instead. And you can still back out. Up until we walk in the door."

"I'm not backing out. Let's get me something to wear."

When he pulled up at the Mazza Gallerie on Wisconsin Avenue, she gave him a surprised look. "Discount shopping on Rockville Pike would be fine."

"I want you to look like you could eat Raymond Conrad for lunch. So let's go to Neiman Marcus."

"Eat him for lunch? Where'd you get that?"

"From my father."

He strolled into the evening wear department of the high-priced store like he owned the place, then settled in a chair while the saleswoman helped her select several outfits, which she tried on for his approval.

It was clear he liked her in the slinky black pants with a gold and black top. But when she tried to pay for them, he pulled out his credit card.

"This is too expensive for you to buy," she told him.

"Right, it's expensive. And I picked it. So I'd like to pay for it."

Seeing the fierce look in his eye, she stopped objecting. Yet she couldn't help feeling that accepting a thousand-dollar outfit from a man moved the relationship to a new level.

They headed back toward his house. When they reached Columbia, he turned off and headed for the mall parking lot.

"You need something else?"

"Yeah."

She let him steer her upstairs to the second level, then down the walkway to a pet shop. Bypassing the ferrets in the window, he strode to the back, where he found the dog collar display.

She stared at him in disbelief. "You can't be serious about Kevin's suggestion."

"It's a nice touch, don't you think?" he asked as he took down a black leather collar with metal studs.

Holding it up to his neck, he asked, "How does it look?"

"Uncomfortable."

"Yeah."

A clerk approached them. "Can I help you?"

"We want something suitable for Rocky, our German shepherd–husky mix."

Savannah made a strangled sound as the clerk started showing them models.

"This one might do," Lance said, picking up a thinner leather collar. "Let me try it on."

The clerk gave him a startled look.

"I never put anything on Rocky that I wouldn't try myself," he said, buckling it around his neck. "How does it look?" he asked Savannah.

"Fine," she managed.

They left with the collar. Not until they were almost to the escalator did she say, "You don't have to carry this quite so far."

"We're after realism," he answered, giving her a wicked grin.

"What are you thinking about now?" she demanded.

"Nothing in particular."

"I know that look."

He only shrugged.

When they got to his house, he suggested that she take a nap. Just the mention of the word made her realize that she'd better get some sleep before their dangerous night ahead.

Gratefully, she went into the guest room and closed the blinds. Then she pulled off her pants and climbed under the covers, still wearing her knit top, panties, and bra.

She fell asleep almost as soon as her head hit the pillow. And she wasn't sure how many hours later Lance woke her by slipping into bed beside her.

Her eyes blinked open. "Is it time to get up?" she asked, starting to sit up.

He pressed down on her shoulder, keeping her horizontal. "Not quite. I thought I'd come in and get us in the mood for tonight."

"Oh?" she murmured, knowing something fundamental had changed between her and Lance. She might be worried about his more-than-human traits, but that hadn't made her turn away from their intimate relationship.

He was wearing a T-shirt and boxers, but his legs were bare. When he turned her to her side and pressed his front to her back, she felt the unmistakable shaft of his erection against her bottom.

"Do you have a thing for this position?" she asked.

He chuckled, then bent to kiss her neck. "I guess I must."

She closed her eyes, enjoying the feel of his lips as he stroked them along her jawline, then to her ear.

He was good with his mouth and tongue. And his hands. And also his legs, she thought as he rubbed his hair-roughened calf against her smooth one, then walked his toes along her ankle.

While he nibbled at her earlobe and probed her ear with his tongue, he slipped his hands under her knit top and cupped her breasts, making her nipples rigid before brushing back and forth against them.

Her heart rate and her breathing quickened. Closing her eyes, she threw her head back so that her cheek could press against him. He turned his face, kissing her there.

"Nice," he whispered.

She purred her agreement.

"You are so damn sexy," he growled.

"So are you."

She moved back against his hard body, enjoying the chance he had given her to be with him before they left on their dangerous mission.

When his hand slid lower and pressed over her clit, she moved her hips urgently against him, silently telling him she wished he'd get rid of the panties.

He didn't take the hint. So she reached down to do it herself.

"Don't."

"Lance . . ."

He eased away from her, leaving her hot and frustrated. She turned to face him. "What game are you playing exactly?"

"Like I said, getting us in the mood. People who come to the Eighteen Club are usually turned on by the idea of being there. I want us to project that same sexual energy."

Outrage bubbled inside her. She had thought he was going to make love to her. But he had left her with fire coursing through her veins. "What are you doing— paying me back in advance for going as my slave?"

"I hadn't thought of it that way."

"You're topping from the bottom," she muttered.

He laughed. "I guess you got that out of a book. You can throw your S&M terminology around tonight."

Before she could swat at him, he was halfway to the door.

"We need to get ready."

Still strung tight with sexual arousal, she swung her legs out of bed.


AN hour later, Savannah sat very still in the backseat of Erica's Mercedes, holding tight to Lance's hand.

As they pulled up to the Castle's main entrance, she slid him a sidewise glance. The last time they'd been here, she had been dressed like a member of the assassin's guild and Lance had been a wolf.

They hadn't talked a lot about the wolf. And for long stretches of time, she managed to forget about it. Then it would come leaping back into her mind.

Like Erica, she was wondering about long-term relationships. If Mrs. Wentworth thought her situation was complicated, she'd be astonished to hear Savannah's problems.

Like, did she want something permanent with a man who roamed the woods at night as an animal? Did she want her sons to have the same trait?

How did his genetic heritage affect his humanity? Did he have a savage streak that she hadn't seen? She needed to ask—when she worked up the courage.

Logic told her she was crazy to stick with Lance Marshall. Yet the moment he'd slid into bed with her a little while ago, she'd been hot and needy.

He brought her back to their present situation with a casual comment directed at the front seat.

"How are you all doing?"

"Fine," Kevin and Erica answered.

Since Kevin was driving, Erica had steadied her nerves with a couple of martinis before they left the house.

He glided past the front door, where many of the guests at the club opted for valet parking. Instead, he pulled into one of the spaces several yards down the driveway, where they could make a fast getaway if they needed to.

Before they climbed out, Lance addressed everyone in the car. "Remember, we're Samantha and Larry."

They all murmured agreement.

"No last names unless you have to give one."

"Yes."

As they assembled in the driveway, Erica gave them a brilliant smile. Probably the liquor was talking when she said, "I've been so looking forward to showing you around my club."

"And we're just as eager," Savannah answered.

They stepped up to the doorman, who passed them through into the lobby.

Savannah had hoped they'd have a little time to get their bearings, but when she felt Erica stiffen, she looked up.

A slender, good-looking man with a touch of gray at his temples was striding toward them. Raymond Conrad, Savannah guessed.

He held out his arms. After a slight hesitation, Erica went into them.

"I was so glad to hear you were coming back to see us," he said. "And bringing friends." He stepped away from the older woman and gave Savannah and Lance a long look.

"Yes, this is my friend Samantha. And her slave, Larry. Samantha, Larry, this is Raymond Conrad who does such a beautiful job here."

"Erica has told us so much about the club," Savannah said.

"I'm so glad to have you here. But I didn't catch your last name."

"We'd like to keep it on a first-name basis," Savannah answered. "At least for now."

"We prefer to have the full names of our guests," he answered.

So much for that ploy.

"Samantha Carter and Larry Marsh," she said, hearing the edge of nerves in her own voice. But that might not set off any alarms with Conrad. Probably he was used to people being on edge when they first came here.

"We thought we'd enjoy the nightclub," Erica said quickly.

"Our more public room? Or our more secluded facility?" Conrad asked.

"Your more exclusive club."

"Excellent. And we have some special entertainment you might like tonight," Conrad said. "Some of our staff will be acting out a scene in the theater."

"Perhaps," Erica murmured.

Lance looked like he wanted to say something, but he kept his lips pressed together—like a good slave, Savannah noted.

"I hadn't heard that you had shows," she said to Conrad.

"Well, Kevin has participated in some," he told her.

Kevin nodded tightly, and Savannah wondered what message Conrad was sending to him. That he was still an employee?

Another couple came in, and Conrad excused himself to greet them.

"Do you mind if I stop at the men's room?" Lance asked.

"That would be fine," she said, since they had arranged beforehand that he'd ask to be excused, so he could have a chance to look around.

Still, now that they were inside the Castle, the thought of being separated sent a small shiver over her skin.

She'd been here five minutes, and she knew she didn't like the place. It felt like some presence in the walls was watching her—tugging at her emotions.

No, that was crazy, she told herself. Yet she couldn't shake the feeling. And she had to wonder if there really were drugs being piped into the air—even in this part of the club.

"You can join us at our table," Erica told Lance. "The room is right down there," she added, pointing to their left.

Erica, Savannah, and Kevin followed a man dressed

like a medieval courtier down a corridor and into a great hall which looked like it had been transported from a French castle.

Oriental carpets softened the stone floor. Guests sat on low couches and pillows grouped around wooden tables. Serving wenches in shockingly low-cut gowns and bare-chested men in revealing tights, with red sashes at their waists, attended the guests.

Tapestries hung on the stone walls and curtained off many of the tables. Still, as Savannah followed her hostess across the room, she felt the interest of the men and women relaxing in the fantasy setting.

She was somebody new, and she understood that they were appraising her. What kind of sexual kinks did she like? Would she enjoy the atmosphere of the club? Would she come back? Would she end up sexually involved with one of the people watching her?

She wanted to fold her hands protectively across her chest, but she kept them swinging at her sides as she followed Erica to a table for four. The two women took the low couch. Kevin sat on a cushion at Erica's feet.

There was another cushion near her own feet, and she wished that Lance would hurry up and occupy it.

Craning her neck, she looked toward the door. But he was nowhere in sight.


LANCE crossed the black marble bathroom. He'd used the urinal and washed his hands, just in case someone was making home movies in the men's room.

He'd come down a long hall from the main entrance. And he'd studied the layouts that Kevin had given him.

He had a reasonable idea of where he was in the building, but as he stepped out of the bathroom, he hesitated, feeling unaccountably edgy.

He'd planned to explore the club. Now that he was here, his self-protective instincts told him he should go back and join his party. But he had put Savannah at risk by coming here. And it better not be for nothing.

So he turned in the other direction, heading for the back of the Castle. The hall was wide, with doors at regular intervals. Most were closed. But as he passed one, he saw what might have been a well-appointed office in an upscale investment firm or a real estate office.

A secretary was sitting at a computer. What kind of interesting records were on the hard disk? Would he maybe discover a history of Charlotte Nichols's visits to the Eighteen Club?

He'd like to find out, but when the secretary glanced up, he walked briskly by on the thick carpet, like he had every right in the world to be there.

Farther down the hall was another door that said "Staff Only." He hesitated, then moved on.

He was about to step around a corner, when he heard a door open. Flattening himself against the wall, he peeked around the wall and saw a man step out of a narrow doorway. When the door shut, it disappeared, looking like part of the wood paneling.

Lance held his breath, wondering what he was going to say if the man came toward him. But the guy turned in the other direction.

When Lance was alone in the hall again, he started toward the spot where he'd seen the door close. Even from a few inches away, it was almost impossible to spot.

He ran his hand along the wall and detected a line where a seam met the fixed paneling.

Leaving the hidden door, he walked farther down the corridor and saw a large room with a stage at one end. Facing it were love seats and some comfortable easy chairs. Lighting and sound technicians were at work, probably getting ready for the show Conrad had mentioned.

Lance was just about to turn around and go back the way he'd come, when he felt a large hand land on his shoulder.

"I got a report that a slave was wandering around on his own back here. What the hell do you think you're doing?" a grating voice demanded.

# CHAPTER
# TWENTY-FOUR

KNOWING THAT HE'D pushed his luck one beat too far, Lance went very still. "I guess I turned the wrong way when I left the little boys' room."

The hand on his shoulder twisted. Instead of resisting, he let his captor spin him around, and he found himself facing a large man wearing a dark suit. He might be nicely dressed, but he moved like a street fighter. And he had no compunctions about how he addressed a slave.

The man fingered the riding crop hanging from a strap at his waist as he looked his captive up and down. "What are you, a dick brain?"

Lance felt his skin bristle. It would be so satisfying to scare the shit out of this bozo. But leaving him limp and bleeding on the floor wasn't an option. So he managed to answer, "I guess so."

"I haven't seen you at the staff lineup. Did you come with a guest?"

"Yes. She's in the medieval nightclub."

"Well, I guess she doesn't want her boy toy damaged."

"I should go join her."

"Yeah, well, we'll just do that together. 'Cause if I find you running around loose again, I'll have to tan your hide."


SAVANNAH tried to hold up her end of a conversation about modern artists with Erica. But she found herself looking toward the door again. Lance had been gone much longer than she'd anticipated, and she was starting to worry.

A flash of movement on her right brought her attention back to the nightclub. A serving girl had gone down on her knees to set drinks on the table between two men who relaxed comfortably among the cushions. When she set down her tray, one of the men pulled her onto his lap, bending to nibble his teeth against her neck.

As she watched the action, Savannah felt a dart of heat go through her. Apparently Lance's little trick earlier in the evening had worked. She was balanced on a fine edge of sexual tension, responding to the stimuli around her. And it seemed she was going to stay that way until he could do something about it.

Presumably she wasn't the only one. She felt a current of tension in the room. Because the management was pumping happy gas into the air?

It wasn't difficult to believe that. From the moment she'd stepped through the door of the Castle, she'd felt strange.

Kevin leaned against Erica's thigh and stroked a hand along her leg. Another visual stimulus Savannah could do without.

When a waitress approached them, Erica ordered white wine for herself and soda water for Kevin. Savannah did the same for herself and her slave.

She hoped she looked relaxed as she settled into the soft sofa back, because she felt every nerve in her body stretched taut.

Glancing up, she saw someone approaching their table. A muscular man, who might have been a nightclub bouncer, was leading Lance by the arm.

Lance's jaw was rigid as he allowed himself to be marched across the room.

The man wore a dark suit, but a riding crop hung from a loop at his waist.

"Is this your slave, ma'am?" the man asked politely.

"Yes. Has he done something wrong?"

"He was wandering around one of the back halls. He claims he got mixed up about how to find his way back to the front hall."

She managed a laugh. "Well, he's directionally challenged. But I keep him around because he has other talents."

"You could have him publicly flogged, if you want to teach him a lesson," the guard said, fingering his whip as he spoke.

Savannah forced a little smile and swept her lazy gaze over Lance. "Do you think you should be publicly flogged?" she asked in a sweetly suggestive voice.

"If you say so, mistress."

She pretended to consider it. "I think you'd like that, wouldn't you?"

"Yes," he bit out.

"In that case, we'll wait until we're alone to take care of your punishment."

"Yes, mistress."

"Down on your knees," she said, aware that some of the people at other tables were watching the little drama—some with obvious amusement at Lance's plight.

He did as she asked, glaring at her.

"You may sit," she said.

He sat by her feet.

Another female guest, with the long blond hair of a twenty-year-old and the face of a fifty-year-old came over to their table.

"I see you have a rather surly slave," she said in an amused voice.

"Sometimes he doesn't know when to mind his manners," Savannah answered.

"If you need any assistance disciplining him, I'd be glad to help," the woman offered.

"No, that's okay."

The woman gave them an appraising look, then went back to her own table.

Savannah struggled to breathe normally. She'd just gotten a lesson in the lack of privacy in the Eighteen Club.

Lowering her voice, she murmured, "Nice place."

"I must have been in a fog when I first came here," Erica murmured.

\* \* \*

RAYMOND Conrad stood on the balcony overlooking the more private of his nightclubs. He'd come up here almost as soon as Erica and her guests had walked down the hall. The slave named Larry Carter had been missing. Then one of the guards had escorted him into the room. Conrad couldn't hear the dialogue on the floor below, but he gathered that the man had been wandering around on his own.

He'd gone to the men's room. Had he gotten confused about finding his way to the nightclub? Or had he taken the opportunity to poke his nose in where it didn't belong?

Curiosity? Or something more?

"Samantha Carter and Larry Marsh." He said the names aloud. Neither of them meant anything to him. But the woman had looked familiar. "Samantha Carter."

He stared at her, trying to figure out where he had seen her before. Or did she just look like someone else? He wasn't sure. And this wasn't the best angle to observe her.

Erica had said she was an artist. He hadn't heard of her. But then he was pretty busy with the club, and he didn't keep up with every obscure personality in the arts.

He stared down at the foursome, considering the interaction among them. They appeared to have settled in. But he didn't like the way Samantha Carter kept looking around—like she was nervous.

And Erica didn't look all that relaxed, either.

Last night he'd been sure that she was out of here for good. Then tonight she'd brought in a couple of guests.

Who were they, really? Private detectives? The cops? That wasn't likely. He had a good relationship with the D.C. police.

He walked quickly down the steps, then back to his office. First he Googled Samantha Carter. There was a character on a TV program called *Stargate* with that name. An actress. A softball player, a writer. No artists that he could discover.

So he went to Larry Marsh and found a Ph.D. professor, an athlete, a musician, a rear admiral. None of the Larry Marshes or Samantha Carters lived in the D.C. area. Although they could have been visiting from out of town, none of them seemed to be the right age. And the photographs that he found didn't match.

He picked up his phone and made a call. "Keep an eye on the Erica Wentworth party. Particularly her guests. And report back to me on their activities."

"Yes, sir."

SAVANNAH watched Kevin's hand tighten on Erica's leg, and she stopped talking abruptly, probably because she realized it was a mistake to say anything negative about the Eighteen Club while she was in their nightclub.

Lance jumped in to fill the sudden conversation void. "Where are the shows held?"

"Usually in a room on this floor," Kevin answered. He shifted in his seat. "Sometimes they ask for audience participation."

"But you can decline, can't you?" Savannah asked.

"Yes."

Their drinks arrived. Savannah took a sip as she looked around the room. When she spotted a man in the doorway, she froze, fighting a sudden sick feeling in the pit of her stomach.

\* \* \*

LANCE felt Savannah go rigid.

"What?" he whispered.

"Over by the door, I just saw Frank Thompson."

He looked in the direction Savannah had indicated and saw a man with dark hair silvering at the temples. A server escorted him to a table, where he sat down alone.

"Oh, great," Lance muttered, then thought for a moment. "He doesn't know you've cut your hair. If we're lucky, he won't recognize you."

Erica leaned toward them. "What's wrong?"

"She just saw Thompson," Lance growled. "Maybe we should get out of this room before he realizes who she is. But wait until his view of us is blocked."

"We could go down the hall and watch the show," Kevin suggested.

"All right," Savannah agreed quickly.

They waited until some other guests were between them and Thompson, then stood. When Erica and Kevin took their drinks, she and Lance did the same.

Lance kept his body between her and Frank, and she turned her head in the other direction as they exited the room.

Kevin took the lead, heading for the room at the end of the hall, but he stopped before they reached the door, looking apologetic. "The shows can get a little rough."

"Maybe we can leave after a few minutes," Savannah murmured.

"If we sit in the back," he answered.

"Pardon us," a male voice interjected.

She stepped quickly aside so that a man and woman could enter the room. The woman was dressed in a skimpy halter and miniskirt. The man wore a silk shirt and gray slacks. From their manner, she guessed they were master and slave girl.

The room held seating for about seventy-five people. And it was dimly lit. A plus as far as Savannah was concerned.

The four of them took two small couches in the back, and she watched the rest of the crowd come in, hoping that Frank wouldn't be among them. There were all kinds of combinations. Some couples, like the man and woman who had pushed past them, seemed to be dominants with submissives. Some seemed to be of equal station.

And there were also well-dressed single men and women, who tended to move toward the front of the room where they could get the best view of the stage.

Low music played, something modern and edgy, and Savannah caught a sense of anticipation in the air. Some couples talked. But mostly the audience waited in silence for the performance to begin.

When the lights dimmed a few degrees more, the hum of anticipation deepened.

A spotlight fell on the left side of the stage, and Savannah felt a tingle of fear as two burly men, naked to the waist and wearing black tights, pushed a structure onto the stage.

Lord, what was going to happen?

She saw a wooden platform with posts standing up at all four corners. Interlocked metal rods formed a kind of roof.

Then the lighting changed, and she realized that a woman stood in the center of the platform. Her hands were bound to a pole running above her head. And her

ankles were shackled to rings on the floor of the platform.

A length of silky fabric hung over one shoulder and
pooled downward between her legs to the center of the
platform. Apparently that was her only garment.

Curtains at the back of the stage rolled to the sides, revealing large television screens, like at a lecture or a
sports event. When they snapped on, they were all various
views of the woman on the stage. One showed her butt.
Another showed her breasts. Another was trained on her
face. And Savannah felt her chest tighten when she saw
that the final camera was on the platform, pointing upward between her legs.

Savannah's gaze went to the close-up of the captive's
face. She looked scared—but excited.

And that excitement rippled through the audience.
Dozens of men and women were riveted on the captive
and the larger-than-life images of her face and body.

Savannah wanted to get up and rush out of the room.
But she forced herself to stay where she was, because
fleeing would reveal too much.

Perhaps she had made a small sound because Lance
reached for her hand and clasped it tightly.

Another man, naked to the waist and wearing black
tights, stepped onto the stage. He wore a Lone Ranger–
type black mask.

With a flourish, he held out his muscular arm toward
the woman. "This is Jewel. Isn't she lovely? And I am
her master for this performance."

Murmurs of acknowledgment echoed through the
audience.

The master approached Jewel and smiled at her as he
caressed her breasts through the silky fabric draped over

them. Then, slowly, he pulled the length of material off of her.

Savannah watched, feeling as though the fabric were sliding over her own flesh.

When Jewel stood naked before the audience, the master walked slowly around her, looking at her body from all angles, reaching to stroke her shoulder, her hip, her butt, each touch mirrored on the television screens.

Savannah slid a glance toward Kevin. Conrad had said Kevin had participated in this show. And it must have been in the part Jewel was playing.

As the master walked behind her, another spotlight flashed on, illuminating a rack of implements Savannah hadn't seen before. From the selection, he picked up a bullwhip. When he cracked it in the air, the woman winced. When he brought it down on her bottom, she moaned.

He gave her six vigorous strokes, each one making the woman—and Savannah—suck in a sharp breath. Then he stopped to walk to her side.

Taking her face in his hands, he gave her a kiss before starting to speak.

"Does the whipping turn you on?" he asked.

"Yes," Jewel whispered.

"Speak up."

"Yes," she answered in a louder voice.

"And do you like having all these people see what I'm doing to you?"

"Yes."

He stroked the inside of her thigh, then thrust two fingers inside her, the action spotlighting on one of the television sets. "Do you need to come?"

"God, yes."

"Good. That's good. I like having control over you. I like making you wait. And maybe I'd like to have someone from the audience help me discipline you. I'm wondering if I should pick a man or a woman."

He moved behind her again, selecting another whip, and Savannah turned to Lance. "I don't want to see any more of this."

"Okay," he answered immediately.

He stood, and they exited the room. Erica and Kevin followed them.

Erica looked disappointed at being pulled away from the performance.

"I—" Savannah started to speak, then stopped when one of the staff came striding up to them—as though he'd been waiting for them to exit the theater.

# CHAPTER
# TWENTY-FIVE

SAVANNAH WANTED TO move closer to Lance. But she decided that acting like she needed protection wasn't a great idea.

"You didn't enjoy the show?" the man asked. He was wearing a discreet gold plate on his suit front that said "Craig Parker, Manager."

She was totally at a loss for a response. But Lance came to her rescue. "Actually, it turned us on," he said quickly. "We were just about to ask Ms. Wentworth how we could get a private room, but we didn't want to bother anyone else."

Parker looked at Savannah. "Is your slave speaking out of turn?"

"No. Not at all. I let him do the heavy lifting," she managed to say.

"I believe we can arrange a room for you," the manager said.

Lance turned to Erica. "Why don't you two go back and enjoy the show? And, uh, we might be here rather late. So maybe it would be better if you left without us."

Erica's eyes filled with concern. "How will you get home?"

"I'm sure we can call a cab," he said smoothly, and Savannah suddenly felt trapped. She wanted to scream at him that that wasn't a good idea. But she bottled up the words.

"I can take Erica home and come back for you," Kevin said.

Savannah gave him a grateful look.

"Sure," Lance answered. "Thanks." He looked like he wanted to say a lot more. But he only watched as Erica and Kevin went back to see the rest of the show.

Savannah felt her nerves stretch taut as she glanced at Lance. She'd been so full of bravado—determined to avenge her sister's death. He'd warned her what the atmosphere would be like inside the Castle. She'd only half believed him. But after less than an hour, she wanted to scream at him to get her out of here.

Another staffer approached them, smiling graciously. This one was also a manager, named James Olson.

"I understand you'd like one of our private rooms," he said.

Lance remained silent, and she knew that as the dominant, she should be the one to make the arrangements. Clearing her throat, she said, "Yes. We'd like a room equipped so that we can act out a scene, something like the one at the performance."

"What sort of setting would interest you?"

Pretending to be considering delicious alternatives, she thought back over the books she'd read and finally said, "A dungeon. With a bedroom attached."

"Very good," Olson said. "If you'd like to wait in the lounge, I'll check the availability of rooms."

He escorted them to a small, plush lounge area, and she hoped he'd return and tell her there was nothing appropriate available.

CONRAD picked up the phone on his desk.

"This is James Olson."

"Is there a problem?"

"You asked to be kept informed about the Wentworth party. Mrs. Wentworth and Kevin Amsterdam are watching the show. But the other two said the show aroused them, and they'd like a private room."

"What kind of room?"

"A dungeon. With a bedroom attached," Olson answered.

Conrad leaned back in his seat. "Do we have something available with good video coverage?"

"Let me check."

Conrad waited while his manager consulted the master list of room assigments.

"We have room 22."

"Just a moment." Conrad went back to his computer and brought up the room on his computer screen. He could see the placement of all the furnishings and the hidden video equipment.

"That looks like a good selection," he said. "I'll want the video feed on my computer here."

The two guests had said they wanted a room for some private fun. If they were planning something different, he'd find out pretty quickly.

SAVANNAH sat sipping her drink. Like all the other settings she'd encountered in the Eighteen Club, the lounge was plush and comfortable—with some twists.

Above the bar was a flat-screen television. Another was on the opposite wall.

They were both showing the same film—something that she'd label as soft-core porn. There was no real intercourse, as far as she could see. And no full frontal male nudity, so you couldn't tell if the guy was hard or not.

But the man and woman in the South Seas hut were doing a pretty good imitation of a couple engaged in intimate activities.

"What's taking so long?" she asked Lance.

"I guess they want to make sure we've got a fantastic room," he muttered. The way he said it set her teeth on edge.

She took another sip of wine, glancing at the couple on the video screen. They had left their hut and were sporting in what looked like an artificial lagoon.

"Ms. Carter?"

Savannah didn't respond. Then Lance touched her arm, and she realized she was being addressed.

Looking up, she saw James Olson standing by their table. "I have a dungeon setting available right away," he said.

"That would be wonderful," Savannah murmured, picking up her wineglass.

"Follow me."

He took them to the end of the hall, where a man dressed as a French courtier stood at attention.

He might be wearing a comic opera uniform, but he definitely looked like he could handle himself in a fight.

They walked past him, then down a set of stone steps, and she felt like she was descending into the fifth circle of hell, where the guard at the top of the steps would block their exit if they tried to escape.

When she shivered, Lance draped his arm over her shoulder and pulled her against his side.

They stepped into a wood-paneled corridor, following the Castle manager past several doors until he stopped in front of room 22. Unlocking it, he led them inside and switched on a light.

They were in a dimly lit, stone-walled room with a wooden table in the center of the floor and various wicked-looking implements hanging on racks on the wall. Although the lights were electric, they imitated flickering torches.

"The bedroom and bathroom are through this way," he said, as though he were a bellman showing them around a hotel suite as he led them to a room with a curtained canopy bed that looked like it might have been transported from a Scottish castle. Through a door was an incongruous modern bathroom with a soaking tub large enough for two.

"The dungeon is very well equipped for anything you have in mind. We have a hoisting device"—he pointed to a set of ropes and pulleys on the wall—"and the table has a very nice feature." He walked over and demonstrated. "There are several trapdoors in the surface. So if you want to strap your slave facedown for punishment, you can still get to his penis and testicles. Or his nipples."

"Yes, right," she answered, hearing the thin sound of her own voice.

To her relief, the man finally left them alone, and she stood staring at Lance, wondering what they were going to do now, since Kevin had told them someone could be watching them.


CONRAD leaned toward the television screen, observing the couple in the middle of the room. She looked as if she wasn't sure why she was there. He looked as if he was prepared to have a good time.

He took her in his arms. She clung to him, and he stroked his hands over her back and shoulders. When she lifted her face, his lips came down on hers, and they exchanged a hot, hungry kiss—like a couple who had been longing to be alone all evening and finally had their wish.

Maybe they really did want privacy. Or maybe they knew that they were being watched.

The man brought his lips to the woman's ear, nibbling on her. Was he speaking, too, in a voice too low to be heard by the microphones?

Conrad reached for the volume control.


SAVANNAH clasped her arms around Lance's waist, holding him close. It was a relief to feel his arms around her. And a turn-on, too. Because even if she hadn't liked the show they'd seen upstairs, it had affected her on a subconscious level.

Maybe it was the same for him, because all his attention was focused on her now. So—could she make him forget about exploring the Eighteen Club?

He stopped nibbling at her ear and spoke in a voice she could hardly hear. "Are you okay?"

"Yes. Now," she said aloud, because if anyone was listening, there was no harm in those brief, positive syllables.

He hugged her more tightly, and she found his lips again. They drank hungrily from each other. Unable to keep her hands still, she slid them down his back to his hips, pressing him against herself, feeling his erection leap to meet her body.

"La . . . Larry," she sighed. "I need you. . . ."

"God, yes," he answered, his hand moving between them, finding her breast through the silky fabric of her shirt and stroking back and forth across the pebbled nipple.

She moaned her pleasure, then took his hand, tugging him toward the bedroom.

They could stay in this room, warm and safe, giving and taking from each other. Then they would leave. And never come back.

In the next moment, he shattered her illusions.

Bringing his mouth close to her ear again, he said in a barely audible whisper, "I'm going to leave you here, and go exploring."

"No!" she almost shouted, then realized that she'd spoken the syllable aloud. In a whisper she added, "Exploring is dangerous. Stay here and make love with me. You want that as much as I do."

He heaved in a breath and let it out in a rush. "Yeah."

"Come into the bedroom."

He lowered his voice against her ear. "We can't. I have to see what's in the building. I found a hidden door in the wall upstairs. I'm sure there will be one next to this room."

She moved her mouth to his ear. "I want to get out of this place. I have a very bad feeling."

"Give me twenty minutes," he said aloud, then walked to the rack of implements along the wall. After studying the equipment, he said, "Wow! What a fantastic room. And all these toys! Sometimes you let me pick. Let me do that now. I loved the way that bullwhip sounded upstairs. It was so sexy cracking through the air. Please, use one like that one on me. And for extra added excitement, can we do it in the dark?"

He had just told her what he intended. She knew she wasn't going to change his mind, so she cleared her throat and delivered a line they'd used in private.

"Are you topping from the bottom again?"

"Yeah. Don't be too hard on me for that."

"I'll take it out on your hide," she said in a shaky voice.

"Good." He cracked the whip in the air several times, then brought it down hard on the table, demonstrating what he wanted her to do.

Then he pulled off his shirt.

"Do you want me on my stomach or my back?" he asked.

"Your stomach. But let me open that trapdoor under your cock first."

"Oh, yeah!" he agreed, sounding enthusiastic.

"Let me set this up." He squeezed her hand, then let go and strode into the bedroom, where he turned on the bathroom light. Then he closed the door, so that only a sliver of illumination escaped from the crack along the edge of the rug.

Back in the dungeon, he took her hand again, then turned off the light. They stood in the darkness, their eyes adjusting.

"Okay?" he asked.

"I can hardly see."

"That's the idea, sweetheart. I'll be able to hear the whip. And you won't be sure where the lash is landing."

"Oh, neat!" she muttered.

"Get used to the darkness while I take off the rest of my clothing."

"Okay."

He walked to her again and gave her a tight hug and a quick kiss on the lips.

Mouth against her ear, he said, "Put my wallet into your purse, and sling the strap across your chest—in case we need to move fast."

She took the wallet from him and stuffed it into her evening bag. "You said twenty minutes," she reminded him in a shaky voice.

"Yeah. That's about all I can take. But you've got to space out the strokes a little."

"Right."

"And, uh, are we following your usual rule? I'm not supposed to talk unless you give me permission?"

"That's right," she answered, knowing why he'd asked the question. He'd taken care of the video camera problem by turning off the lights. But since he wouldn't be in the room, they needed a reason why nobody would hear his voice.

"Make me hot, baby," he growled. "Make me burn."

"Oh, I will."

As she stood there in the middle of the room, clutching the whip handle in her hand, Lance opened the door a crack, then slipped out, leaving her alone. She wanted to scream at him to come back. Instead she lashed out with the whip, hitting the wall, then turning and hitting the edge of the table as she fought to steady herself.

WITH the lights off, Conrad could see almost nothing in the room. Too bad they didn't have infrared cameras. But in his experience, few couples who came to the Castle wanted to play in the dark. They wanted to see each other's bodies. See the expressions on each other's faces.

But there were some people who didn't follow that prescription. Like the ones who were into sensory deprivation, for example. Sometimes a top would bind a sub up like a mummy so he could see and hear nothing.

A brief flash of light angled across the screen. Then the scene went black again.

Conrad leaned forward, studying the black screen and cursing. Then he heard the woman's voice.

"Lord, this is sexy," she said. The exclamation of delight was followed by the crack of the whip in the air before it came down on a firm surface. The man? Or had she hit the table?

"I like this trapdoor idea," she purred. "Let's see how this is affecting you. But I'm warning you. Don't you dare come until I give you permission."

Conrad cursed. With the lights off, he couldn't see a damn thing on the screen. Maybe he should go downstairs into the passageway beside the room and look directly through the spy panel.

* * *

LANCE fought back a dart of panic. He'd been so sure
that there would be tunnels down here like the one he'd
discovered up on the main floor. And he'd formulated a
plan based on that conviction.

Now that he was in the hallway, the paneling along
the wall felt seamless. And he thought he heard footsteps on the stone stairs.

Shit!

Quickly he moved to the side of the door, sliding his
hand over the wall.

To his relief, he finally felt a crack in the wood. And
when he pushed, he felt the surface give way. A narrow,
practically invisible door swung inward, and he stepped
quickly into a dimly lit passageway.

Out in the hallway, footsteps came closer and he held
his breath. But whoever it was went on past.

He looked to his right and saw what was probably a
panel like a one-way mirror. But the other side was dark.
Through a speaker, he could hear Savannah talking—
talking to him.

The whip cracked, and she murmured, "I hope you
like the sting of that lash."

"Yeah, baby, I do," he whispered. "Good going."

He turned to the other side of the hallway. There was
another window with a view into a room so totally un-
like the dungeon that he blinked. It was decorated like a
young girl's bedroom with a canopy bed, frilly green
and white spread, white furniture, and a candy pink rug.

A girl wearing a long cotton nightgown sat in the
middle of the spread. Her blond hair was done up in two
ponytails. She was licking on a large lollipop. But as

Lance gave her a better look, he saw that she was probably in her early twenties. Standing beside her was a man wearing a Victorian dressing gown. He fondled one of the girl's ponytails, then slipped his hand down her neck and over the front of her nightgown.

"Do you like it when Daddy visits you at night?" he murmured.

"Oh, yes."

"Put down your lollipop. Daddy has something much nicer for you to suck on."

He opened the front of his dressing gown, revealing an enormous erection. With a hungry look, he lay down on the bed beside the girl.

Lance grimaced and turned away, then hurried down the passageway. As he rounded the corner, he heard a door open.

Jesus!

He ran lightly along the passage, then came to a set of steps leading downward. To more private rooms?

Something seemed to tug him downward—a voice, sounding in his head. *Come down and see the show.*

He started down. Then he stopped short. Something was down there. Something calling him. And if he went down to the next level, he was in big trouble.

*Come down.*

*COME down. Come to me.* Savannah heard the voice calling in her mind, invading her consciousness.

"No," she said aloud.

*Come to me. You are frightened. And you are angry. I can help you deal with those emotions.*

"No," she said again, fighting the pull of something she didn't understand. "Who are you?" she gasped out.

She didn't really expect an answer. But the voice in her head murmured, *Boralas.*

Boralas. She'd heard that name. Charlotte had said it to her shortly before she'd died.

"Leave me alone!" she cried out.

When the voice invaded her mind again, she raised her arm, making the whip bite the air around her with a cracking sound before it slammed down onto the table.

*Do not resist me. You want to come to me. You want the satisfaction I can give you.*

Again she cracked the whip. Harder, trying desperately to ignore the seductive voice. The voice of Boralas.

LANCE heard the voice, too, calling him.

Fear jolted through him. Not for himself. For Savannah. It wanted him. But it wanted her more.

He knew suddenly that he had to get back to her. But he couldn't simply retrace his steps, because whoever was in the passageway would see him.

He kept going, turned to the right, and figured he was in a tunnel in back of the room. Lighted windows gave a view into other chambers, but he ignored them. When he came to the next corner, he dashed down the corridor, then skidded to a stop at the end of the passageway. He had gotten into here, but he didn't know how to get out.

Footsteps followed behind him. He was trapped, unless he could figure how to unlock the door from the inside.

He fumbled along the panel, his fingers desperately searching for the hidden mechanism. Finally, his hand found a catch and he depressed the spring. The door swung open, and he pushed his way out. He was in the main corridor again, one door down from room 22.

Sprinting for the room, he turned the knob and bolted inside. In the shaft of light from the open door, he saw that the dungeon was empty.

Shit!

He pounded into the bedroom, but Savannah wasn't there, either—or in the bathroom. Oh, God, what had happened to her?

# CHAPTER
# TWENTY-SIX

LANCE STOOD IN the middle of the room, clenching and unclenching his fists.

He'd left Savannah alone here—left her in danger—because of his own selfish need to gather information about the Eighteen Club. And before he could discover anything besides the hidden passages, he'd known she was in trouble.

His mind supplied a logical explanation: someone had come down here, found that she was alone, and carted her off for interrogation.

He rejected that theory. Something had called him. And called her. And she had followed the voice.

He returned to the hallway, but before he had taken ten steps, he saw the door in the paneling begin to open.

He flung himself into the next room, praying it was

empty. It was, and he held the door open just a crack so he could look out.

Raymond Conrad walked by, his face set in a grim line.

Had he given orders to have Savannah brought to him? And now he was looking for her?

The man opened the door to the dungeon and looked in. Then he stepped inside. When he came out, he trotted to the stairway.

After he had disappeared, Lance stepped into the hall again.

*Come to me. That's right. You want to come to me. Open your mind. Let me give you everything you want.*

The voice was calling him. And calling Savannah. His life mate. And he had to save her from whatever it was leading her to—her destruction. If he knew anything, he knew that.

He forced himself to stand quietly and listen for the silent, seductive voice, although his blood was pounding so hard in his ears that he could barely hear anything.

But he focused with every cell of his concentration— then quickly started down the hall again. When he reached the stairs, he felt an icy cold wafting upward from the basement. Savannah was down there. He knew it.

He wanted to call her name. But he was afraid that would only give him away. So he slipped off his shoes and went quietly down.

RAYMOND Conrad assembled several of his senior staff in his office.

"Where are Erica Wentworth and Kevin Amsterdam?"

"They've left, sir," Olson told him.

"The two people they brought in—Samantha Carter and Larry Marsh—requested a private room. But they're not down there. They must be wandering around the premises. Find them."

"Yes, sir."

"I'll go to the TV monitor room." He turned to Olson. "You and your men search the building."

"All floors?"

"Except the basement. Put a guard at the top of the steps. But I don't want anyone going down there without my express orders." He was thinking about Boralas crouched in his rock-bound cave. His silent partner, who was spinning out of control. He didn't want to send any of his men near the being.

LANCE reached the lower level, deep in the earth. Again, he was in a hallway. From a room at the end of a corridor, he could hear angry voices.

Savannah! And someone else. A man.

What the hell was going on?

He crept closer, drawn by the voices and the murmuring in his head, tugging at his brain.

*Join us. Come and join the party. You want to be with us. You want to watch what happens.*

He felt his throat clog. Suddenly it was hard to breathe.

When he came to a heavy wooden door, he pulled it open and saw a stone chamber beyond.

Savannah was standing rigidly next to one wall, facing a man who stood just as stiffly. It was Frank Thompson. And they were shouting at each other, their harsh words bouncing off the walls of the stone chamber.

Behind them, a strange reddish glow emanated from a crack in the far wall. Lance couldn't see it well, because when he tried to look directly at it, his eyes burned.

He forced himself to endure the pain and saw writhing, pulsing movement. Something was back there. Something that had no form he could name.

Jesus, what was it?

And what the hell was going on? He didn't understand. But he knew that his life mate was in mortal danger. And he knew he had to save her.

Yet his legs wouldn't carry him forward. Not now. All he could do was stand and listen.

Savannah's voice rang with anger. She was speaking to Thompson. "Don't lie to me. You seduced my sister."

Her former husband answered with a harsh laugh. "You have *that* bass-ackwards. She seduced me."

"You're lying!"

"No. She came to me. She said you'd described me as an uptight brute. And she was going to show me there was a lot more to life than fucking in the dark. She taught me how to have a great time in bed."

Savannah gasped. "You're lying!" she shouted again.

"You know I'm not."

"Why did you kill her?"

"I didn't kill her. She went crazy. She came to me, raving about a monster in the basement of the Castle. She was screaming at me. Hitting me."

"And what did you do to her?"

"I defended myself."

"You lying piece of shit."

"You little hypocrite. When we were married, you lay in bed like a limp rubber doll and deigned to let me fuck you. What the hell are you doing here?"

"You were horrible. Self-centered. All you cared about was your own sexual climax."

"Because you acted like you couldn't stand for me to touch you. So I did it as quickly as possible."

"Me? Our miserable sex life was my fault? I was a scared virgin on our wedding night. I didn't know anything about sex. And you taught me it was all about your pleasure. You acted like I was your personal servant in bed. And the lord of the manor the rest of the time."

"Your father told me you knew your place. He was wrong."

The light behind Savannah and her ex-husband pulsed and surged like flames leaping from a bonfire that had suddenly been showered with lighter fluid.

"Why were you stalking me?" Savannah shouted.

"I knew you'd blame me for her accident. I had to find out what you'd do, you bitch."

"And you wanted the diary!"

"You bet!" Thompson flung himself across the room, grabbing Savannah and shaking her. "Where is it?"

Lance struggled to charge to her rescue, but some force he didn't understand kept him out of the room, away from Savannah and Thompson.

*No. Let them fight. Their anger feels so rich. So powerful. Does her anger make her strong enough to defend herself?*

Savannah made a sound that held more fear than anger as she tried to fight the man off. But he had the advantage of size and weight.

He knocked her to the ground, coming down on top of her as he lifted his hands, closing them around her throat.

Her scream choked off, and her eyes glazed with terror as she fought to pull his hands away.

But he hung on with maniacal strength.

Lance bellowed in fear and frustration. He felt as if his muscles had turned to stone. Or maybe it was more like being held in a force field. All he knew was that he couldn't move. He could only watch in sick horror as Thompson choked the life out of his mate while the awful light in the room surged, filling the whole chamber with an unearthly glow.

He knew with terrible certainty that no one could come to her rescue. She was going to die, and he couldn't do a damn thing about it.

He couldn't get through the barrier. Not as a human. But maybe he had an alternative. Maybe that thing in there couldn't reach the wolf's mind.

He had already discarded most of his clothing. He had only to tear off his pants and undershorts—which he did as he said the ancient chant of transformation.

"*Taranis, Epona, Cerridwen,*" he shouted, the words sharp and desperate in the chill air. After repeating the phrase, he went on to the second half.

"*Ga. Feart. Cleas. Duais. Aithriocht. Go gcumhdai is dtreorai na deithe thu.*"

For a terrible moment he thought it wasn't going to work. The foreign presence in his brain seemed to be fighting to stop him from changing to a wolf.

Or maybe that was only his imagination—born of his desperation to get through the process.

To his relief, the familiar gray hair popped out along his flanks, then covered his body in a thick, silver-tipped pelt. The color—the very structure—of his eyes changed as he dropped to all fours. He was no longer a man but an animal. And the invading force in his brain receded to a background buzz.

Released from the force that had held him on the other side of the doorway, Lance howled his rage as he flung himself into the room, leaping on the man's back, biting his arms and shoulders.

Thompson screamed and let go of Savannah's throat, and she started coughing.

*Are you all right? Tell me you're all right.* He could only scream the words in his head because the wolf couldn't speak.

Thompson turned, throwing up his arms and lashing out. But he was no match for the maddened animal that began to tear at him.

Savage anger coursed through Lance. He wanted to kill this man. But Savannah's hoarse voice brought him back from the brink.

"Lance, no."

He raised his head and looked her in the eye. He ached to kill, but he wouldn't do it in front of her.

He gave the man a final shake and let go. Wide-eyed, Thompson skittered across the stone floor, putting as much distance as he could between himself and the wolf.

Savannah sat up and blinked as though she was just coming back to herself. She looked wildly around, focused on the place where the red glow emanated, and gasped.

Lance couldn't speak. And he knew that if he changed back to human form, the voice in his mind would suck him under again.

He bowed his head, butting against Savannah's side.

*Get up! Get up!* he silently screamed. *We have to get the hell out of here!*

She still looked dazed. He tugged on her sleeve, trying to move her toward the door.

Hoping like hell that Kevin had come back and was waiting outside for them, he kept tugging, and she seemed to snap awake. Pushing herself up, she stood on shaky legs.

In a corner of his mind, he saw that her purse was still strapped across her chest. Good, because he didn't want to have to go back to the dungeon for his wallet.

The red glow surged and filled the room, and as they approached the doorway, Lance felt the color thicken around them, holding them back.

Savannah stopped short.

He broke through. Half in and half out of the room, he tugged at her sleeve.

When her gaze shot to him, he tugged harder. The silk fabric gave way with a ripping sound. Springing back into the room, he pushed her into the hall, then urged her toward the steps, staying in back of her and pushing against her bottom to make her keep going.

CONRAD stood in the video room, looking at the ten screens that displayed various views around the interior of the Castle. There were fifty cameras in the building, many in the private rooms. But there were also cameras in hallways, the lounge, and the nightclubs.

As each room came into view, he took a look. He saw couples engaged in various sex acts or S&M scenes.

He studied a couple in bed, the woman on top, bouncing up and down on the guy's cock. For a moment, he thought it might be Samantha Carter. Then he caught a look at the man's face. It wasn't Larry Marsh. So he switched off the feed to that room.

He would have liked to cut off the video from all of the private suites, but he couldn't take a chance, in case they had ducked into one of the rooms.

So he kept scanning through the scenes, switching off cameras when he was sure he hadn't caught the fugitives on-screen.

He scanned the hallways and the nightclubs. Still no sign of the missing man and woman.

But he stayed where he was, and finally his vigilance paid off. He saw Samantha Carter slowly walking up the stairs from . . . from the basement. She looked dazed and confused.

The hair on the back of his neck stood up. What the hell had she been doing down there? If he'd had a view of the room where Boralas lurked, he would have put it on the monitor. But he'd never dared to wire that chamber for sound or video.

He leaned forward, trying to figure out what he was seeing. Larry Marsh wasn't with her. Instead a large dog followed her up the stairs.

He felt goose bumps break out on his skin. Was it really a dog? Or was it a wolf? And what the hell was it doing inside the club?

He reached to unlock his lower right desk drawer and pulled out an automatic. Holding the weapon down by his pants leg, he ran from the room and toward the stairway at the back of the building.


AS Savannah reached the top of the stairs, she gasped and stopped short. When Lance saw one of the guards blocking the entrance, he leaped past her and onto the man, knocking him to the floor.

The guard screamed and struggled. Lance grabbed the shoulder of his jacket and tugged him toward the stairs, where he tumbled downward.

The wolf didn't have to push at Savannah now. She was dashing for the second flight, her high heels clattering on the stone risers. He wanted to tell her to kick them off.

He heard running feet coming toward them, but all he could do was keep going.

Another man tried to grab Savannah as she careened into the upper hall. Once again the wolf came to her rescue, snapping and snarling and forcing the man to back off.

Someone screamed.

"Jesus. A wolf. What the hell is a wolf doing in here?"

Savannah made for the door. Thank God, she was almost home free.

Then Raymond Conrad stepped into their path with a gun in his hand. Raising the weapon, he took aim at the animal charging toward him.

# CHAPTER
# TWENTY-SEVEN

GUESTS HAD HEARD the commotion, and several people were almost on top of the animal.

If Conrad fired, he risked hitting one of his patrons.

Savannah stopped short. The wolf snarled at her. *Run. Get the hell out of here.*

She glanced wildly at him, then flew through the front door, almost knocking down the attendant who had turned to find out what was happening behind him.

Lance followed into the night, and they pelted down the driveway.

Jesus, where was Kevin? And what the hell was he going to think when Savannah appeared with a wolf?

As far as Lance could see, their only option was to keep going down the driveway and hope that the farther they got from the Castle, the less likely Conrad was to create a disturbance.

Did he have someone posted out here, waiting for them? Would he call the D.C. police and claim they'd committed some crime inside the Castle?

Lance had no way of knowing. He could have run faster, but he held back, keeping pace with Savannah.

He heard her breath coming in gasps. How much longer could she keep up their frantic pace—in her strappy black shoes?

A moment later, he knew that was the least of his worries. Along the driveway, a car swerved out from the shadows and stopped right in front of them, blocking their escape route.

The driver's door swung open, and the wolf braced to fight whoever had intercepted them.

In front of him, Savannah had stopped short, her breath coming in gasps.

"Get in," the man behind the wheel called out. His gaze zeroed in on Savannah. "I'm Lance's brother. Get into the backseat. Quick."

She reached for the handle and pulled the door open, then scrambled inside. The wolf clambered in after her, and she jerked the door shut as they sped into the night.

Savannah sat with her head thrown back, panting. Lance laid his head in her lap and licked her hand.

When she stroked the top of his head and scratched behind his ears, he pressed more firmly against her.

He ached to ask if she were okay, but he still couldn't speak.

"I'm Grant Marshall," his brother said from the front seat. "And I guess you must be Lance's life mate."

Savannah sucked in a sharp breath. "Life mate?" she demanded. "What does that mean?"

"Oh, shit. Uh . . . sorry about that," Grant mumbled as he made a sharp right turn. He might have headed for Connecticut Avenue; instead he wove his way up and down several residential streets.

"I guess we're not being followed," he said, then looked back over his shoulder at Lance. "I'll stop in the park, and you can change. I've got sweatpants and a T-shirt up here."

Lance waited while his brother turned onto Broad Branch Road. Pulling to the shoulder, he reached to open the back door. Then he got out and handed the wolf a shopping bag.

With the handles of the bag clamped in his teeth, Lance trotted into the woods, then disappeared behind an outcropping of rock.

Quickly he pushed through the ritual of change, almost slurring the words in his mind. As soon as he had returned to human form, he pulled on the sweatpants and T-shirt. As he hurried back to the car, twigs and rock dug into his bare feet, but he ignored the pain.

Climbing into the car, he slammed the door shut and reached for Savannah. She moved back, giving him a questioning look.

"What the hell did your brother mean about my being your life mate?"

In the front seat, Grant swore. "Jesus. Sorry, I just assumed . . ."

"Yeah, right," Lance growled. "We didn't get around to talking about that yet."

"Maybe you'd better explain it to me now," she said, punching out the words.

He turned his head to glare at his brother. Grant had just saved their asses, and now all Lance wanted to do was land a few good blows on his brother's head and chest. Grant had overstepped the bounds of werewolf behavior—by a couple of country miles.

Still, Lance struggled to pull himself back, because he recognized where his anger was coming from. The alpha male werewolf exerting his domination.

"We'll talk about it later," he muttered.

Savannah opened her mouth, but before she could say anything, Grant began to speak, his voice gritty.

"Lance doesn't want to talk about it in front of me because my wife—my life mate—was murdered."

"Oh, Lord, I'm so sorry," Savannah said.

"I thought I could never love again—never be truly alive again. Then I met a woman who had the guts to change my mind. I fought my attraction to her every step of the way. But she brought me back to life."

Grant's heartfelt confession was too much for Lance. He had come close to losing Savannah tonight, and he now had a small taste of what his brother had gone through.

He pulled Savannah into his arms. "I need to know that you're all right," he growled. "I need to know that Thompson didn't damage you—and neither did that damn thing in the basement."

For agonizing heartbeats her body remained stiff. Then she relaxed against him, and he gathered her closer, stroking his hands into her hair, up and down her back. Embarrassed to show so much emotion in front of his brother, he glanced toward the front seat, but Grant was looking straight ahead.

Still keeping his hold on Savannah, Lance struggled

to get control of his voice. When he thought he could speak without crying, he said, "Let me look at your neck."

He turned on the dome light, then tipped Savannah's head back. He could see marks where Thompson's fingers had dug into her flesh.

"The bastard," Lance muttered.

"It wasn't his fault," Savannah whispered. "He was suffering from the same problem as me."

"Which was . . .?" Lance demanded.

She swallowed painfully. "That thing in the basement—Boralas—called us down there *to see us fight*. No—to *feel* us fight—to feel him kill me."

"Boralas? It has a name?"

She ran a shaky hand through her hair. "It told me. And Charlotte did, too. My sister said that word, before she died, only I didn't know what it meant. She was unconscious in the hospital. But she struggled far enough back to consciousness to say that one thing. That was a couple days before she died."

"Jesus," Lance breathed. "So you think it drove her off a cliff—the way it called you to the basement?"

"I think so. Then, when she was already so weak and sick, it reached out to her again, and finished her off." She shuddered.

Lance held her tightly. "I felt the thing's power. I heard it calling you. And me. That's how I found you. Then it wouldn't let me get to you. It made me stand there and watch Thompson choke you," he said, his voice barely under control.

She raised her head and said, "And you figured out that changing to wolf form might mean that it couldn't reach your mind."

"Yeah."

She clamped his hand more tightly. "Thank God you were right. Otherwise, Frank would have killed me."

After a few moments, Grant cleared his throat. "Do you mind telling me what the hell all of this is about?"

"First things first," Lance answered. "I'd like to know what you were doing in the driveway of the Eighteen Club waiting for us."

Grant looked into the backseat for a moment, then swung his gaze to the road again.

"Remember when I called you a couple of weeks ago? Antonia thought something was going on down here." He sighed, then looked at Savannah in the rearview mirror. "My wife reads tarot cards. She kept doing readings for Lance, and they all predicted that his life was going to change. I thought it meant he'd meet—" He stopped and started again. "He'd meet the woman he was going to marry. Antonia thought it was more than that. She was afraid something bad was going to happen to Lance." He heaved in a breath and let it out. "She wanted me to come down here, but the men in my family don't work well together."

"Lance told me that," Savannah said.

"Okay—well, I tried to stay out of it. But Antonia kept getting more and more upset. Finally we drove down to Maryland."

"Both of you?" Lance demanded.

"Yeah. She's back at your house." He looked at Savannah again. "She's pregnant, and I'm not taking her anywhere dangerous."

"I understand," she answered.

"That still doesn't explain how you ended up at the Eighteen Club," Lance said.

"You left your cell phone at home. I checked your last call. It was from Erica Wentworth. I called and told her I was your brother, and she told me she and Kevin had left you at the Eighteen Club and they were worried about you. Kevin was going back. I told him that it would be better if I did it."

"Thanks. We would have been in deep shit if you hadn't been waiting for us."

"So are you going to tell me what's going on?"

Lance relented. "Would you believe there's a gateway to hell in the basement of the Eighteen Club? Complete with fire and brimstone shining from a crack in the wall where an evil presence is hiding?"

"That's a little hard to swallow," Grant answered.

"The monster in the basement can take over your mind," Savannah whispered. "It gets into your brain and makes you do and say things that you'd never do and say on your own."

"Jesus," Grant muttered.

"If you want proof, go down in the basement," Lance added. "And hope you get out alive."


BACK at the Eighteen Club, Raymond Conrad felt like the floor had dropped out from under his feet.

He called Olson into his office. "Is the building cleared yet?"

"Not quite. Some guests resented being interrupted— even when I used the cover story that we have an electrical emergency."

"Let me know when all the guests are gone."

"Yes, sir."

"How many staffers are still here?"

"I've sent home all the people who work as slaves, servers, and in the beauty salon. Only the security men are still in the building—and patrolling the grounds."

"I want a full security detail on duty."

"When are we reopening?"

"When I say so," Conrad snapped.

His manager looked down at the floor. "Sorry to overstep."

Conrad ignored the apology. "I want the back door secured, so that the only way into the building is through the front entrance."

"Yes, sir."

"And I don't want to be disturbed."

"Yes, sir."

He waited until the man had bowed his way out of the room. Then he stood and walked to the far wall of his office. Pushing on the paneling, he opened an entrance to one of the hidden passages. He seldom used that route in and out of his office. This evening, he walked down the narrow hallway and then to a flight of narrow stairs.

As he stepped into the room where he always met Boralas, he felt his own dread choking off his breath.

A man lay on the floor, facedown. Rushing forward, he rolled the limp body onto its back and saw Frank Thompson. He was dead, his face contorted into a ghastly mask of pain.

"What happened?" Conrad gasped.

*He is dead.*

"I can see that. What happened to him?"

*He was the lover of Charlotte Nichols.*

"Tell me what happened down here. Tell me something I don't know!"

*He was once the husband of the woman who called*

*herself Samantha Carter. She is also the sister of Char-*
*lotte Nichols. He recognized her in the nightclub. Her*
*real name is Savannah Carpenter. And he was surprised*
*to see her there. That was how I got the idea to bring*
*them down to my cave.*

"You should have told me who she was."

*I am telling you now. But I wanted to feel their emo-*
*tions when they confronted each other. She goaded him.*
*And he tried to kill her. But the wolf saved her.*

The wolf. Christ.

"How did it get in here?" he demanded.

*The wolf was the man. Larry Marsh.*

"What the hell are you talking about?"

*He changed into a wolf.*

Conrad whistled through his teeth. "I don't believe
you."

*I never lie to you. I saw it. It was interesting, watch-*
*ing him transform. There are people in my world who*
*can do it. I did not know there were any here.*

Conrad tried to wrap his head around the information. It sounded like Boralas was going crazy. But he already knew that. Crazy. Or drunk with sucking the
emotions out of people.

*You must bring Savannah Carpenter back here and*
*make her tell you the name of the man-wolf.*

"Listen, you'd better explain that part."

*You have a word for it. Werewolf.*

"Jesus! No."

*They will come back to hunt me. You must stop them.*
*But the wolf has morality. He wouldn't finish off*
*Thompson. I had to do that.*

Conrad winced. "And what the hell do I do about the
body?"

*I will drag him into my world—like when we get rid of the slaves who die here. Nobody will know what happened to him.*

"We've never done that with a guest. Somebody must have seen him here tonight."

*You can say he left. Only two people can prove what happened—Savannah Carpenter and the wolf-man. Bring them back here.*

"Yes," he whispered, feeling trapped.

When he had formed the partnership with Boralas, he had never imagined anything like this. As he hurried back to the secret stairway, he felt the world collapsing in around him.

AS they rode home, Lance leaned toward the front seat.

"You have a phone with you?" he asked Grant.

His brother handed him the instrument, and Lance punched in the Wentworth number.

Erica answered.

"This is Lance. I'm using my brother's phone. I want you to know that we got out of the Eighteen Club okay. And Grant picked us up."

"Thank God," she breathed. "We were worried."

"Thanks for working with Grant."

Kevin came on the line. "Can you tell us what happened?"

"We ran into some trouble in the basement. I don't want to talk about it over the phone."

"Does this have something to do with Conrad's silent partner?" Kevin asked.

"His silent partner? Who is that?"

"Mr. Boralas."

Lance's fingers clamped around the phone. "What do you know about him?"

"Just that Conrad has mentioned him. He used to stay in the background. I get the feeling he's making some of the major decisions now."

"Yeah. I think he was behind what happened to us," Lance answered. "And my advice would be for you to stay away from the club."

"You got it," Kevin agreed.

Lance hung up.


SAVANNAH sat huddled in the backseat, listening to Lance and his brother talk. Everything had happened so fast, and she was still trying to come to grips with it.

Lance had risked his life to save her. Now that she was thinking straight, she understood that.

But he had risked something else, too. He'd changed to wolf form in the hallway outside the room where Boralas had summoned her and Frank.

The demon, or whatever it was, must know about Lance—must know he was a wolf. And if it knew, Raymond Conrad would know, too.

"Boralas is coming after us," she said, suddenly admitting the terror that had been simmering inside her, unspoken. What are we going to do?"

He wrapped a protective arm around her shoulder. "We'll figure it out."

They pulled into the garage, and everybody got out. As they started toward the inside door, it opened, and Savannah saw a striking woman standing in the doorway, her face turned toward them.

"Grant?" she called out, although her husband was already striding toward her.

"Right here."

She and her husband clasped each other tightly and clung for long moments. Finally, she turned to the rest of the group.

She looked to be in her late twenties, although a streak of white at her forehead split her shoulder-length dark brown hair, drawing attention to her lush, shiny curls. But Savannah was more interested in her blue eyes.

It took several seconds for her to realize that Antonia Marshall was blind.

# CHAPTER
# TWENTY-EIGHT

"DID GRANT SAY you were a tarot card reader?" Savannah asked. The moment the words were out of her mouth, she knew how dumb that sounded.

But Antonia was probably used to the question. Unfazed, she said, "I learned to read the cards long before I lost my sight. Now I feel the braille markings in the corner, and I know what card each one is. Then I see it in my mind."

"Oh. I'm sorry—I'm being rude. I'm Savannah Carpenter."

"Lance's—" Antonia stopped short.

The unspoken phrase hung in the air: *life mate.* That's what Antonia Marshall must be—the life mate of a werewolf. And she didn't seem to be suffering from the condition. In fact, she looked radiantly pregnant.

Her husband kept his arm around her, and Savannah saw the strength of the bond between them. "I'm sorry we took so long getting back here," he told his wife.

"You can't force a supernatural creature to conform to your timetable," Antonia said.

"How do you know what he is?" Savannah managed.

"From the cards." She moved her shoulder in a small shrug. "Well, not just the cards. I know things." She gave Savannah what appeared to be a penetrating look. "Does that worry you?"

"No," she managed.

"I sense that you're being polite."

"I . . ."

Antonia opened her arms. "Come here. I think you need a hug."

Savannah felt awkward, but she moved into the other woman's embrace.

"You didn't have much love in your early life, did you?" Antonia said.

"You sense that?"

"I feel it as a sadness. But you have us now. The men in this family might rub each other the wrong way sometimes, but the women stick together."

Savannah swallowed. She wasn't sure she wanted to be part of this weird family. But did she really have a choice?

They all walked into the living area and sat down.

"Tell me what happened," Grant's wife said.

Savannah gave a brief account of the evening.

Antonia made a clicking sound. "You and Lance came through it—together."

"Yes."

"We can make some plans in the morning. But now you're exhausted," Antonia said to Savannah.

"Do I look that bad?" she asked, then stopped short, remembering that she'd asked the question of a blind woman.

"I hear it in your voice. You've been through an ordeal. And you need to recharge your batteries."

"Yes. Thanks." She started down the hall, then realized Grant and Antonia had probably taken over the guest room.

Lance was apparently thinking the same thing, because he steered her toward his bedroom. And she found someone had moved her overnight bag to the dresser.

"I'll come back later," he said. "You sleep."

"What are you going to do?"

"Call and get some help from my brothers and cousins."

"I thought you couldn't work together. You seemed pretty prickly with Grant."

"Yeah. A family problem. But I don't think you and I can handle this by ourselves."

He left her alone. She stripped off her ruined silk pants and top, then pulled on a T-shirt and collapsed into bed—and was asleep almost instantly.

THE Eighteen Club was finally cleared of all customers. Now there was nothing for Raymond Conrad to do but wait tensely by his telephone. When the call came, he snatched up the receiver.

"Do you have the Carpenter woman?"

"She's not home."

"Shit!"

"Do you want us to go to plan B?"

"Yes."


SAVANNAH awoke to darkness and the knowledge that Lance had just climbed into bed.

When she turned toward him, his arms wrapped her close and his mouth came down on hers in a savage kiss.

As she stroked her hands over his shoulders and down his body, she discovered he was naked. And when he moved against her, she knew how much he wanted her.

His hands glided over her body, possessive, arousing, urgent, rekindling the fire he had sparked before they'd left for the Eighteen Club.

She hadn't had time to think about the two of them. Not after the shock of the "life mate" comment. All she knew at this moment was how much she needed him.

When he rolled up her T-shirt and sucked one nipple into his mouth, she moaned her pleasure.

And when he wedged his erection at the juncture of her legs, she rocked against him.

As he broke the contact, she sobbed out a protest. But he was only moving far enough away to tug off her panties.

He pulled them down her legs and she kicked them away, then gasped as his fingers stroked through the slick, swollen folds of her sex.

"Now. Please, now," she cried out.

He came down on top of her, covering her body with his, plunging into her, his movements as frantic as hers. Seconds later, climax rocked them.

They lay locked in each other's arms, in a sweaty heap, panting.

"When I saw Thompson with his hands around your throat, I about went crazy," he whispered.

"I'm sorry."

"About what?"

"Getting you into trouble—at the Eighteen Club."

"You forget how we met. I was already prowling around the Eighteen Club. I thought it would make a good story."

He rolled to his side, taking her with him.

"But I got you involved in my investigation of Charlotte's accident." She snorted. "And for what? All the time Charlotte must have been laughing her head off at me. She knew my marriage was a failure. And she was a better lover for Frank than I ever was."

"Maybe she didn't think of that herself. Maybe it was one of Boralas's games."

She clutched his arm. "Do you think so?"

"Why not? It's as good an explanation as any."

"And now we can't just walk away from the Eighteen Club, can we?" she asked, voicing her earlier fear.

"No."

"Boralas will come after us, because we know the Castle's secret."

"Yeah."

"Oh, God. I wish it weren't true."

"My brothers and cousins will help us."

"We'll put them in danger."

He sighed. "I'm afraid we already have. Just because they're close to us."

She couldn't hold back a moan.

"But we'll come up with a plan of attack." He curved a hand over her shoulder. "Conrad doesn't know our names. That buys us some time."

"Okay."

He switched on the bedside lamp, and she blinked in the sudden illumination. When she could focus on his face, she saw his determined expression.

"You and I have to talk."

"About what?" she asked cautiously.

"What I should have told you before." His breath hitched. "When the men in my family get to be thirty, they start looking for a mate. I didn't want a mate, and I thought that drinking those noxious Chinese herbs would save me. Maybe it did for a few years—but I think I just hadn't met the right woman."

"What if I don't want to be that woman?" she murmured.

He reached down and took her hand in his. "I'm trying to be honest. I think the bond between us is too strong to break."

She flopped to her back. "I would have liked a choice!"

"So would I!" He climbed out of bed and she watched him walk naked to the window, push up the sash, and bend to step out. He disappeared into the early morning. She couldn't see him, but she heard him chanting in the darkness.

She lay rigid in the bed. If the circumstances had been different, she might have climbed out of bed and left. That wasn't an option, not after this evening at the Eighteen Club.

When the phone rang, she jumped.

Disoriented, she snatched it up. "Hello?"

"Savannah!"

She recognized the voice on the other end of the line.

"Savannah, this is Kevin."

"I know. What's wrong?"

"They want you. They thought you were here."

"What? Who?" she asked stupidly.

"Conrad's men. I fought one of them off and told Erica to lock herself in the bedroom. But they'll get in. I'm afraid they're going to torture us unless we tell them where you are."

"Oh, God," she moaned.

"I can take it. But Erica can't. And . . . and if they tell me they're going to hurt her, I won't have any choice but to cooperate."

"I know. I know. I'm so sorry I dragged her into this." She took several shallow breaths, fighting for control. "Tell them what they want to know."

"What about you?"

"We'll handle it."

"Savannah—" The phone went dead.

She pulled on her T-shirt and found a pair of pants in her luggage.

"Grant, Grant," she called, "we have to get out of here."

He met her in the living room, where he'd apparently already been talking to two other people—a tall man who looked like Lance and Grant and a young woman with dark blond hair.

The man turned to her and said, "I'm Lance's cousin, Ross Marshall. And this is my wife, Megan Sheridan. We got here a few minutes ago. What happened?"

"Conrad's men went after Kevin and Erica—the two people who got us into the Eighteen Club. They want us."

"Shit!" Grant exclaimed.

"Lance is out in the park. Can you find him?"

"Yes."

"We have to get out of here. We can meet at—"

"At the Marriott Courtyard in Columbia," a voice said behind her. She whirled to see Lance standing in the doorway, wearing a pair of sweatpants.

"What—what are you doing here?"

"I saw the lights and figured I'd better come back."

Antonia came out of the guest bedroom. "Are they coming for us?"

"Yes."

"I was afraid of that."

"Why didn't you say something?"

She turned her head toward her husband. "Sometimes what I fear never comes to pass."

"Like when you were afraid I'd kill myself?" he asked.

"Exactly."

Lance's voice cut through the private conversation. "We have to leave now."

Grant and Antonia had not unpacked. Neither had Ross and Megan, who had dropped their children off with their friends Jack and Kathryn Thornton before coming over.

"Adam and Sara are on their way here," Ross said.

"Adam—your brother?" Savannah asked.

"Yes. The forest ranger. And his wife has . . ." he stopped, then plunged ahead, "psychic powers that can fight the thing in the basement of the castle. We have to call them and warn them not to come here."

"I'll call them on the way to the motel," Lance said.

He looked at Savannah. "Can you drive so I can talk on the phone?"

"Yes."

Lance fetched the emergency overnight bag he always kept in his SUV, while Savannah quickly scooped up the few things she'd unpacked. In under ten minutes they were out of the house and speeding in three cars up Route 29 toward Columbia.

Savannah's head was spinning. Maybe the men in Lance's family had trouble working together, but it looked like they could manage in an emergency.

In the car, Lance gave Savannah directions to the motel. "If I can't get Adam and Sara on the phone, I'll have to come back here and tell them about the change of plans."

"No! That's too dangerous."

"Not for a wolf lurking in the woods," he said. "And even if it were, I can't let them walk into a trap."

# CHAPTER
# TWENTY-NINE

SAVANNAH COULD HEAR the phone ringing.
When a male voice answered, Lance looked like an
enormous weight had been lifted off his chest.

"Adam, where are you?"

"At the rental car counter at BWI airport. We're
about to head for your house."

"Don't do it! The bad guys are on their way there
now. So we've changed plans. Meet us at the Marriott
Courtyard in Columbia." He gave him directions, then
hung up.

"Thank God you caught them," she breathed.

"Yeah." He reached over and found her hand. "We'll
get through this."

"Conrad moved up our timetable."

"It was too much to expect that he'd give us a reasonable amount of time."


THE Marshall family assembled at the motel. Lance and Savannah had taken a suite where everybody could gather in the living room.

She looked around at the determined faces, understanding that these men and women had committed themselves to saving her from Boralas and Raymond Conrad. Well, not just her, she reminded herself, but Lance.

He had told her about the relationships in his family. Now she watched each of the men, including Lance's younger brother, Logan, striving not to dominate the conversation. Ross was apparently a natural facilitator; he dealt very effectively with the small brushfires that sprang up.

"We've lost the element of surprise," Lance's cousin Adam said. He had been a National Park Service ranger and now ran a private nature preserve in Wayland, Georgia.

"Which means that the quicker we go in there, the better," Lance said.

"But the building is full of guards—waiting for us."

"What if we create an emergency?" Grant asked. "Like a firebomb or something?"

"That would make it difficult for us to function when we got in there," Ross answered.

"A diversion, then," Savannah suggested.

Lance's eyes narrowed. "What do you have in mind?"

"I go in the front door and tell Conrad I want to talk to him. You guys go in the back."

"I don't want you anywhere near the place," Lance growled.

"I think we do need a diversion," Sara agreed.

"You're not going there, either," Adam told his wife, just as adamantly as Lance.

"I'm sorry," she murmured. "But you're going to need me. That monster in the basement has psychic powers. And it's not from this universe."

"How do you know it's not . . . from here?" her husband demanded.

"She and I have discussed it," Antonia broke in. "I know the natural world. I know what exists here and what doesn't. And the thing you are describing is impossible."

"But it's real!" Savannah objected.

"Of course. And it found a door from its home into our universe," Antonia insisted.

Megan looked at Lance. "Did you call Sam and Olivia?" Sam Morgan was the brother of Adam and Ross but he had changed his last name when he'd fled a bogus murder charge in Baltimore years before. His wife also had psychic powers. That branch of the family lived in California.

"Yes. But we have to head for the Castle before they get here."

"Wouldn't it be better to wait?" Megan asked.

"We have to assume Erica and Kevin are being held there. And the longer we wait, the more chance that Boralas or Conrad will kill them," Savannah answered.

There were murmurs of agreement around the room.

"Right now, I'm the only one who can fight Boralas

on the psychic level," Sara said. She looked at Savannah. "It had you in its power, right?"

She swallowed. "Yes."

"Tell me everything you can about it. How you felt when it called you to its lair. How you broke the spell."

"I didn't. Lance came into the room as a wolf and saved me. Otherwise my ex-husband would have choked me to death."

"So this being, Boralas, can control people's actions?" Sara clarified.

"And create illusions. I thought I was standing in the bedroom of the house where Frank and I lived. I don't know what *he* thought."

"What happened to him?"

"I was going to kill him," Lance bit out. "Savannah stopped me, but we haven't seen him since." He slung his arm around Savannah's shoulder and pulled her close as he told the group his recollections of the night before.

"How are we going to fight it?" Megan asked when he'd finished.

"The wolves can attack it," Adam said.

"I'm betting the wolves can't hurt it," Sara answered. "It will take psychic power to drive it back where it came from."

Everyone was silent as they tried to decide how they would get into the Castle and out again—alive.

"Erica and Kevin complicate the problem," Adam said.

"We can't leave them there!" Savannah shot back.

"I wasn't suggesting it."

After they discussed and discarded several plans, Ross's wife, Megan, the doctor, cleared her throat.

"I have an idea," she said, "but it's risky."

"Let's hear it," Lance said.

They all listened. Then Savannah made a suggestion. And the other women added their thoughts.

"Too dangerous," Grant muttered.

"I don't think we have an alternative," Antonia said.

Savannah shook her head. "I can't let anyone take that kind of risk."

Sara gave her a direct look. "You're not asking. We're volunteering. At least I am."

The other women in the room quickly joined in.

AT the Eighteen Club, Raymond Conrad paced back and forth across the stone floor of the cavelike room where Boralas dwelt.

"Kevin couldn't watch my men torture Erica. For all the good that did us."

*He loves her. I can feel it.*

"Well, don't get too wrapped up in that," Conrad snapped. "When we got to Lance Marshall's house, they'd cleared out. Either they were smart enough to go into hiding, or Kevin warned them."

*He called them,* Boralas said, the tone of his mental voice flat and matter-of-fact. *I picked that up from his mind.*

"Oh, great."

*They will be here soon,* Boralas said. *They cannot afford to wait. But we will be ready. Every minute I am in your world, I grow stronger.*

THE assault team waited until dark before driving to the Eighteen Club, once again in three cars.

They parked at the end of the block and the men slipped into the woods. Ten minutes later, five wolves, four of them wearing backpacks, approached the building through the screen of trees.

Savannah drove her car to the bottom of the driveway and waited, praying that the posthypnotic suggestion Antonia had given her would block her real thoughts from Boralas. Nervously she checked her watch. At exactly nine thirty, she pulled up to the front door of the Castle and got out. An armed guard was waiting for her.

Although her heart was pounding so hard that she felt like she was going to faint, she managed to keep her voice steady when she said, "I have a proposition to make to Raymond Conrad."

The guard looked skeptical.

She had rehearsed what to say if he didn't offer to take her into the building. "I'm alone. Lance doesn't know I've come. And I'd feel better if we went inside where he can't see me."

He hesitated a moment. "I can't let you inside without searching you."

"I understand."

She handed over her purse, waiting with her pulse pounding while he went through the contents. Then he patted her down, enjoying the feel of her curves.

But he found no weapons.

After speaking into a walkie-talkie, he ushered her into the front hall. Five guards materialized around her. How many were in the building?

She stood on the marble floor, trying to look like she wasn't going to jump out of her skin, and trying to keep her thoughts on the surface of her mind, as Antonia had told her she would. Still, this was the most problematic part of the mission. If the thing in the basement figured out what she was doing, then the game was up.

Silently, she repeated over and over, *You're here to save Erica and Kevin. You feel horribly guilty about what happened to them. You're going to tell Conrad that you'll keep silent about what happened.* She repeated the words, over and over, like a mantra.

When Conrad finally appeared, she pressed her hands to her sides.

"Thank God," she whispered.

He gave her an assessing look. "You're glad to see me?"

"I'm worried about Erica and Kevin. Will you take me to them?"

"What makes you think they're here?"

"Kevin called me. This is the message he gave me." She reached into her purse and wrapped her hand around the lipstick tube that they'd put together in the afternoon. It wasn't ordinary lipstick.

Instead, it was designed to deliver knockout gas— something like the gas that had been used against the Chechen rebels who took over a Moscow theater and held the patrons hostage.

Savannah had already been given a dose of the antidote.

But before she could pull out the tube, Conrad's face changed, and she knew in that terrible instant what had happened. Despite Antonia's mental suggestion, Savannah had focused on her real mission, and the thing in the basement—Boralas—had picked up her intention.

Now it was speaking a silent warning to the owner of the Eighteen Club.

"You bitch." Conrad lunged for her, but she ducked away, crashing into the guard who stood behind her.

The man grabbed her arm, and she thought that she had failed before the rescue operation had even gotten started.

But the lipstick was already in her hand. With the tube still in her purse, she pressed the catch on the side.

Immediately, gas began hissing into the bag, then out through the opening.

"Get it!" Conrad shouted.

Someone yanked the bag from her hand, and she sobbed out in frustration.

But as the man reached for the tube, five dark shapes charged through the door. They were Lance, Ross, Adam, Logan, and Grant—all in wolf form. And all protected by the antidote.

The guards drew their guns. A weapon discharged and one of the wolves staggered back.

"God, no!" Savannah screamed.

He pushed himself up, and she could see that the bullet had only grazed his shoulder.

The other wolves snapped and snarled at the men. But before the battle was over, the guards began dropping to the floor, overcome by the gas. They lay in a heap, Conrad among them.

*No! Stop.*

The command rang in her head, and she knew it was Boralas, switching his full attention to her. Gritting her teeth, she struggled to keep her focus.

*Take one of the guns. Turn it on yourself.*

"No!" she screamed, fighting the command inside her head that was far stronger than the suggestions Antonia had given her.

One of the wolves hurried toward her. It was Lance, her mate. She would have known him anywhere.

Her mate! The thought reverberated in her head. Her life mate. How could she have denied that for so long?

She managed to get the pack off his back.

*Stop. You don't want to hurt me. You want to be with me. I am your true lover. Not the man-wolf.*

"No," she whispered, but this time the protest carried little conviction. She was losing. With a moan, she started for the end of the hall—toward the stairs.

One of the other wolves intercepted her, and she pounded at him with her fists. But he pressed his weight down on her.

Then she heard something metal being rolled across the floor. That was followed by a hissing sound, and she knew that one of the wolves had discharged more of the gas into an air-conditioning register. Soon it would spread throughout the Castle.

"No!" she moaned, fighting against the wolf who held her. He could have hurt her, but he only kept her pinned, and she started to cry in frustration.

She wanted to go to Boralas. And the wolf wouldn't let her up. If she had had a gun, she would have shot him.

*Find a weapon. Get away from him.*

She looked wildly around. Spotting a vase on the table in the hall, she tried to get to it so she could hit the wolf over the head.

Just then, Sara, Adam's wife, came charging through the door. Like the other members of the family, she had been inoculated against the gas. She knelt beside Savannah, cupping her hand over her shoulder.

Immediately Savannah felt a burst of energy flood

into her. Her mind cleared, and she looked gratefully at the woman who had come to her rescue.

Sara looked at the wolf. "It's okay. You can let her up."

The animal backed away. It was Ross.

Sara's voice brought her back to their present danger. "I can feel it," she whispered. "Trying to invade my thoughts and give me orders."

Savannah nodded. Reaching out her hand, she knit her fingers with Sara's.

"Together, we can fight it."

Savannah hoped it was true. She wished now that they'd waited for Sam and Olivia Morgan.

"I . . . don't know. It's strong." Even as she said it, she felt the monster's thoughts sliding into her head again.

*Go away. If you stay here, I will fry your brain cells.*

Boralas sent her a lash of pain, then another and another.

She lay on the floor panting. And she knew Sara felt it, too, because the other woman's face went white.

"I think we have to work fast," Sara whispered.

They stood up, wavering on their feet. Five wolves stood looking at them. They were protected by their animal form from the worst of the assault.

Without warning, flames roared up around them, and Savannah gasped. Sara's hold tightened on her hand. "It's an illusion," she muttered. "He's trying to drive us away. We have to go down there to his lair."

The fire seemed to consume the furniture, the marble floor, the walls. Yet the floor didn't collapse. And when the women didn't run from the building, the illusion snapped off as suddenly as it had flared up.

"You made a mistake!" Savannah shouted aloud. "You just confirmed that you can't affect the physical world."

*But I can affect you.*

As though someone had shot at her with a nail gun, she felt iron spikes digging into her brain. Screaming, she let go of Sara's grasp, sinking to the floor again as she raised her hands to her head, trying to ward off the pain.

In a blur, she saw Lance leap toward her. His body came down over hers, as though he could somehow shield her.

She reached for him, slinging her arms around his neck, hanging on for dear life. And the contact helped.

Then Sara and Adam were beside them, pressing close. And that helped to push away the pain.

But she had learned one thing for sure. She and Sara were never going to make it to the basement to confront the monster.

She sat there panting. Then a noise in the hall made her head swing around in fear as she braced for an attack from more guards.

IT wasn't the guards; they still lay sprawled on the floor. Megan and Antonia were coming toward them, pregnancy making Antonia's gait awkward. But she held firmly to Megan's arm as the other woman led her forward.

Howling in fear and anger, Grant charged toward the women, blocking their path with his wolf's body.

Antonia knelt to stroke her hand over the fur of his back. "Grant, don't stop me. Even outside, I knew what was happening in here. They can't fight the monster alone. They need my power. And if you don't let me help them now, he'll just learn from each encounter—and grow stronger."

The wolf howled again, then pawed the floor.

"Please. Trust me."

His head bowed, Grant let them pass. Even without any psychic abilities, Savannah felt his fear and pain.

She and Sara rushed toward the other two women. Megan helped Antonia up, and this time all four of them held hands. Savannah felt energy surge through her, from the two psychics—and from the power of their combined wills.

They took a moment to let the mental power flow among them, collecting and pooling in one joined consciousness.

She sensed the other women's thoughts.

Sara had fought like this before to save herself and Adam. Antonia might be blind, but she saw things that other people couldn't see. And Megan had an iron strength that had helped her survive capture by a serial killer.

The energy of their combined power surged.

"Let's do it!" Savannah shouted, and they pushed toward the steps.

Four wolves went with them. Ross stayed behind to look for Erica and Kevin.

The Castle was filled with an eerie quiet as they hurried down the steps.

Savannah felt the temperature drop as they descended farther into the earth.

They passed the floor with the dungeon where she and Lance had been just the day before. Lord, it seemed like a century ago.

Then they started down the last flight—to the level where Boralas waited.

Before they reached the last step, Antonia shouted, "No!" and tried to pull them back.

# CHAPTER
# THIRTY

SAVANNAH FELT HER heart leap into her throat as a
guard stepped around the corner, gun pointed at them.
Obviously he had been waiting for just this moment.

"Hold it right there!" he growled.

They stopped in their tracks, and Sara's hand tightened on Savannah's.

"How . . . ?" she managed, then realized the ventilation system for the Castle must not reach this floor—so
the gas hadn't penetrated down here.

In the next moment, the guard screamed and dropped
his gun as though it had suddenly turned white hot.

And Savannah figured out that Sara had hit him with
some kind of energy bolt.

While the guard was whimpering and cradling his
hand against his chest, Megan reached to scoop up his

gun. As she stepped back, one of the wolves rushed the man, knocking him on his butt. Savannah saw it was Adam who stood over him, growling.

"Any more men down here?" she demanded.

When he pressed his lips together, the wolf lunged at his throat, snapping and snarling.

"No. Get him away from me!"

"I'll have him rip out your vocal cords if you don't cooperate. Who else is down here?"

"Nobody!"

But was it true?

Their only choice was to leave Adam guarding the man, while they pressed on.

Savannah had described the layout of the basement to the other women. They hurried down the hall, to the chamber where she and Frank had confronted each other.

Through the doorway, she could see a red pulsing light.

Boralas.

And suddenly she felt his mental fingers probing at her mind again.

When she had been here before, she had been focused on Frank. Now she forced herself to study their enemy.

Was he really in the room? Or was he in some other place, peering at them through a doorway into another universe?

"What do you see?" Antonia asked.

"A red glow."

"I feel it."

"And a doorway."

"Is it small?"

"Just a sliver, I think."

"And I think Boralas is only partly in this world. If we can close the crack, it will have to go back," Antonia murmured.

"We hope," Savannah answered.

She studied the crack in the wall from which the red glow emanated. It seemed like such a narrow opening. All they had to do was make it go away.

Sara's hand tightened on hers. And so did Antonia's. And she knew Megan was clenching Antonia's other hand. The four women held fast to each other as they stepped into the room, facing the monster who lurked in the Castle basement like some ogre from a children's fairy tale.

"Leave this place!" Sara shouted. "Go back where you came from and leave this world alone!"

*Make me.*

"Give me your energy," Sara whispered to the small group that dared to challenge the creature, and Savannah opened her mind to the request. She could feel the other women doing it, too.

Sara sent a lightning bolt surging toward the beast. It shrank back. Then, in the next moment, it sent a burst of pain toward them, and Savannah knew that it had been waiting for this moment—waiting to trap them here.

Involuntarily, they staggered back, and Sara's next volley was weaker than the last.

What had they been thinking? There was no way they could fight this thing.

"Don't let him frighten you," Sara whispered. "Work with me."

They pooled their energy again, sending another bolt toward the monster.

When it turned the blast around and sent it back, they all staggered from the impact. Antonia would have sunk to her knees if Savannah and Megan hadn't held her up.

"Fight!" Sara shouted. "All we have to do is push him back, then close the sliver in the rock."

Suddenly it seemed like an impossible task.

Grant and Lance rushed forward, snapping and growling at the opening. And for a moment, the beast shrank away. Then it sent a blast at the two wolves, and they staggered on their feet.

Savannah felt Sara desperately trying to focus their efforts. But she knew it was a losing battle.

And behind them, they heard an army clattering down the stairs.

"God, no!" Savannah gasped. They had been here too long. While they'd been fighting, the knockout gas had worn off, and the guards were awake.

The women whirled, breaking the contact with each other—and the chain of power. The beast took the opportunity to blast them.

Conrad charged into the room, followed by five of his guards.

"No!" Savannah cried.

The wolves would have sprung at the owner of the Eighteen Club, but the guards held them off with guns.

What was going to happen now? Would Conrad throw them to the monster?

Conrad's frantic words reached her ears but hardly registered on her mind.

"I'm here to help you. Please. Let me help you," he begged. "Let me help you drive it back—while we still can."

Savannah was sure she hadn't heard that right.

"Why? How?"

"Why? Because that thing had my mind in its control. But when I woke up, I understood what it had been doing here at the Castle." He looked from Sara to Antonia. "And you're here to fight it on its own terms, aren't you?"

"Yes," Antonia answered.

"Let me help. Let me make up for what I've done."

In response, a roar came from the monster.

"I know how to defeat it. Quick, before he gets back into my mind," Conrad gasped out.

Savannah didn't know whether to believe him. Could he really have changed sides? But Antonia didn't hesitate. She held out her hand to him. "Yes!" she shouted. "Yes!"

The guards turned and ran away. Their footsteps echoed in Savannah's ears as the other women joined together again, with Conrad between Sara and Savannah. He squeezed her hand as they faced Boralas, their minds united in one effort.

The beast roared out its rage and fear.

And from the other side of the stone, they saw something else. In the red glow, shapes moved. A young woman and an old man.

"What—?" Savannah gasped.

There wasn't time to focus on them. But Savannah felt the woman's energy—coming from the other side of the crack—fighting with them.

Sara directed the stream of power that flowed from their side of the barrier into the crevice in the stone. They saw the red glow surge—then begin to ebb.

Savannah heard a scream inside her head, and she knew it was the creature screaming in anguish as the doorway closed.

But just before the opening sealed, the monster gathered its power and sent one last bolt of energy through— all of the power concentrated on Conrad.

He made a gurgling sound, pulling away from the women and clutching his chest as he slumped to the floor.

For a moment, there was utter silence in the room.

Detaching herself, Savannah knelt beside Conrad. He wasn't breathing, and when she felt for a pulse at his neck, there was nothing.

"Is he dead?" Sara whispered.

"Yes. Why did that thing kill him and not us?" Savannah asked.

Antonia answered, "I sensed they were connected in some way we can't understand. Conrad had been around it for years. He was more vulnerable to it than we were. And it was enraged at his betrayal."

Savannah nodded. Then, because she needed to believe they were finally safe, she said, "It's over. Thank God."

But safety was just another illusion.

Even as she spoke, she felt a grinding sound as the floor beneath them began to shake.

"What is it?" Antonia gasped. "What's happening?"

Savannah understood in that terrible moment that the rules had changed again. The building felt like it was caught in an earthquake, and she knew it was no magic trick. When the monster pulled back, it had shifted the bedrock, and the Castle was going to disintegrate around them.

"Hurry!" she shouted. "We have to get upstairs."

Savannah caught Antonia's hand again and led her toward the exit.

They stayed connected, and the wolves hung back, behind their mates.

She wanted to shout at Lance to go ahead. He had a better chance of getting out alive.

But he remained in back of her.

A chunk of rock fell in their path, and Antonia stumbled. Savannah pulled her up, helped her over the obstruction.

When they reached the floor above, they saw the guards were nowhere in sight. Probably they were already out the door, Savannah thought as huge chunks of rock fell from the walls, breaking the paneling and revealing some of the tunnels between the rooms.

Plaster fell from the ceiling. The floor swayed as they dashed down the hall, and she knew they had too far to go.

Her breath coming in harsh gasps, Savannah dragged Antonia along, aware of the wolves keeping pace with them. One of the animals dropped back.

Moments later, a naked man was beside her. It was Grant. He scooped Antonia into his arms and ran ahead.

When she looked around, she saw Lance had changed back to human form and was beside her, one hand joined with hers and the other with Megan's, urging them along, while Adam scooped up his wife and sprinted ahead.

A stone landed right behind Savannah. Then one came down in front of her. The whole building was going to fall.

Putting on a burst of energy, they hurtled toward the door, but she knew they weren't going to make it.

Just as she prepared to die, the shaking around them stopped. Another woman was standing in the hall, her arms raised.

"Hurry!" she shouted. "I'll hold it as long as I can."

Savannah guessed this must be Olivia, the other life mate with powers—arriving just when they needed her.

"Wait!" Savannah screamed. "We have to get Erica and Kevin!"

"No—we have them!" Ross shouted from the upper stairs as he and a man who had to be Sam Morgan led the two dazed captives down.

They all pounded through the front door and down the drive and into the night.

All except Sam, who waited just outside the door for his mate.

As she ran to him, Sam grabbed her hand and led her to where the others stood. With Savannah's car between themselves and the building, they watched in horrible fascination as the structure began to fold in on itself.

In a little over a minute, the Castle was gone— reduced to a pile of rubble.

Savannah felt dazed. Lance took her in his arms, holding her close. All around her the men of the Marshall clan were doing the same—holding tight to their mates—as Kevin was cradling Erica.

Sam raised his voice. "Hey, guys, you might want to cover your butts." He picked up the knapsack he'd grabbed and began distributing sweatpants.

Erica stared at the men. "Why are they naked?" she gasped.

"That was the best way to sneak around the castle,"

Lance said, and Savannah hoped Erica and Kevin wouldn't examine that premise too closely.

"What . . . what happened?" Erica gasped, staring at the pile of rubble.

"We attacked Boralas with gas," Savannah said, giving a plausible reason for how they'd fought the battle, since she didn't want to give away anyone's psychic powers.

"He pulled the Castle down," Lance said. "And maybe we want to get the hell out of here, before the cops arrive," he added. "We can meet back in Columbia—in case Conrad left some of his men at my house." He looked at Erica. "You and Kevin, too. We need to make sure your place is safe before you go back there."

"Thanks," Kevin said. "Thanks for getting us out of there. I thought we were finished."

Erica looked around. "What happened to Conrad?"

"The monster in the basement zapped him," Savannah answered. "But we'd better leave now and talk later."

"I'll follow you," Sam said.

Savannah turned to him. "Could you follow one of the others? Lance and I need to make a stop."

"Sure."

Still shaky from the mental combat, she asked Lance to drive again, and once they were seated in her car he looked at her expectantly. "You said we need to make a stop?"

"Just drive up Connecticut Avenue," she said. "I'll tell you where we're going."

He did, and she looked at the side streets. When they came to Fessenden, she asked him to turn right.

Older houses and large trees lined the street of the sleeping northwest D.C. neighborhood. She pointed to a maple with low-growing branches. "Park over there."

He looked at the tree in confusion. "What's special about that sugar maple?"

"It gives us some privacy. And I want to kiss you."

His foot bounced on the gas pedal. Then he eased into the space under the tree, cut the engine, and stamped on the brake.

When he reached for her, she came into his arms.

"Thank God you're all right," they both said at the same time.

Then his lips claimed hers, and for long moments, neither of them spoke.

Finally she lifted her mouth a fraction of an inch and said, "Lance, I love you."

"I thought I'd never hear you say that."

He brought his lips down on hers again, and they devoured each other, clinging tightly. She felt his solid body, breathed in his scent.

"You said your family couldn't work together," she said. "It's not true. You're a fantastic team."

He swallowed. "Not just the guys—the women. I knew that, even when I resented Antonia's interference."

"Right. The women. I can't get over them." She swallowed hard. "For the first time in my life, I feel like I have a real family. Lance, I learned a lot tonight. Well, not just tonight. I learned what it means to really belong. To you—to the Marshall clan."

"And for the first time in my life, I feel complete. I didn't know how alone I was until I fell in love with you."

"When was that?"

"I wouldn't admit it then. But it was before I took you to the Watergate."

He bent to her again, his mouth moving over hers, his hands questing, sending fire through her blood. But when she realized he was dragging her pants off, she tried to pull away.

"Lance, we can't. Not here."

"Oh, yeah? Watch me."

He had her naked from the waist down in seconds. And since he had on only sweatpants, it was easy to drag them out of the way, then lift her into his lap.

"Lance, what if someone sees us?" she gasped.

"I'll rip their throat out," he muttered as he brought her down onto his erection.

They were both so hot and needy that it took only a few frantic strokes to bring them to a thundering climax.

Then she sagged against him, holding tight to her man—to her werewolf.

"My life mate," she whispered.

"God, yes." He hugged her to him. And she allowed herself a few more precious minutes in his arms.

"We'd better get back to the motel, before they wonder what we're doing."

He laughed. "I think they know."

"Are you trying to embarrass me?"

"No."

"Brand me?"

"Yeah. For starters."

They walked into the motel suite holding hands. The knowing looks from everyone in the room made Savannah's cheeks heat. But she held her head high. She belonged to Lance Marshall, and she wanted the world to know it—starting with this group of people.

She'd bonded with all of them in a way she'd never expected. They were her family now.

Erica and Kevin sat in the corner, looking a little lost in the Marshall crowd. Probably they knew there was something strange about this group of men and women, but they didn't know what. While Lance was putting on his shirt, Savannah crossed to them and sat in the chair beside Erica.

"I'm so sorry Conrad kidnapped you," she said. "But in the end, he helped us."

The older woman looked shocked. "What? Why?"

She clasped Erica's hand. "It was something like what happened with you and Kevin. The monster . . . Boralas . . . pushed Conrad to do things he wouldn't have done on his own. But he finally realized it—and he came down to hold off Boralas while we . . . gassed him," she said, using their cover story again.

Logan, the youngest of the Marshalls present, stood and looked around at the others. "I need to leave. I doubt that Conrad's men know who I am."

"I assume they're out of a job," Lance agreed, clearly giving the younger werewolf his own space.

"I'm out of a job, too," Kevin said. "As far as the Castle is concerned."

"That gives you more time to finish up your accounting degree," Erica murmured.

He gave her a long look. "Are you trying to get rid of me?"

"Oh, Lord, no. Not if you want to stay with me," she answered.

They got up and walked onto the balcony where they

could have some privacy. When Savannah saw them embrace, she smiled. It looked like things were going to work out for them, and she was glad.

The other out-of-town members of the clan began leaving for home, with the women promising to keep in touch and the men shaking hands awkwardly.

Savannah and Lance and Ross and Megan ended up at Lance's house.

"I have you to thank for getting this group together," he said to his cousin.

"I enjoy dragging the Marshall clan into the twenty-first century."

Savannah hugged Megan. "And I have to thank you for giving my future children a much better chance in life."

"My children, too," Megan answered. "If you need any help or advice—call me. I'm only a half hour away."

The two men looked at each other, and Savannah suspected they were glad the thirty minutes gave each of them their own space.

Megan and Ross left, and finally, she and Lance were alone.

When she caught him watching her, she asked, "What?"

"I'm still having trouble believing that you're here—with me."

She crossed the room and wrapped her arms around his waist. "Believe it." Tipping her head up, she asked, "Are you still going to write about the Eighteen Club?"

"I don't think so. I think we're safer not focusing any attention on us—and the Castle."

"I believe that's right."

"I'll have to put one of my other projects on the front burner." He bent to nuzzle his face against her hair, then asked, "So, can you use the lower level as an art studio?"

"Yes."

"And share it with my exercise equipment?"

"If you're working out, that's going to be distracting. I'm going to think of you holding on to that chinning bar for all you were worth, while I was cutting off your clothes."

He laughed. "Oh, yeah?"

"You don't sound too worried."

"I was thinking we deserve a little R&R, after getting out of the Castle alive."

"Who is going to end up holding on to the bar?"

"We can flip a coin. And the winner gets to choose."

"Agreed," she murmured, pulling his head down for a long, lingering kiss.

Turn the page for a special preview of
Rebecca York's next novel

# NEW MOON

Coming soon from Berkley Sensation!

**THE FOREST AT** night was his playground, his domain. And werewolf Logan Marshall ran for the sheer joy of taking in his kingdom. A lithe gray shape, he was one with the night, the wind ruffling his fur and the sounds and scents of the night tantalizing his senses.

Tomorrow he would go back to work, focusing on the project that had brought him to this patch of Maryland woods. Tonight he ran free. Or as free as a man could be who must try to fit into two very different worlds.

His campsite was a mile back, in a patch of woods scheduled to be demolished by developers in the next few months. It made him sick to think that next year this magnificent stand of oaks and maples would be no more, and the forest creatures who lived here would lose their homes. But tonight he could enjoy the ripple of the wind in the trees and the moonlight dappling the leaves.

He was two miles from camp when a new sensation crept into the edges of his consciousness. No ordinary human would have noticed the subtle difference in the night air. But the werewolf was blessed with senses that no man, except his brothers and his cousins, possessed.

He stopped short, lifting his head and dragging in a deep draft of the humid air. Unfamiliar scents tickled his nose. It was as though a door had opened, letting in dank air that had come from some other time and place. In this one patch of woods, he sensed a rip in the very fabric of the universe. The notion was out of kilter with reality.

A rip in the fabric of the universe? Yeah, right.

Yet he knew it wasn't impossible. Hadn't the Marshall clan fought a monster from another world? A creature that had lurked in the underground reaches of a private club in Washington, D.C., where the rich and powerful had come to indulge their sexual appetites— egged on by the monster who fed on their emotions.

They had killed the creature. Not the werewolves— the strong women of the Marshall clan who had joined their mental energy in battle. He had left while they were still celebrating their victory, because watching the other werewolves and their wives had made his chest tighten. He had never told his married brothers and cousins that he envied them. They would have laughed and advised him to enjoy the time he had left as a free man.

But he'd met no woman who could have been "the one." So he kept to his bachelor existence, carving out a name for himself as a landscape architect who specialized in native plants. This was what he was doing camp-

ing out this weekend, gathering plants ahead of the bull-
dozers.

Only now he knew something was wrong. Some outside force had disturbed this patch of Maryland woodland. A man might have backed away from the danger.
The werewolf knew he had to investigate. Or was the
compulsion coming from within his own mind?

A command below the level of his wolf's hearing
seemed to pull him toward the unknown. And he obeyed,
taking one step forward and then another when deep inside he knew that he should turn and run for his life, for
his sanity.

Disaster struck like a sharp-toothed animal lurking
in the underbrush, only no animal could possess the
steel jaws that suddenly snapped around his ankle. The
pain was instantaneous—and excruciating. It knocked
him off his feet, and he went down, howling as he rolled
to his side, leaves and debris clinging to his stiff fur. For
long moments, he was unable to move. The agonizing
bite of the claws in his flesh was mirrored by savage
claws in his brain.

He had to . . . He had to . . .

It was impossible to complete the sentence. He was
caught in a snare, and the saw-toothed teeth that dug
into his flesh did more than hold him fast. They made it
almost impossible for him to think.

As waves of pain radiated through him, he tried to
gather some semblance of coherence. He knew on some
deeply buried level that he must free himself or die. He
lay panting, gathering his strength, struggling to focus
on wrenching himself away. But when he tugged against
the thing that held him fast, a burst of agony shot up his
leg, searing his nerve endings.

He couldn't yank his foot out of the trap. And his wolf's paws could never pry the steel jaws off his leg. He must change back to human form. And to change from wolf to man, he must say the words of transformation in his mind. But in his present foggy state he couldn't even be sure what they were. All he could do was lie there in the leaves with his eyes closed and his breath shallow, feeling his consciousness slipping away. He would die here in this patch of woods. Or perhaps fate had something worse than death in store for him.

A long time passed. Or perhaps it was only seconds stretched out to hours by the pain. His eyelids fluttered closed and he drifted on a sea of agony and disorientation. A noise somewhere close by made his eyes snap open again. Blinking, he saw a shape coming toward him through the forest. For a moment, he was sure he was hallucinating.

He saw a wolf.

Thank God! One of his brothers, Lance or Grant, had come to set him free from the terrible pain. Squinting, he tried to figure out who had come to his rescue. But the size seemed wrong. And the coloring was off, too; more whitish than gray. Or were his senses fading?

He stared at the animal. Could it be a real wolf? From where? The forest? A zoo? There were no wild wolves in the eastern part of the United States, as far as he knew. Only his own relatives.

The animal was pretty. And delicate. A damn pantywaist of a werewolf, if he was any judge of character. So who was this guy? Nobody he knew in the Marshall clan.

Yet the animal trotted toward him with purpose, as though it understood he was in trouble and had come to help. It stopped a few feet away, sniffing at him and sniffing at the trap, obviously wary of the thing.

"Don't worry," he wanted to say. "It's already got me. It can't grab you, too."

Gravely, the wolf circled him. He watched the wary eyes, the tense body. Then it moved in, nuzzling insistently against his face as though trying to get his full attention.

He nuzzled back because the contact was comforting. But there was little more he could do. The wolf made a frustrated sound, then grabbed his neck in strong teeth and gave him a shake.

*What the hell do you want me to do?* He couldn't speak, only ask the question in his own mind.

He kept his focus on the other wolf as it paced back and forth, then moved a few yards away. When it looked like it was going to leave him here, he felt a surge of alarm jolt through him.

*No,* he silently screamed. He had always thought of himself as strong. But the trap had sapped his will. Not just from his body. From his spirit, as well.

Logan's gaze stayed focused on the white wolf, and what he saw made him doubt his own sanity. He saw the creature go through a transformation. Not from wolf to man but from wolf to naked woman.

Impossible. He must have slipped into a fog of unreality.

Yet the naked woman was no illusion. And he knew that she would either free him or leave him there to die.

# Rebecca York's
romantic paranormal "thrillogy"

## Killing Moon
0–425–19071–4
The first book in a sizzling paranormal series about a man's secret passion, a woman's dangerous desire...and a werewolf's curse.

## Edge of the Moon
0–425–19125–7
A police detective and a woman who files a missing persons report become the pawns of an unholy serial killer in a game of deadly attraction.

## Witching Moon
0–425–19278–4
A Georgia swamp is the perfect place for forest ranger Adam Marshall to hide his werewolf nature.
But when he finds himself irresistibly drawn to biologist Sara Weston, their future is threatened by a coven of witches with a score to settle with the locals.

## "Rebecca York delivers page-turning suspense."
—Nora Roberts

# Penguin Group (USA) Online

*What will you be reading tomorrow?*

Tom Clancy, Patricia Cornwell, W.E.B. Griffin,
Nora Roberts, William Gibson, Robin Cook,
Brian Jacques, Catherine Coulter, Stephen King,
Dean Koontz, Ken Follett, Clive Cussler,
Eric Jerome Dickey, John Sandford,
Terry McMillan, Sue Monk Kidd, Amy Tan,
John Berendt...

You'll find them all at
**penguin.com**

*Read excerpts and newsletters,
find tour schedules and reading group guides,
and enter contests.*

Subscribe to Penguin Group (USA) newsletters
and get an exclusive inside look
at exciting new titles and the authors you love
long before everyone else does.

**PENGUIN GROUP (USA)**
us.penguingroup.com